Books by Lynn Steigleder

Rising Tide

Eden's Wake

Deadly Reign

Terminal Core

DEADLY REIGN

LYNN STEIGLEDER

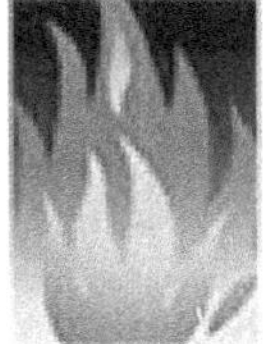

SOUL FIRE
PRESS

an imprint of
Christopher Matthews Publishing

Boston, Massachusetts

Deadly Reign

Editor: Jeremy Soldevilla
Cover design: Neil Noah

ISBN 978-1-945146-18-3
ebook ISBN 978-1-945146-20-6

Published by
Soul Fire Press

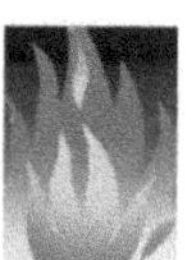

an imprint of
CHRISTOPHER MATTHEWS PUBLISHING

http://christopher matthewspub.com
Boston

Printed in the United States of America

For Mary Fredette, my newest assistant, typist extraordinaire, grammatical wizard, muse, occasional nemesis, and buddy who, for whatever reason, puts up with me. Together we read this book numerous times during the rewriting process. I think I'll keep her.

Acknowledgments

To the living God, the One who never lets me down, who provides through His Son Jesus, a chance for life eternal in paradise. To one of His most precious gifts to me, my wife, Donna, who takes wonderful care of me, is patient, kind, dedicated, fun to be with, takes her wedding vows seriously, and puts up with me.

The Story So Far

Set adrift in an endless sea, Ben Adams can see no escape from his prison. A powerful hurricane has destroyed his habitat, killed his best friend, Pete, and left him alone, floating in a cramped decompression chamber.

Due to unseen forces, Ben is compelled to search for an unknown signal he comes to realize as "C-7." This realization comes in the form of a series of pulses on his otherwise unresponsive communication system. Before time runs out, he manages to contact a passing ship, the *Morning Star*, and is rescued. However, his eleventh hour saviors turn out to be less than honorable. The ship's crew are modern day pirates, led by the corrupt and murderous Captain Evans.

Despite their initial distrust, Stewart, Vinny and Skull befriend Ben, taking him into their confidence. Ben learns that the ship has been under the control of an unseen force that guides the vessel. Ben also discovers the captain's ward: a beautiful, young woman named Eve and quickly falls in love with her.

While Evans is consumed by an evil metamorphosis, Stewart, Vinny and Skull, along with Ben and Eve, form an alliance against the captain. They attempt to uncover the strange events occurring onboard the ship.

The ship reaches its next destination: an island that appears on no charts and is populated by a primitive, yet advanced civilization.

Jhorr, their leader, embraces the *Morning Star's* crew and confines Evans until his transformation reaches its necessary stage of completion. It is here that Ben learns the object of his obsession. 'C-7' is a ship's transport container.

The crew, along with the newly-transformed Evans (now called Eleazor), once again boards the *Morning Star*, headed toward their final destination.

Upon reaching the container, the doors open, revealing a vast seascape, a new world totally covered by water.

As Ben, Eve, and Eleazor cross the threshold, water begins pouring from the new world, filling the old.

As their old world fills, the container doors close and disappear into the surrounding scenery. They find refuge in a new domain as the water continues to recede, leaving a landscape complete with flora and fauna. Ben, Eve and their inept ward, Eleazor, fight from the beginning to survive. Eleazor soon realizes his transformation into the personification of evil, taking Ben and Eve captive. Belac (the couple's guide in this when) rescues the doomed pair and provides counsel for their journey. Ben discovers people thought deceased in his former world and allies himself with the new arrivals. This proves disastrous and drives a programmed Ben and friend, Pete, back to Belac. The Andor (a powerful ancient artifact) is the enticement for two factions: one demanding world domination and the other determined to forge a peaceful existence. Unthinkable beings battle a fierce contingency of humans in a struggle to retake control of the Andor. Ingenious solutions keep the humans, including Belac and his men, one step ahead of the demonic horde. Against all odds, the humans recapture the Andor and destroy or scatter their enemies . . . for now.

As you travel with The Three, you will encounter different components of time and space. Parallel Dimensions exist simultaneously apart from one another within the same timeline. Each dimension can consist of totally different environments. Even though they may share many of the same characters, no dimension's development is influenced by another until travel between dimensions is realized.

Existing within timelines are specific placements of time referred to as whens. The characters' location and reasons for being remain relative to their current place in time, or their whens. There are instances where a character may interact with The Three (Ben, Eve and Pete) as an old individual. Later in the series, the same character may appear as a young child. This person, whether young or old, may retain memories of his former self. This is accomplished by way of parallel dimensions, timelines and whens crossing paths determined by the Great One.

As this is the third book in the *Rising Tide Series,* a Glossary has been added at the end of the book to help readers refresh their memories of important characters and objects that appear throughout the series.

Chapter 1
Parallel Dimension I

"I haven't been on one of these things since I was a kid," Pete said.

"You're one up on me," Ben replied, " 'cause I never have."

"Ditto," Eve said, "and why did I get the feisty one?" Her mount whinnied, rocked its head, and pranced sideways, eager to run.

"Just pull back on the reins," Pete said, "he'll come around. You've got to let him know who the boss is."

"This monster?" Eve said. "One of his feet is bigger than my head."

"He doesn't care about the size of your head," Pete said.

Ben smiled. "I guess the next time I tell you to saddle up, you'll be a little more inclined to comply."

"Don't count on it," Eve said.

"So, little man," Pete asked, "where are we headed?"

"Bout all I can tell ya is thata way," Ben said, pointing a finger straight ahead down the deserted path.

"Hmm," Pete grunted.

"When you figure out a little more," Eve complained, "let me—"

"Shh," Ben interrupted, holding up a hand and pulling his horse to a stop.

Eve's horse bucked, nearly throwing her to the ground.

"Stop, now," she demanded. Her mount threw its head back and obeyed.

"Good, girl," Pete whispered.

Ben waved his hand, "Quiet!"

He motioned everyone off the trail and under cover into the foliage beside the road.

"What is it?" Eve whispered.

"Just wait," Ben said.

The sound of massive footfalls shook the ground. The noise increased until dust and debris flew into the air as the assembly thundered by.

Eve gazed upon the barrage of nothing as it passed, turning into a resonance that faded into silence. She turned to Ben. "I know I heard them, but there was nothing but shadows."

"Ah, yeah," Ben stammered. He turned to Pete. "You saw that, right?"

"Well, I saw nothing that would compare to what I heard." He rubbed the side of his face. "In fact, I didn't see anything," he nodded in Eve's direction, "except shadows."

Ben threw his leg over his mount and stepped onto the ground, "I want you to tell me in your own words, what just passed by."

Pete dropped from his horse, as did Eve. He pulled the reins over its head and held them in one hand. "It was big, and there were flags or pieces of cloth trailing behind."

"I recognized the same thing," Eve chimed in. "It was like a herd of rhinoceroses with a pile of rags on top."

Ben nodded several times. "I saw the same thing, and whatever they were riding, it wasn't of the equine variety."

"What do you think they were?" Eve asked. She moved the reins in her hands back and forth.

"Don't know," Ben replied, "but they weren't human."

"What makes you say that?" Pete asked.

"They sat too low in the saddle," Ben said. He chuckled, "As if we had saddles."

"What do you mean?" Eve asked.

"Look at the direction the sunshine originates," Ben said.

Pete and Eve, both puzzled, looked toward the setting sun.

Ben extended a finger toward the yellow light. Moving the digit along the path, he passed it in front of himself and off in the same direction as the retreating aberrations. "It's low in the sky and shining straight down the path. It would have been behind the riders as they came through."

"So?" Eve replied.

Ben sighed. "Their shadows would be cast on the ground in front of the pack."

"Again," Eve repeated, "so what?"

Ben fumed, his jaws clenching tighter until pops and clicks could be perceived as enamel abraded enamel.

"The shadows would have appeared taller than they were," Pete said.

"Exactly," Ben said, relaxing, "and I saw nothing above the head of whatever they were riding, so . . . "

"So," Eve interrupted, "they were short enough that their heads didn't extend above their mounts."

"Good girl," Ben exclaimed.

Eve opened her mouth to speak, only to be interrupted as another storm of noise made its way down the trail toward The Three.

"Get down," Ben cautioned, motioning for all to drop to a squat position.

Eve lowered her head, squinted, and listened. After a few seconds, she rose and looked at Ben. "They're slowing down," she whispered.

Ben gestured with his hand for Eve and Pete to squat lower and turned his attention to the commotion on the trail.

A group of twelve horsemen came to a halt in front of the three crouching travelers. Eve's horse snorted, blowing air through his vibrating lips. The man leading the pack jerked his head to the left and dismounted as did the remaining eleven.

Ben reached to his shoulder and eased an arrow from his quiver. Before the arrow cleared its holder, twelve projectile points extended through the foliage aimed in his direction. He dropped the arrow and lowered his hand.

"Still," a stern voice commanded.

"Ah, honey," Eve said, "maybe you shouldn't move."

"I'm already frozen," Ben replied.

"Stand and come," the voice commanded again.

The Three rose and pushed through the brush, following the retreating arrow tips, and stood on the road facing the twelve horsemen. Twelve were aiming, not longbows, but crossbows.

The leader was a tall blond man, pacing back and forth in front of The Three, tilting his head from side to side. After several revolutions, he stopped in front of Ben. His long hair, bound in a ponytail, trailed halfway down his back. His face was clean-shaven except for a Van Dyke that ended six inches below his chin. The man smiled. "How is my brother Belac?"

"Your what?" a surprised Ben sputtered.

The blond man extended his hand. "My brother; I believe you share an acquaintance with him."

Ben stared at the outstretched hand and then raised his head and focused on its owner's smiling face. He placed his hand into the blond man's hand. "Well, yeah, but how do you know us?"

"Belac sent word you would be coming," the blond man said.

"We just left," Pete said. "How did you get the message so quickly?"

"By way of a runner," the blond man said, "Belac's grandson."

"You don't suppose . . ." Eve said looking at Ben.

I'm sure Belac has grandchildren other than Jhorr, Ben thought, furrowing his forehead. *But come to think of it, he never mentioned any.* Ben shook his head. "Nah, it's too crazy," he mumbled. He turned his attention back to the blond man. "How did you know we were the right people?"

"You number three;" the blond man said, "two men and a woman. Also, you are wearing such clothes as Belac."

Ben scanned the blond man from head to toe. "You're wearing denim."

"My brother is much behind the times," the blond man said. He shook his head. "Forgive my lack of manners; I am Caleb."

"And I'm . . . "

"You are Ben," Caleb interrupted. "We identify each of you by name."

"Shoulda known," Ben said.

"The light grows dim," Caleb said, peering into the darkening sky. "Please follow me to our village."

Ben mounted his horse then asked Caleb, "Who were the riders that came down the road ahead of you?"

Caleb whirled to face Ben, his face bent into a mélange of concern. "You have seen others?"

"Well," Ben said, "they were invisible except for their shadows."

Caleb threw a wary eye and a nod toward his men and then glared at Ben. "We will leave now." He climbed aboard his mount. "Come, we should not tarry."

"But who were they?" Eve insisted.

Ben placed a hand on her shoulder. "Not now."

Eve sensed her husband's concern and then nodded without protest.

"We must make the village before the light disappears," Caleb said. "It is for your safety. We will speak of this occurrence at a later time."

The trip to the settlement was uneventful, depending upon how one defines the term "uneventful." There were no catastrophes, battles, unseen riders, or anything to waylay their journey.

"Did you see that?" Eve said, breaking the silence.

"What?" Ben asked. "All I've seen are different shades of green."

"No," Eve insisted, "it was right over there." She pointed to a small dark opening leading into the deeper foliage.

A pointed nose with a black bulbous end protruded out of the hole, moving left to right, up and down, and then repeating the sequence. A small creature about twice the size of a guinea pig emerged. It checked its surroundings as it moved. Before Eve could determine the color of the creature, a bright flash moved through the air, taking the small mammal with it. Tuffs of white and jade-colored hair floated to earth, the only evidence that the furry victim had ever existed.

Caleb smiled. "Another one gone."

Eve looked at him.

Caleb, noticing her confusion, explained. "The tendor is a small creature that carries disease and destroys our crops." He nodded toward the area where the tendor was evaporated.

"He was seized for nourishment by a karron, which are one of our greatest allies in this battle."

"How can he move so fast?" Eve inquired, now engrossed in a simplistic daily occurrence.

"I wish I could answer your question," Caleb replied, "but I have no explanation for the fire that emanates from this flying creature, giving it such great speed."

"Jet propulsion in a living thing?" Ben asked, unsure if those words had come from his own mouth.

Before discussion could begin, the party arrived at the village.

Chapter 2

"The buildings," Eve exclaimed.

"I see," Ben said, "they're not made of sod." He looked at Eve. "It's like we've traveled years ahead in time, and it's been less than twenty-four hours since we left Belac."

"Never imagined I'd see a real building in this world," Pete said.

Ben shook his head in amazement. "Well, there it is, stone walls and all."

Caleb dismounted. "Come with me," he urged. "Your horses will be fed and hydrated." He entered a stone structure along with one of his men.

Ben, Eve, and Pete followed. They walked into a modest rectangular shaped room; the interior walls were the opposite side of the stone exterior with no other adornment. Caleb sat at a small but sturdy table, his companion to his right. Ben, Eve, and Pete sat opposite the already seated men. A yellow orb, hovering in the corner, illuminated the room.

"Tell me once again of the riders," Caleb said.

"Like we said the first time," Ben began, "we heard them, but saw nothing except shadows as they passed."

Caleb nodded. "It is as I feared. The ones you have seen are the menace that moves to serve Orac."

"Who is Orac?" Eve asked.

"A large and formidable being," Caleb replied. "We consider him to be demon possessed."

"How large?" Pete asked.

Caleb stood and placed his hand several feet over his head. "Orac stands this tall," he said.

Pete's eyes widened. "That's over eight feet."

"More like nine," Ben replied.

Caleb spread his arms as far as they would reach. "This is his shoulder breadth, if not further."

"Nine feet tall and six feet wide," Ben mumbled. He looked at Caleb. "Orac, why is he here?"

"To turn the world to chaos," Caleb said. He looked sternly at Ben. "He is here for you."

"For us!" Eve exclaimed. "Why does he have a bone to pick with us? We have done nothing to him." She looked at Ben and then at Caleb. "How could he even know about us?"

Ben wrinkled his forehead. "We're part of the prophecy."

"No," Caleb replied. "You *are* the prophecy."

"*The Book of the Chosen*?" Ben inquired.

"Yes," Caleb replied.

"What do you mean, we are the prophecy?" Pete asked.

"There are many future events foretold within the pages of the sacred book," Caleb said. "The passage of The Three is but one."

Ben closed his eyes, clenched his teeth, and shook his head. "I can't believe I'm going to ask this, but, can you tell us what we have to look forward to?"

"But of course," Caleb replied. He lowered his eyebrows and contemplated a moment. "At least that which I am able to relay; however, first we should eat." He clapped his hands, and a man entered with a tray filled with meat, vegetables, and bread.

"This is the first time a man has served us," Eve said.

"We reckon that all should serve," Caleb said.

Eve nudged Ben with her elbow. "Forward thinking," she mused.

"I've noticed," Ben said. He patted her cheek. "Don't get used to it."

The man set a plate in front of each one at the table, along with a bronze knife and a two-pronged fork. He placed a wooden cup at each setting and filled them with water. Laying a cloth on top of the plates, he said, "Enjoy," and left the assembly.

Chapter 3

Pete burped and covered his mouth. "Sorry."

"It is good to see your fulfillment," Caleb said.

Pete nodded.

"Caleb," Ben asked, "what did you mean by, 'what you are able to relay'? Can't you tell us everything?"

"Only what has been written," Caleb said.

"Only what's been written," Eve repeated. "How could it not have been written?"

Caleb turned toward Eve. "For the deeds are yet to be done."

"So we're fulfilling prophecy as we go?" Pete asked.

"In a manner of speaking, yes," Caleb said.

"Tell us what you know," Ben said.

"Very little;" Caleb replied, "only that you are here and you will face Orac."

"That's all?" Ben said.

"Yes."

"Why can't whoever's going to write whatever it is that we're going to do go ahead and write it?" Pete suggested.

"And with a happy ending," Eve added.

"Again, dear ones," Caleb said, "stories cannot be written until the act is done, and I know not who will pen the adventure."

"*Adventure*;" Ben repeated, "I don't think I like that word."

"What about the riders?" Pete asked. "Why couldn't we see them?"

"They are fledglings," Caleb began, "having come into existence a short time ago."

"The essence of the tamar?" Ben whispered.

Caleb looked at him and continued. "As they mature in their purpose, they will come to be seen by The Three, but not by all."

"Why us?" Ben asked.

"It is from the Great One," Caleb said, "to aid you in your struggle to defeat Orac."

"*Struggle*;" Ben said, "there's another one of those words I don't like to hear."

"It is what it is," Caleb said, "and will not be easy." He looked around the table at The Three. "Struggle may understate what you truly face."

Ben leaned back in his chair, sighing and rubbing his hands against his legs. He turned his head toward Eve and Pete. Eve chewed her thumbnail while Pete sat motionless.

"What of the Andor?" Ben asked. "Belac told us of its importance, as far as victory in battle, to the combatants who possessed the artifact."

"Ha, ha," Caleb chuckled. "My brother, always the one to speak quickly before all is known. You see at that time, Belac giving such a reason was pure speculation. He was not sure of the Andor's purpose. The Andor is a vessel which holds ten edicts from the Great One, the cleric's staff, and a container of food that fell from the sky to feed the people."

"Good to know," Ben said. "He also said the artifact would play an important role in our mission's conclusion."

"This I cannot answer, Ben Adams, but I think that may not be the case."

"Makes perfect sense to me," Pete said. "It follows our itinerary to the letter."

Chapter 4

A huge fist slammed down onto the table, turning it to splinters. "Why are they not here?" the owner of the fist screamed.

"In time," the small, bearded man replied, "in time." He wrapped his petite digits around the massive hand. "You should relax; everything is in place."

The giant looked down at the small man; he smiled and knelt. "Nilrem, you always know best."

"Orac, dear Orac," Nilrem replied, lifting his hands and caressing the giant's face. "Patience is your ally. You must embrace this notion for anything otherwise will send you to ruin."

"I will try," Orac said, standing once again. "But what of the riders, should they not have arrived by now?"

"They are new to this world," Nilrem said. "They will arrive when they arrive."

Orac walked to the window and laying his crossed arms on the sill, looked out. "The sky grows dark. I think the water should fall soon."

"That would bring disaster," Nilrem said, a concerned look now crossing his face.

"Why?" Orac asked. "The ground grows dry. The moisture would be a welcome relief."

"Concern yourself with other things," Nilrem said. "There is much before you."

Orac turned and looked at Nilrem. "I know what I am ordained to do, but I do not wish to do so."

"We discussed this at great length," Nilrem said. "I thought we had reached a mutual understanding." He stared back at the giant. "Is that why the outburst?"

"Nilrem," Orac said, "you are as a father; however, this thing you have bidden me do is not right to pursue." Orac moved from the window and placed his hand on the small man's shoulder. "If I must do this, then I want to proceed with all haste."

"There, there;" Nilrem said, patting Orac's hand, "you will see it is the right thing to do." Nilrem turned toward the shattered table. "Please control your temper. Furniture makers to construct larger than normal pieces are few and far between in this day, and the pieces that remain are necessary."

Orac produced a humble smile. "I will guard against such outbursts."

The sound of thundering footfalls could be heard outside the stone structure.

"Ah," Nilrem said, "it would appear that your wards have arrived."

Chapter 5

"The karron;" Ben said, "tell us about this rocket-powered bird you claim to have."

"We will speak of such unessential matters at a time that is more fitting," Caleb replied. "With immense respect, I withhold such information, as there are much more pressing matters we must concern ourselves with first."

"Fair enough;" Ben said, "then tell us more of the riders. Will we have to face them to defeat Orac?"

"The riders are there to do whatever Orac bids them do," Caleb said.

"So if Orac deems that we're in the way, he'll send them after us?" Eve asked.

"That would seem so," Caleb said. "However, I fear that you would be considered, as you have said, in the way."

"At least that's how we should approach this whole scenario," Ben answered.

"I agree," Pete said. "We should hope for the best but prepare for the worst."

"I am glad to see you are eager to face the challenges that lie before you," Caleb said. "I see that my brother has instilled in you three, the heart of a warrior."

"That and much more," Ben replied.

Eve looked at Ben. "You're thinking of Jhorr, aren't you?"

Ben smiled and nodded. "Caleb," he asked, "what challenges lie before us?"

"If I could tell you of each confrontation you will face, I would, but these things I do not know. What I know is that this task will harbor its own difficulties." He stood and backed away from his chair. "You will use everything within your being to secure victory. Only the Great One knows the outcome."

Ben sighed, "Why can't we ever spend a normal day together?"

Eve kissed him on the cheek. "This is a normal day for us, sweetie."

Pete chuckled. "At least that's the way it's gone so far."

"The evening wanes," Caleb said. "Allow me to show you to your sleeping quarters. We will talk further in the morning."

Caleb gathered The Three, led them outside and walked across the street to a single story stone dwelling. "I apologize for the modest accommodations. Please sleep well. I will awaken you in the morning."

Constructed of stone, the room measured twenty by thirty feet from floor to ceiling, with a stone partition dividing the room in the middle lengthwise. A single bed, made from a stout wooden frame with a mattress covered in cloth and an unknown stuffing, sat on the side of the partition. A larger bed sat on the far side of the divider. Both were laden with pillows and folded covers made from the same fabric as the mattress. A housecoat type garment lay for Eve on a small bench in the corner.

"Please don't apologize," Eve said. "This is more than adequate."

"Caleb," Ben asked, "is there someplace to . . . uh, you know . . .?"

"Yes," Caleb said. "Forgive me for not showing you sooner." He motioned to Ben. "Please follow me." The two men walked what amounted to a city block and stopped in front of a community restroom and bathhouse.

"Here is where you will find relief and cleansing," Caleb said. "Once again, I apologize for the distance you must travel to accomplish such a necessary task, but we have no other such facility."

Ben waved his hand. "This will be fine." He took a deep breath. "In fact, I'll make use of this facility right now."

"I will take my leave and see you in the morning."

"Goodnight," Ben said.

Caleb nodded and turned to leave.

Ben entered the room and placing his hands on his lower abdomen, bounced up and down.

♦♦♦

Eve yawned. "Pete, I'm going to bed. Ben will be back soon, and I'm too tired to wait up for him. I have no doubt that he'll talk Caleb's ears off before he returns."

Pete nodded, yawning in answer to Eve's suggestion of sleep. "Ditto."

Eve lay back on her pillow. She could hear Pete snoring. Thoughts of the day, launched with the riders, leapt into her mind.

These aberrations brought about uneasiness, determined to rob her of sleep. With the security Caleb and his men brought to this lopsided equation, Eve soon matched Pete breath for breath.

Eve sat up and yawned, spreading her arms wide. A single beam of sunlight pushed between the curtains, cutting through the room. It illuminated the millions of dust particles suspended in the air, mimicking a star-studded micro galaxy. Eve yawned again and reached over, patting the other side of the bed and realized there was no one lying beside her. She jerked to the right. The covers were undisturbed.

He hasn't been here all night, she thought. A wave of panic spread through her as she jumped from the bed and wrapped the housecoat around her. "Pete," she yelled, running to the other side of the partition.

He moaned and then fell silent. "Get up," she insisted, shaking him.

"What?" Pete said groggily, opening his eyes. "What are you going on about?"

"Ben," Eve pleaded, "he's not here; he didn't come back last night."

Pete shook his head and sat upright. "What do you mean?"

"Get up now." she pleaded. "We've got to find Caleb."

Chapter 6

After Ben had relieved himself, he walked outside, briefly pausing to look up toward the sky.

"Beautiful night," he whispered, and then headed back to his room. As he walked, he began to sense he wasn't alone.

"Why," he moaned, "every time I'm by myself this goofy feeling that someone is following me pops up, and what do you know? Okay, what is it this time?" Ben turned around and spread his arms as if to invite the unknown in for a visit. It took a minute, maybe two, but in the end, he wasn't disappointed.

Ben sat in a shallow cave, wondering what had happened. *One minute I'm walking back to my room, and the next I'm whisked away by something unseen and deposited here.*

He stood and walked toward the entrance, running into an invisible barrier. He took a step back and moved forward, hitting the obstruction with more force. This time it pushed back, knocking him to the floor. Ben could sense an intelligence emanating from the barricade. He climbed back to his feet. "All right!" he barked. "Tell me what I'm doing here, because I have had enough of this."

A slight man appeared and walked through the entrance. "Ben, I see you are awake." The small man bowed. "I am called Nilrem."

"My friends call me Ben. You can call me Mr. Adams, and I haven't been asleep."

Nilrem chuckled. "What makes you think you are not among friends?"

"For starters, a friend wouldn't kidnap another friend in the middle of the night, drag him to this forsaken place, and then leave said friend in the middle of nowhere to be imprisoned by an invisible jailor."

"Perhaps;" Nilrem said, with a hint of something akin to arrogance, "however, I know of no other more acceptable tactic one would use to get said friend to this place." He paused, staring at Ben. "Would you have come willingly?"

Ben snorted. "Since you didn't ask, I guess we'll never know."

Nilrem grabbed his belly and laughed. "I guess not." He smiled at Ben. "You must be hungry?"

Ben cocked his head. "I could eat; although I'm not sure I want anything from you."

"You suspect the worst," Nilrem said. "Please come with me, and I will show you different."

Ben paused, pondering this stranger's invitation. He finally nodded and followed Nilrem out of the cave.

The foliage changed from a sparse, grassy groundcover to a thicket of short, tree-like plants with large leaves. A notion entered Ben's mind as they walked: *I'm not so sure about this whole situation; it may be time for me to take a leave of absence.*

He was walking about six feet behind Nilrem, pushing a possible plan of escape through his head, when the little man turned to speak. "Keeping up back there?"

Ben stammered. "Why yes, no problem at all."

Nilrem smiled. "Good," he said cheerfully and continued his trek.

Ben looked at the back of his leader's head. There was something wrong with that smile of his. He glanced left and then right. *Time to bolt!* Ben slowed his progress, allowing Nilrem to move further away. When he was out of sight, Ben made his move. A second later, he stopped dead in his tracks.

Whatever invisible force had Ben in its clutches, soon caught up with Nilrem. The bearded little man continued to walk, paying no attention to the commotion behind him. *Or was he?* Ben thought. The entity continued to push him along until he walked again as if nothing had happened.

"At this juncture, Mr. Adams, even though you are not officially a prisoner until our business is concluded, leaving is not an option," Nilrem said without turning around.

I can see that. Ben cringed but said nothing.

Chapter 7

"Caleb!" Eve exclaimed. "Ben didn't come home last night. I don't know where he could be!"

Caleb frowned. "It begins sooner than I had hoped."

"What begins?" Eve insisted. "And what about Ben?" She began to move erratically, looking back and forth, not knowing which way to go.

Caleb moved in, grabbing her upper arms. "Eve," he said, looking into her eyes, "you first have to calm yourself and concentrate."

"How can I concentrate when my husband is missing?" Tears began to run down her cheeks. "This is like last time."

"You must," Caleb implored. "It is as simple as that."

Eve wiped her face and with a burst of determination brought herself somewhat under control. "Okay," she said, trembling, her eyes fixed on Caleb, her breaths coming in shallow spurts, "what do you mean by, it begins sooner than you had hoped?"

"Time," Caleb replied. "The battle has begun, and I have had no time to prepare you."

"We've gotten used to flying by the seat of our pants," Pete said.

Caleb eyed Pete curiously and nodded understanding. "First, we must update your weapons."

Pete's forehead creased in distain. "I'm not so sure I want to trade my bow for one of those pea-shooters that you guys carry."

Caleb tensed. "Our pea-shooters, as you refer to them, are small enough that both may be utilized." He sighed, taking on a more relaxed posture. "You may come to find it an invaluable tool."

"No harm giving it a try," Pete said.

Caleb nodded. "I will make the preparations."

Having begun to bring herself under control emotionally, Eve began to speak, "This is all fine and dandy," the irritation in her voice beginning to grow again, "but what say we find Ben before we go shopping?"

"The search will begin after the morning meal," Caleb said.

"No," Eve protested, "Ben could be long gone by then."

Caleb raised his hand. "We are no good to Ben without the proper nourishment to strengthen our bodies for the journey." He extended his hand toward last night's meeting place. "Please."

Eve shook her head in resolve. "You're just like Belac."

After the morning meal, Eve, Pete, Caleb, and three additional horsemen gathered in the settlement's center square with two pack horses loaded with provisions. A small animal similar to a dog sat below Caleb's mount. The creature was sleek and sable, resembling a large meerkat. His two-foot-tall frame was punctuated by a long, bushy tail. Its snout jutted comically from its face, and rounded, mid-length ears protruded from the top of its triangular-shaped head. But the defining feature was its disturbing eyes. Yellow and piercing, the sclera began in the front and curved around the side of its head. As the animal sat in the square, he scanned the area, his pupils making the trek from one end of its elongated socket to the other. At the sound of a horse's neigh, one eye turned to look while the other continued monitoring the riders.

"Do you see that?" Eve stammered.

"If you do, then I do," Pete replied.

"Ah," Caleb said, "allow me to introduce Seeka."

The creature looked up at Eve and Pete, seeming to smile and nod.

Eyes bugging, Eve looked at Caleb. "What is it?"

Seeka cocked his head looking at Caleb. "Not to worry my friend," Caleb said. "She meant no animosity." Satisfied, the animal sat down on its haunches.

"It understands you," Eve said, further mystified with the creature.

"Seeka understands you as well," Caleb replied, "and is not so sure he likes the new name you have given him."

"What new name?" Eve asked.

"It," Caleb replied.

Eve gasped. "I didn't mean to imply—"

"He understands," Caleb interrupted, "nothing more need be said."

Eve looked at Seeka. The creature made a short yip.

"Wow," Eve said. "Can he speak?"

"No," Caleb replied, "not in any language you would understand; however, he can communicate in his own way."

"What is Seeka?" Pete asked, phrasing his question so as not to offend the creature.

"He is a nuckta," Caleb said. "His race is now extinct. As far as is known, he is the last of his kind."

"How could his race be extinct?" Eve asked. "This world isn't old enough to have born a race of beings and then brought it to the point of extinction."

"Did my brother not explain the passage of time in this world?" Caleb asked.

"Well, yeah," Eve replied.

"Mayhap I should explain once again," Caleb said.

"Please," Eve replied.

"Time applies to the situation you are experiencing," Caleb began. He squinted, searching for words they would understand. "Even though our years number more than each of your years, this also relates to your present circumstances."

"I'm not sure we're following you," Pete said. He looked at Eve. "I am speaking for both of us, aren't I?"

Eve answered with a dumbfounded nod.

Caleb dismounted. Seeka whined, extending his neck. Caleb smiled and scratched the animal's throat.

"How shall I put this?" Caleb mumbled. His eyes brightened, and his gaze turned to Eve and Pete. "You spent many days with Belac but a short time ago," Caleb said.

"Yes," Eve replied, nodding in agreement.

"If you were to return to the place where Belac and his people dwelt, you would find no one there and no trace of their existence."

"Where have they gone?" Pete asked.

"They have long since lived their lives and now cease to be," Caleb said.

"That can't be right;" Eve protested, "we just left."

"I know the words I have spoken are difficult to understand," Caleb said. "As my brother once conveyed, time passes differently in this when."

"This when?" Pete asked.

"Time, as I have said," Caleb replied, "is relative, and in this when, it is relative to each of you."

"Caleb," Eve said, "you're talking in circles."

Seeka lowered his head. Caleb ran his hand down the creature's nose and then mounted his horse. "Whenever the three of you encounter individuals in this when, time passes at a consistent rate for each of you. But when apart from The Three, time becomes increasingly relative, because our presence is no longer necessary to your quest. We then live our lives to fruition. In your time this equals a mere blink of an eye." He pulled his mount's reins and turned to Eve and Pete. "We must now find Ben."

"Seeka," Caleb said. The creature looked at Caleb, making clicking noises. Caleb clicked in response. The strange creature nodded and trotted out of town.

"Now we follow," Caleb said.

Chapter 8

Ben swallowed. "You want to tell me what I'm doing here?" He looked at his surroundings. "Wherever *here* is."

The building was constructed from stone, very much like the ones in Caleb's settlement, save for no windows. A massive wooden door with black iron hardware barred the only exit. Ben sat on a rock with a wooden plate in his lap.

"Of course," Nilrem said. "Would you care for more to eat?"

"No," Ben replied, "just information."

Nilrem smiled, "I wish to talk with you and possibly enlist your assistance."

"Uh huh," Ben said, standing. "No thanks. The last time someone wanted to enlist my help, I nearly lost everything close to me, including myself."

"Please hear me out before you refuse," Nilrem pleaded.

"Don't waste your breath," Ben said. He walked toward the door. Before he could reach it, an invisible hand grabbed him and placed him in front of Nilrem once again. "So now I'm your prisoner. What happened to 'friend?'"

"No," Nilrem said. "Heed what I say and after that, if you still wish to leave, then you may go."

"All right," Ben said, plopping back down on the rock, "make it quick."

"Thank you, my words shall not disappoint." He motioned toward the door, and a large rock sitting in the corner now levitated on its own. It placed itself down several feet from Ben. Taking a seat on the kinetic boulder, Nilrem began, "No doubt you have heard of Orac?"

Ben nodded.

"What were you told of his presence in this world?"

"You obviously know;" Ben countered, "so you tell me."

"I can see that the prophecy has spoken true."

Ben raised his eyebrows. "You know of the prophecy?"

Nilrem leaned closer to Ben. "How else would I have known to host an assembly with none but you?"

"Have you seen *The Book of the Chosen*?" Ben asked.

"I should ask you the same."

"Well, no," Ben said.

"Then allow me to tell you what has been withheld." Nilrem stood, moving toward Ben. "The passages which tell of The Three are within its pages; however, there are other readings of which you have not been told."

"Like what?" Ben asked.

"The curse that has also been written concerning the same three."

Ben sat up straight, Nilrem's comment piquing his interest. "What about the curse?"

"Not far into *The Book of the Chosen*, the one known as Nacor commits a great offense unto his father. As a result, the father curses the son's lineage."

"Why?" Ben asked. "What did Nacor do that would make his father curse his own bloodline?"

"That is it."

"What's it? You answered my question with an erroneous statement that makes no sense at all."

"No, no," Nilrem said. "You answered your own question."

"How so?" Ben asked, now curious how this game of questioning would end.

"Bloodline."

"And . . . ?" Ben said, growing irritated.

"You disappoint." Nilrem crossed his arms and frowned. "After all, you are one of The Three."

"I've had about enough of you talking in circles," an infuriated Ben scoffed, fed up with Nilrem's absurd line of interrogation.

"Very well," Nilrem calmed. "Nacor ignored his father's warning and had taken an Andonite woman for his wife."

"Andonite?" Ben lowered his eyebrows. "Why would his father have any say in who Nacor married?"

"In that day to intermingle with an Andonite was forbidden to keep the bloodline pure."

Ben rubbed his temples. "Whatever. I don't care about Nacor, his father or who either of them married." He looked at Nilrem, "They could have married each other if they'd wanted to," he said, raising his voice. "Just tell me what any of this has to do with me."

"It is the curse that concerns you." Nilrem sat back down, folded his hands, and placed them on his lap.

Ben stood, now incensed. "Look, you kept me here to listen to your rhetoric. If that's all you have to say, then I think I'll leave now." Ben walked toward the door.

"Are you not concerned about the curse?" Nilrem inquired in a condescending tone.

Ben whirled around. "Not if you're going to make me guess. Just let me go; I've grown tired of amusing you."

"Please Ben, come, sit, and I will tell you of the curse."

Ben sighed, shook his head, and returned to his seat on the rock facing Nilrem. "Get on with it," Ben said.

"I will tarry no longer," Nilrem assured. "The father's admonition stated that Nacor's descendants would bow down and serve his brother's descendants all their lives, being nothing more than slaves underfoot."

"Again," Ben said, now exasperated, "what does that have to do with me?"

"Nacor's father, known to all in that day as Paterasis, would translate to father of The Three in your speech."

Ben squinted and stared at Nilrem. "Continue."

"Nacor was the youngest, the twins, Raham and Dahor were Nacor's elders by two years, and the firstborn, Colossac, which means—"

"Large one," Ben said.

"Good, your response now justifies the stigma that precedes you." Nilrem hesitated, allowing Ben to ponder this information before he continued. "The prophecy of the giant leading The Three has been passed down since this time."

Ben's mind raced, piecing together the puzzle this slight man laid before him. His eyes once again connected with Nilrem's.

"Slaves to Orac?" he added, questioning his own statement.

"It is as you say." Nilrem paused, staring at Ben. "However, there may be a way."

"Let's not play any more games. Just give it to me and give it to me straight."

"I would act as liaison between you and Orac," Nilrem said, "as a neutral party, of course."

"Why?" Ben looked at Nilrem. "What's your stake in this?"

"No other than not wishing to see my world thrown into turmoil."

"What makes you think Orac would consider talking with me?" Ben inquired, determined not be taken in as he had been by Eleazor.

Nilrem raised his eyebrows, his excitement evident. "He was entrusted to my care these past thirty cycles."

Ben chuckled. "I guess you'd know then."

"It would seem," Nilrem admitted.

"So what do you propose to avoid this confrontation?" Ben asked.

"That you join with Orac as a willing participant in his appointment as ruler, instead of being forced to aid him as a slave," Nilrem replied.

"Not much of a choice," Ben said.

Nilrem produced a grim smile. "Much better than the alternative."

"Which is?" Ben asked.

Nilrem sighed. "Slavery or death."

Ben thought a moment, "I guess it wouldn't hurt to hear Orac out."

"Good, I will take you to meet with him."

"What's wrong with here?" Ben protested.

"It will be much safer where I am taking you."

"Safer for whom?"

"For all concerned." Nilrem extended a hand toward Ben. "Please, come with me."

Ben looked at the ground, shaking his head. "When am I going to meet someone that can stay in one place?"

Chapter 9

"Are you sure Seeka can find Ben?" Eve asked.

"If he is still alive," Caleb said, then immediately added, "I am sorry. I did not mean to imply that Ben is anything other than well."

Eve briefly allowed herself to think the worst and then pushed it from her mind. "That's okay. I was just wondering how your creature tracks his prey."

Caleb smiled. "Waves of energy specific to each of us exude from that particular individual. This is how a nuckta finds its intended."

Seeka stopped, stretched his neck, and shuddered. Turning to look at Caleb, he clicked three times and increased his pace.

"We must follow," Caleb said. "Seeka has located our quarry." The group increased its pace to a gallop. After several minutes, the nuckta stopped at a lone stone structure.

Eve was the first off her horse. "Ben!" she yelled, as she ran toward the building. The massive wooden door lay open. She passed through into an empty room. The rest soon joined her.

"I thought you said Seeka would find him," Eve protested. "There's no one here."

Seeka rubbed against Caleb's leg, who reached down and stroked the nuckta's head. "He has been here."

"How do you know that?" Eve grumbled.

"Seeka sensed the concentration of energy left in this place," Caleb said. "When an individual lingers, that person's energy will focus upon that place, leaving their essence."

"Then where is Ben?" Pete asked.

"I do not know," Caleb replied, "but we will be able to follow his trail from here."

Eve walked around the room looking in each corner, pausing at the stone seats.

"Ben has been here," she said, emphatically turning to Caleb. "He has been here. We must leave at once."

"In time," Caleb said.

"What do you mean, 'in time?'" Eve protested. "We've got to leave now!"

Caleb raised a hand to quiet her. Seeka sniffed around the room. He crawled upon the rock on which Ben had sat and began to click. Caleb responded in like fashion. He moved his gaze from Seeka to Eve. "That time is now."

"What is he doing?" Eve exclaimed.

Seeka had stopped and began to turn in circles, unsure of which way to go.

"Didn't you say he found his prey by energy waves?" Pete asked.

"Yes," Caleb replied.

"Then why was he sniffing around the stone building?"

"Seeka uses many techniques," Caleb said. "The foremost being the energy each of us conveys."

"So what does this mean?" Eve asked, her voice growing in irritation. "Has your pet lost the trail?"

"Calm down," Pete said. "This won't do anyone any good, especially Ben."

Caleb glared at Eve. "Seeka belongs to no one. He is his own."

"I'm sorry," Eve said, "but we can't just sit here doing nothing."

"Something is interfering with the power signature," Caleb explained. "It is up to Seeka to rectify."

"Well this is just great," Eve complained. She dismounted and moved away from the rest, eyeing Seeka with contempt as she passed. The animal glanced at Eve, then began to follow. Eve paused and immediately felt a nudge against the back of her leg. She turned and looked down. "What do you want?" she grumbled.

Seeka whimpered.

Eve stared a moment and then smiled. Kneeling down, she touched the sable colored fur on the animal's head. Seeka placed his front paws on Eve's knees, pushed his head under her chin, and nuzzled his nose against her. Eve began to rub his neck. "I know it's not your fault," she said. "I guess I needed someone to blame."

Seeka gratefully accepted the attention and began to hum.

Eve chuckled, "A cat with vocal cords."

Seeka licked Eve's cheek and then began to move slowly backward, bobbing his head up and down. When he had reached a distance of six feet, he sat back on his haunches and stretched his head toward the sky, swaying his neck, first to the left and then to the right. After several moments he stopped, lowered his head, nodded at Eve and winked.

Eve jerked and stood in amazement as a yellow ball appeared, hovered above Seeka, and then settled over the creature. "The orb," she whispered.

The orb began to pulsate and spin. A white cloud encompassed the nuckta. It grew and then dissipated. Seeka was gone. The orb followed, fading into nothing.

Caleb now stood beside Eve.

"Where did he go?" she exclaimed.

"I do not know," Caleb said, shaking his head. "This is something I have not seen until now."

"He wanted to tell me something," Eve said, "but I couldn't understand." She thought for a moment, and then looked at Caleb, "Is he okay?"

"Most likely," Caleb replied. "I suspect this was a tactic to locate Ben."

"What do we do now?" Eve asked, concerned with Caleb's lack of understanding of his companion's methods.

Caleb raised his eyebrows, asking himself the same question. "Until Seeka returns, we wait."

Chapter 10

The path was now of sufficient width for Ben and Nilrem to walk abreast.

"I don't feel right having come with you," Ben said. "Eve will be worried."

"You left of your own volition," Nilrem said. "You were neither forced nor coerced."

Ben stopped abruptly, squaring his body toward Nilrem. "Is that what you call this little getaway you have so kindly provided? I'll admit a small portion of what you've said is indeed correct. That portion being this leisurely little jaunt from where we were to where we are going." He leaned closer to Nilrem as the volume of his rant increased. "Other than that, to say the least, it's a jovial kidnapping; to imply the worst, we are subservient to a dictatorial autocrat bent on world domination." He paused to take a deep breath. "I'm going to do this on the outside chance that you are telling me anything close to the truth." He stopped speaking and glared at Nilrem. "I'll give you one day to convince me. After that, I'm gone."

Nilrem smiled, "It will not require that length of time." He motioned toward yet another stone structure. "We are here."

As the men entered the building, circling above, a white feathered object extinguished its engines and began a slow descent. As it wrapped its talons around a branch, its organic propulsion system faded to black.

Ben walked into the building and recognized an unseen presence surrounding him. The room was as all of the structures he had seen up to this point, made from stone and constructed in the shape of a dome. It was sixty feet in diameter and rose to a rounded peak of over twenty feet. A single entryway, devoid of a door, was the only way in or out. Nilrem entered the room directly behind Ben.

"Something else is here," Ben said, looking around warily. "I don't know what it is, but I've felt it before." He looked at Nilrem, "Your turn."

"All is as it should be," Nilrem replied, shrugging his shoulders. "What is your question?"

"I've stated my question," Ben said, glaring at Nilrem. "You can drop the charade; you know it's here too." He moved menacingly toward the slight man.

"No closer," Nilrem warned, "lest the unseen misinterpret your advance and come to my aid."

"See there?" Ben said with a smirk, "look at all the trouble we can avoid if we just tell the truth." He turned his back to Nilrem and began to scan the dome walls. "So, tell me about your friends."

"You continue to live up to your calling."

"You forget," Ben said, jokingly peering back over his shoulder. "I'm the Key."

Nilrem's eyes narrowed. "No, Mister Adams," he mumbled, "that is the one thing that I have not forgotten. I was merely beginning to explain to you the source of the presence you have been experiencing."

"Please continue," Ben said.

"Tell me when you initially experienced this presence," Nilrem asked cautiously.

"A couple of days ago when we were on the road leading into Caleb's settlement, a group of riders thundered by. They cast shadows, but nothing more of them could be seen."

"And that was your first experience?"

"Yes," Ben replied. "And every place you've taken me has held a portion of this presence, but it's much stronger here."

"And what did Caleb tell you of the aberrations?"

"Ah, I hadn't had the occasion to ask him yet," Ben lied.

"Strange," Nilrem said. "It seems something of that nature would have demanded your immediate attention."

"It certainly would have," Ben said, "had I not been kidnapped shortly after we arrived."

"I understand," Nilrem said, smiling nervously.

Ben waited several moments. "Are we playing games again, or are you going to tell me?"

"In time," Nilrem said. "First, we have other matters to discuss."

A large hand appeared on the doorframe, followed by another, and then the massive body lumbered into the room.

Ben stared blankly at the huge figure.

"Orac," Nilrem said, "I have been expecting you."

The giant stood upright and smiled at the slight man. His hair was of medium length and mussed. A short-cropped beard decorated his chin. He wore a light colored, long-sleeved shirt, a brown leather vest and denim pants. On his feet were calf-high leather boots.

"Who have we here?" the large one boomed.

"This is Ben," Nilrem replied, "the leader of The Three."

Orac made his way closer to the pair. He stopped and extended his hand.

"I have heard much of you, Ben, leader of The Three. It pleases me to finally meet you."

Ben placed his hand into Orac's. The massive hand wrapped around his, gently squeezing and then releasing.

"Huh . . . good to meet . . . huh . . . you too, I think," Ben stammered, inspecting his hand to make sure everything was still intact.

The giant reared his head backward with a great roar of laughter.

"Calm yourself, small one," Orac implored. "You are among friends here."

Ben warily glanced at Nilrem. "So I've been told." He turned toward Orac, "I'm figuring you're in charge." He looked back at Nilrem. "Let's start discussing those matters."

"Of course," Nilrem replied, "but not here."

"No," Ben demanded, "I will not move from this spot until you tell me what's going on."

Orac looked at Nilrem. "Feisty, is he not?"

"Indeed," Nilrem replied.

"Shall I?" Orac asked.

"No need," Nilrem said. "We will talk here."

"Shall you what?" Ben asked.

"Nothing you need to trouble yourself with," Nilrem said. "There is much to talk about."

"Maybe I bestowed the mantle of leadership on the wrong one," Ben mumbled.

"How is that?" Orac inquired.

"Oh, nothing," Ben said. "At least nothing you need to trouble yourself with."

"As I previously explained," Nilrem began, "the strength of The Three is well noted within the pages of *The Book of the Chosen*. However, the demise of The Three is also foretold. Would it not be more prudent to combine the power of The Three along with the destined leader?"

"You see," Orac continued, "together we would be a nearly unstoppable force. Apart, we would clash, and The Three would be no more."

"You do present an interesting proposal," Ben said. "But it's not my decision alone."

"Are you not the leader?" Nilrem asked.

"I am," Ben replied, "but a good leader weighs the opinion of his troops before making a decision."

"Point taken," Nilrem said. "What do you propose?"

"Allowing me to leave would be a gesture of good faith. In this way, I can talk with my people and bring this to the best possible resolution."

"As I have said," Nilrem replied, "you have always been free to go. I will give you three risings of the Great Light to reach a decision. If by then I have not heard from you, I will presume that you have elected to die."

"Not exactly as I would have put it," Ben said, "but I guess that pretty much says it." He looked at Nilrem. "Three days it is."

Nilrem nodded.

Ben paused at the door and looked back at Nilrem and Orac. "If I do not return, rest assured that our battle will be one to the death."

Nilrem took a step forward, "Three risings."

A pair of yellow eyes at the far end of the room gazed unnoticed at the unlikely trio.

Chapter 11

"I think it best that we return to the settlement at this time," Caleb said.

"That's it," Eve protested. "What about waiting for Seeka?"

"We have waited for some time now. The Great Light grows low in the sky." He touched Eve's shoulder. "Seeka will look out for your Ben, and they both are under the watchful eye of the Great One."

Eve nodded, "Okay. I guess, there is as good as anywhere."

The group left the stone building and began their journey back to the village.

"Pete," Eve said, "what do you think of our latest predicament?"

"Par for the course."

Eve looked perplexed, "What do you mean?"

Pete smiled, "Never played golf, huh?"

"Golf?" Eve inquired. "What is that?"

Pete shook his head. "Never mind. What I meant was that ever since we've been here, we've faced one challenge after another with almost no break in between." His horse puffed, jerking its head to the side. Pete patted his mount's neck and looked at Eve. "The verdict on this Great One for me, at least, is still out, but what I do know is that everything He's been involved in so far has turned out okay." Pete rubbed his chin. "I just have a hard time leaving my fate in someone else's hands. I've always taken care of things myself, ya know."

Eve pursed her lips and nodded. "Even though I've wavered at times, when it comes right down to it, I'm not crazy about relinquishing control either."

The sky had grown dark, and the group moved on in silence until they reached the village.

"Come," Caleb said, nodding toward Eve and Pete. "We will take nourishment."

They walked into the same stone building they had eaten in the night before and seated themselves. Just as the previous evening, a man brought a tray of food and laid it before them. Too famished to do anything other than eat, the ones seated did so in silence.

As the meal neared its end, Caleb spoke, "I trust each of you has eaten your fill?"

Eve and Pete both nodded as they swallowed their last bite of food.

"Very good," Caleb said. He raised his hand signaling to an attendant. The man brought three cups containing a pale green liquid and set one before each of the diners. He placed a pitcher of the same liquid on the table and then excused himself.

Eve and Pete looked at Caleb.

Caleb smiled. "Please," he said, waving a hand toward the beverage, "enjoy."

They complied and found the drink delightful and warming.

Chapter 12

"I exist in one of two states," Ben mused. "Either I'm moving from point A to point B, or I'm lost." He stopped and scanned the path in front of him. "I'll opt for lost this time."

Something nudged his leg from behind. Ben whirled, drew his bow, loaded and readied to fire as he did so. The path behind him lay empty.

"What? I know something—" He noticed the small figure at his feet. He could just make out the shape of an animal in the fading light. The creature made a clicking noise, stood on its hind legs and extended his neck toward Ben, bobbing its head up and down.

Ben lowered his bow. Sensing he had nothing to fear, he knelt closer to the newcomer. Seeka licked his cheek and ran down the path, stopping and returning to Ben. He repeated this several times.

Ben chuckled, "I guess you want me to follow you." He rubbed Seeka's neck. The animal clicked and hummed. "Why not?" he said. "It seems my destiny is to follow someone, or in this case, something." He shook his head, stood and threw his hand forward signaling affirmatively. "Lead on."

A small fireball sped across the sky directly overhead the pair. Seeka jumped up and down, barking somewhat like a dog as he did so. Ben knelt, touching the nuckta on its back.

"Calm down, little fella," Ben said, trying to settle the excited creature. "I think it's one of those jet powered birds I saw earlier."

Within several seconds the glowing avian disappeared. Seeka relaxed, although Ben could still feel a slight shaking in the ruffled nuckta. Ben stood. "Okay, now where were we? That's right, I was about to follow you."

Seeka turned his head away from the glowing bird, glanced at Ben, and with a nod that nearly knocked Ben off his feet, disappeared into the darkness.

Chapter 13

Eve swallowed and yawned, nearly choking on her drink.

"Easy," Pete said, patting her on the back.

Caleb's smile changed to laughter, and then to wonderment. He signaled for quiet. A hush fell over the room. Distant clicks could be heard, growing closer.

Eve's face brightened. "Seeka!" She closed her eyes. "Please let Ben be with him," she whispered. When she opened her eyes, the room was empty. She hurried outside to join the others.

Orbs lit the immediate area. A constant flurry of clicks emanated from the shadows. Seeka emerged from the darkness, bounding toward the group. Eve held her breath in anticipation until what she had longed to see came into view.

"Ben," she exclaimed. She ran toward her husband and fell into his arms.

"Did ya miss me?"

She leaned back and glared at him shaking her head.

Pete moved toward the embracing pair. "Good of you to take time out of your busy schedule to join us."

Ben smiled, slapping his friend on the shoulder. "Until I get a better offer, this will have to do."

Somewhere between the scream and wail of a madman-turned-banshee, a dark figure traveling at a high rate of speed entered the settlement. It seemed to glide just above the ground, unsure of its target.

"Destroy!" Caleb screamed.

Speeding through a barrage of arrows, the creature fell into four pieces with thin strands of tissue holding it together. It hit the ground with a dull thud, a dark purple fluid oozing from its remains.

Eve lowered her bow. "What was that?"

"Another one of those cursed blood suckers," Caleb replied.

"You mean a vampire?" Pete asked.

Caleb nodded and kicked several of the stumps as if he were checking the tires on a used car. "Another one bites the dust," he said and then spat on the corpse.

"What about a wooden stake through the heart?" Ben asked. "I thought that was the only way you could kill them."

Caleb shook his head. "No, you can club them to death with pretty much anything. Their intelligence level hovers around that of a Gibeon rock beetle, so it's not a difficult task." Caleb left the three standing around the dead vamp and returned to speak with Seeka. He knelt on the ground, exchanging clicks with the nuckta. The animal nodded and left. Caleb stood and joined The Three. "It pleases me to know you are safe."

"Thank you," Ben said. "It's good to see you as well."

"It grows late, and I know all are weary," Caleb said. "I think it best you three retire to your sleeping area, and I will have food brought to you, Ben."

"That would be great," Ben said, patting his stomach. "I'm starved."

As the three entered their quarters, a man was leaving, having deposited a tray of food.

"Thank you," Ben said.

The attendant nodded and excused himself.

Ben and Eve sat on Pete's bed, with Pete making himself comfortable on the floor.

"Okay," Eve said, "spill it."

"Spill what?" Ben asked.

"Tell us where you've been," she insisted, "and tell us now!"

"Can I eat first?"

"No! I'm fed up with these little disappearing acts of yours." She picked up the tray of food. "Now talk, or you'll be wearing this instead of eating it."

"Okay, okay," Ben said, making calming motions with both hands. He relayed his story, beginning with the kidnapping the night before and ending with his return a short time ago.

"You don't believe them, do you?" Eve asked.

"Don't know," Ben replied. "What I think we should do is ask Caleb for the book, read it for ourselves, and then make our decision."

"Fair enough," Pete said.

"I guess," Eve agreed.

"Look," Ben said, "I'm doing everything possible to avoid repeating the same mistake as last time."

"Okay," Eve said.

"Now that's settled, do you mind if I eat?"

"Oh, sorry," Eve said, handing Ben the tray.

"Would you two do that on your side of the partition?" Pete asked. "I'd like to go to bed."

"Sure," Ben said. "See you in the morning."

"I know, Seeka;" Caleb said, "however, it is not for me to decide. The terms you imparted were discussed between Ben and the enemy. It must be the choice of The Three and no other."

Seeka frantically clicked a response.

"If they choose the dark path, then so be it," Caleb said. "We will have no other choice but to eliminate Orac and The Three."

Seeka dropped his head in remorse. Caleb stroked the creature's neck. "We will know soon enough."

Chapter 14

"Welcome to the morning meal," Caleb said. "I trust you slept well."

"Yes," Ben answered.

"Where's Seeka?" Eve asked. "I haven't seen him since last night."

"He requires a great deal of rest after his ordeal," Caleb said. "Seeka will join us later."

"As long as he's all right," Eve said. "I just wanted to thank him."

"Seeka is fine," Caleb said. He then looked at Ben. "Tell me of your time away."

"There's not much to tell," Ben lied. "I left the men's room, decided to nose around, and ended up following the road out of town. I wanted to try out my new crossbow, so I headed into the forest. The full moon was so bright it made the night as day. When I tried to return, I got turned around and ended up lost. That little pet of yours led me back."

"Shh," Eve cautioned. "Seeka is not a pet."

"Well, what is he?" Ben asked.

"Seeka is his own," Caleb said.

"I'm sorry, Caleb," Ben said. "I'm grateful for his guidance. I didn't mean to offend."

"Do not concern yourself," Caleb said. "You did not know; although I am curious about your story."

"How so?" Ben asked with a hint of defensiveness in his tone.

"I do not recall the light of darkness being as bright as you have stated," Caleb answered.

"I guess it could have been the orbs," Ben said.

"The companion does not shine outside of the village," Caleb replied.

"Look," Ben exclaimed, rising from his seat. "I don't know the exact answer for why I could see; all I can say is what happened. Now you can take it or leave it, and I don't care which." He remained standing, glaring at Caleb.

"Ben," Caleb said, standing, "I was merely trying to arrive at what happened in your absence. I will accept your account. Please be seated and enjoy your meal."

Ben lowered his head. "It's okay. I'm sorry for the outburst."

Both men sat down, and the meal began in silence.

"So," Eve said, in an attempt to break the tension, "this is very good."

"Thank you," Caleb replied. "I will tell the one who prepares that you were pleased."

"Caleb," Ben said, "I am curious about The Book of the Chosen."

"Yes, Ben," Caleb replied. "What may I clarify for you?"

"I was hoping you would have a copy here that I may borrow." Ben paused. "For study purposes of course."

"Of course." Caleb signaled to one of the attendants. "You may peruse it at your leisure after the morning meal.

Ben nodded. "Thank you."

◆ ◆ ◆

An attendant laid the book before Ben as another cleared the dishes.

"I will leave you three to investigate the hallowed pages and reach conclusions of your own," Caleb said. "There are matters that require my attention. I will return afterwards."

"Thanks again," Ben repeated. He ran his fingers over the rich leather bound book. A single eye adorned the front cover. Illegible text wrapped itself around the eye. Ornate symbols, embossed and overlain with what appeared to be gold, decorated the whole.

"Look at that," Eve whispered. She ran her hands over the raised areas, fascinated by its beauty.

Ben rolled the cover back and moved through the pages. "The passage Nilrem mentioned supposedly originates near the beginning of the book," he said.

Pete sat on the floor with his back against the wall, nodding. Eve paced around the room. "It's been hours," she said. "Don't you think you'd have found it by now if it was there?"

Ben waved his hand without a reply and continued his search.

"Come on," she insisted. "Why don't you . . ."

"I've got it," Ben declared. "It's right here just like Nilrem said."

Pete opened his eyes moving to an upright position. "Got what?"

"Dewey Decimal reckons he's found something," Eve mocked.

"No," Ben said, "Look."

Eve and Pete moved closer to Ben.

"Well?" Pete said.

"Here," Ben said, pointing toward a particular passage. "Paterasis, Nacor, Randor, Colossac, the curse; it's all here."

Eve and Pete both scanned the document. Once finished, they looked at Ben.

"How do you know we can trust this?" Eve asked.

"There's one way to find out," Ben replied.

"How?" Pete asked.

"We look through the book and find the section about our battle with the tamar," Ben answered.

"That's a lot of book to search through," Pete said.

"What other option do we have?" Eve asked.

Ben opened the book in the middle. "The pages are empty!"

Eve and Pete gazed at the vacant sheets in bewilderment.

"Obviously they're not written yet," Pete said.

Ben flipped pages back toward the beginning. About halfway there, he found text. "This is amazing," he said. "Our journey must have been among the last things written."

The three found their way to the beginning of the story and read, savoring each word with great satisfaction. When done, they sat down basking in the wake of their accomplishments.

"Jhorr sure did a great job recording our story," Ben said.

"Yeah," Pete said, "we're almost like heroes."

"Almost!" Ben objected.

"Wait a minute," Eve said. "Just listen to us."

"What do you mean?" Ben asked.

Eve stood and faced Ben. "Don't you remember what Belac told us?"

"He told us a lot of things," Ben said. "You'll have to be more specific."

"Pride," she said. "He warned us of being prideful and how it would lead to our downfall. The Great One empowered us to do everything in the story we just read, and now we're claiming the glory for ourselves."

Ben pondered a moment. His expression turned from smug to one of embarrassment. "That's why I married you," he said, kissing her cheek.

"Why is that?" Eve replied.

"To keep me straight."

Eve smiled and returned the kiss.

"All right," Pete said, "so we've proved that the book is accurate. What do we do about the curse?"

"If you're asking me," Ben said, "we pay a visit to Nilrem."

"Of course I'm asking you;" Pete said. "You're in charge."

"Let's tell Caleb," Eve said.

"No," Ben cautioned. "I don't believe Caleb wants anything bad to come our way, but either he hasn't read that part of the book, or he's hoping for more. It's similar to Belac when we faced the tamar."

"What do you mean?" Pete asked.

"After our battle in the cave," Ben began, "I told Belac that I was sorry we hadn't dispatched more of the tamar than the three we had killed. He indicated that he had hoped for more also, but not to worry because what we'd done was foretold."

"Isn't our story written as we experience it?" Eve said.

"Question nothing that has to do with time in this world," Ben said. "If you think about it, Jhorr was gone, and our task was complete."

"I'm not following you," Pete said.

"If Jhorr wrote that portion of the book," Ben said, "then the story is recorded instantaneously."

"You're right," Pete said. "Trying to assemble any rational timeline in this place would drive you nuts."

"Okay," Eve said, "We go talk to Nilrem."

"I'm in," Pete echoed.

"Good," Ben replied. "Caleb said he'd be gone for a while, so there's no time like the present."

Chapter 15

"This is where I left them," Ben said.

"No one seems to be here now," Eve replied.

"You came sooner than I anticipated," a voice from behind said. The three whirled around to see a very large and a very small figure standing in the doorway. The improbable pair made their way closer to the three.

"It is good to meet with you again, Ben Adams," Nilrem said.

"Yes," Orac echoed, patting Ben on the back. The giant nearly knocked Ben over with each strike.

Ben raised his hand. "Enough, big guy," he said, as he placed his right foot forward to keep from toppling over.

"I am sorry, small one," Orac said.

"No problem," Ben said, with a cough. He looked at Nilrem. "Good to see you."

"I trust you have come to a decision," Nilrem said.

"I think so," Ben said. "Allow me to introduce my friends. This is my wife, Eve."

"An unexpected pleasure," Nilrem said, taking her hand and gracing it with a kiss.

Eve smiled and turned to look at Ben.

Orac placed a hand on her shoulder. "It pleases me to meet you."

Eve nodded.

"And this is Pete," Ben said.

"Ah, the Rock," Nilrem said, pressing Pete's hand against his forehead.

Pete looked at Ben and mouthed, "*The rock?*" He smiled and shrugged his shoulders.

"Now," Nilrem said, "tell me your decision."

Ben nodded. "We're with you."

"Excellent," Nilrem said. "Please tell me what brought you to this conclusion."

"Caleb allowed us to read *The Book of the Chosen*," Ben said.

"And this convinced you?" Nilrem replied.

"Yes," Ben said.

"I am curious," Nilrem said. "What parts of the book did you examine?"

"The passage you relayed concerning the origin of the curse," Ben said, looking a little embarrassed. "And the section containing our exploits proved the book was accurate."

Nilrem smiled. "And these were the only passages?"

"Yes," Ben replied.

"What did your benefactor say about this decision?" Nilrem asked.

"We made no mention to Caleb; we wanted to talk with you first." Ben sighed. "Frankly, we don't know where to begin or where it will take us."

"I will guide you along the path," Nilrem said.

"What about Caleb?" Ben asked. "Shouldn't we enlist his services?"

A grim smile crossed Nilrem's face. "I asked you on the passages you read in *The Book of the Chosen* for one important reason."

"And?" Pete asked.

"The rock," Nilrem mused, "always quick to speak."

"I'm sorry to interrupt," Pete said. "I just want to understand what we're getting into."

"Do not apologize," Nilrem said, "for such is your nature." He smiled and nodded toward Pete. "I will gladly answer your question." Nilrem turned his attention back to Ben. "Had you read further you would have seen the demise of the tall ones. They found The Three, but would not join them in the one true cause."

"I don't understand," Ben said. "Why wouldn't Caleb band together with us, if in fact, it was best for all concerned?"

"I know not," Nilrem said. "Sadly, I read only the truth that is written."

"I don't want to fight Caleb," Ben said.

"Nor do I wish such a thing," Nilrem said, "but alas, there may be no alternative."

"I won't do it," Eve protested. "Caleb has been good to us."

"Do not concern yourself," Nilrem said. "We will avoid a confrontation with Caleb at all costs."

Eve pulled Ben to the side. "We should tell him," she whispered.

"Tell who, what?" Ben countered.

"Caleb," she said, "we owe him that much."

"Not now," Ben said.

Nilrem cleared his throat. "Is there a problem?"

"No," Ben replied, looking at Eve. He turned to face Nilrem. "Not at all. My wife suggested that we should confer with Caleb."

"Do as you wish," Nilrem said, "but know this; Caleb will not join with you and will attempt to sway you from your decision." He looked at Orac and then at Ben. "The choice is yours."

Chapter 16

"I see you have returned," Caleb said, smiling. "The midday meal wanes; come, tell me of your travels."

"Sure," Ben said.

The group moved into what they now called the mess hall, seated themselves, and began to dine on assorted fare.

"Wow," Pete exclaimed. "What a spread!"

"Yes," Caleb said, "the condemned should enjoy a fine meal."

Three heads jerked to face Caleb.

"What does that mean?" Eve stammered.

Caleb reclined in his chair, placing his thumb under his chin and his index finger along his cheek. "Perhaps you should tell me," he replied, his demeanor still jovial.

The three looked at each other, unsure of what to say.

"I'm not sure what you mean," Ben said. He stirred nervously in his chair.

Caleb sat fully upright, glaring at The Three.

"You have given audience to the enemy," he said. "Impart to me what you will."

Ben placed his arms on the table, steadying himself to answer what he perceived as Caleb's challenge. Taking a deep breath and looking at his comrades and then at Caleb, he began. "Caleb, you speak the truth when you talk of our absence." Ben hesitated, searching for the right words. He gathered himself and looked at Caleb. "However, to call the ones with which we choose to ally ourselves the enemy is not at all the correct conclusion."

"Then enlighten me," Caleb replied.

"Caleb . . ." Eve said.

Caleb glared at Eve. "I speak to Ben Adams only."

Eve backed down.

Caleb looked at Ben, his eyes burning with fire. "I no longer require a response," Caleb said. Four of his men entered the room with crossbows drawn, surrounding the table.

"Caleb," Ben said, "give me a chance to explain."

"Have you not made up your mind?"

"Well, yes," Ben said, with some hesitation.

"Then I would ask you to take your leave."

"Don't do this, Caleb," Ben implored.

"Either you are with me," Caleb said, "or against me. It cannot be both ways."

"Please," Eve pleaded.

"Enough," Caleb said. "Escort these three to the end of the village."

The three stood. "Can't I change your mind?" Ben asked.

"I should ask you the same," Caleb replied.

The four men moved in, herding The Three to the door.

Ben turned. "I trust we will meet again," he said, pausing at the threshold. "I can't promise the outcome will be of your liking."

Caleb squinted. "That will be totally up to you, Ben Adams."

Ben nodded. The four men took The Three through the door and to the edge of the settlement. Once there, they bade them a silent farewell.

Caleb stood in sorrow, contemplating the future. A slender nose nudged his hand. He knelt. "Dear friend, what we have feared has come to pass."

The creature whimpered and began to click.

"To banish them was the only course. In no other way would they learn." Seeka replied in nuckta fashion.

Caleb smiled grimly. "If they do not, they become an enemy of the Great One, and therefore, my enemy as well." Caleb stood. "You can be of service, my friend. What I wish of you is to follow. Stay hidden, unless it becomes necessary for you to be seen."

Seeka nodded and clicked, all the while backing away. The familiar yellow ball appeared and encompassed the creature. The orb pulsated until Seeka disappeared.

"Farewell, my friend. Take care of yourself and of the wards I have entrusted unto you." He lingered several minutes after Seeka had gone. "If you fail, my friend, I fear the next passage written in *The Book of the Chosen* will be penned in the blood of The Three."

Chapter 17

"Pretty rude, if you ask me," Pete complained. "He didn't give you a chance to tell your side of the story."

Ben nodded, and the three continued on without speaking.

"Ben," Eve said, breaking the silence, "do you think we're doing the right thing?"

"Little late for that, isn't it?" Ben replied.

"I can't help wondering if we should have stayed with Caleb."

"You heard what he said. Staying was not an option."

"Yeah," was the only reply Eve could muster.

"As abruptly as we left," Pete said, "we had no plans to rendezvous with Nilrem. How are we going to find him?"

"Don't know," Ben said, "but for now we need to find a place to bed down for the night."

The Three came to a small glade. They still retained the horses and supplies Belac shared with them several days before. Within an hour they had a makeshift camp. The Three sat staring into the dancing flames of the fire.

Ben sighed. "Let's get some sleep. No telling what tomorrow will bring."

Ben awoke to a heavenly aroma. "I must be dreaming. I haven't smelled bacon since I was on the *Morning Star*."

"You are quite awake," a familiar, yet out of place voice said.

Ben sprang up, opening his eyes. "Nilrem, Orac, you startled me out of three years' growth."

"I must apologize," Nilrem said.

"That's okay," Ben said, rubbing his face. He pulled himself up, resting on his knees. He looked back and forth, between the sizzling bacon and Nilrem.

"Could I interest you in something to eat?" Nilrem said.

Ben rubbed his hands together. "I thought you'd never ask."

"While I finish cooking the morning meal," Orac said, "perhaps you should awaken your comrades."

"Sure," Ben said. Within minutes the three were watching Orac prepare what looked to be an omelet.

"What kind of egg is that?" Eve asked.

Orac held a large, red, brown, and white, mottled egg. "This is from a creature known as a toleco."

A puzzled expression overtook The Three.

Orac chuckled. "Allow me to clarify. The toleco is a four-footed animal with a thrice-cloven hoof, the flesh of which is inedible. In fact, it would be fatal to you or me."

"That egg is huge," Eve said. "How big is a toleco?"

"The same size as your horse," Orac replied, "but with a disposition much less docile."

"Do you raise them?" Pete inquired.

"Oh, no;" Orac said, "domestication was attempted long ago with no success; now they run wild. During their breeding season, we raid the nests to procure these delicacies." Orac portioned out the meal, handing a plate to each.

"Wow," Eve exclaimed, "calling this a delicacy is an understatement."

"Is there cream in this?" Pete asked.

"No;" Orac replied, "that is the natural texture of the embryo itself."

"Enjoy;" Nilrem said, "for the season wanes, and it will be some time before these are available again." He set his plate down and brushed crumbs from his lap. "Now, there are more important things to concern ourselves with."

"Of course;" Ben said, doing likewise, "you have the floor."

"If I understand you," Nilrem said, "I will initiate."

Ben nodded.

"My first is a question," Nilrem said. He stood facing The Three. "I trust that, since you are here, Caleb has rejected your proposal?"

"Rejected is hardly the word," Ben said. "He refused to listen to anything we had to say. His decision was already made."

"Just the way of the self-righteous," Nilrem replied, shaking his head.

"What do you mean?" Eve inquired.

"My dear," Nilrem began, "some reason that theirs is the only way, without giving credence to another's perception."

"I never thought of Caleb as being that way," Eve said. "He treated us with care and dignity."

"Even the best intentions are often distorted when one puts himself at the head," Nilrem said.

Pete heard a faint growl. "What was that?" he said, whirling toward the sound.

"It would seem that a storm is on the horizon," Orac said.

"A storm of proportions which we have never seen," Nilrem echoed.

"That was no cloud," Pete said. "It was alive."

"Yes," Nilrem said, "alive indeed."

"It's the presence I felt in the dome, isn't it?" Ben asked.

"Yes," Nilrem replied.

"It's also the thing that pushed me in the cave, and the riders we experienced just before we met Caleb," Ben stated.

"Again, yes," Nilrem said. "Now what do you know of this presence?"

"What Caleb imparted," Ben said. "The riders, according to Caleb, were new creations sent to serve Orac. As they mature, Eve, Pete, and I will gradually be able to see them."

"They also will be visible to Orac and me," Nilrem said.

"Caleb made no mention of that," Ben replied.

"He speaks the truth, your Caleb does," Nilrem said. "To your detriment, he kept key portions of the truth to himself."

"The curse?" Pete asked.

"Allow me to introduce your new subordinates," Nilrem said, ignoring Pete's question and rising to his feet.

Surrounding the camp were six massive, translucent figures.

"What are they?" Eve asked, moving closer to Ben.

"The riders," he replied.

"It's hard to determine what they are," Pete said. "They're still closer to invisible than visible, but I'm getting the impression of a rhinoceros." He looked at Ben. "I'm afraid to guess what may ride it."

Eve shuddered. "I choose not to; my curiosity warns against."

"Now, now," Nilrem said, "you will grow to rely on these six with your lives. Please treat them in such a way which keeps that in mind."

Orac walked to one of the creatures and rubbed its head while conversing with the nearly invisible rider standing beside the beast.

"They seem to identify with each other," Ben said.

"Like-minded causes bring with them an air of familiarity," Nilrem said.

Orac left the aberration and joined Nilrem. "They are ready to begin."

"And so it shall," Nilrem said.

"Begin what?" Ben asked.

"The fulfillment of destiny," Nilrem replied.

Ben could feel the riders thunder out of camp. "Would you mind explaining in a little more detail," Ben insisted. "I have a right to know where they're going."

"Dear Ben," Nilrem said, "do not worry yourself over such things. The riders begin to gather reconnaissance on those who would resist the heir to the prophecy."

"You mean Caleb," Ben said.

"Whoever chooses to defy Orac," Nilrem said. "Now, come with me, and I will show you your new quarters."

Chapter 18

Seeka urgently clicked the warning to Caleb.

"Thank you, my friend," Caleb said. He stooped down, taking the animal's head in his hands. "I do not know how to fight what cannot be seen. If this is the last time we shall meet, you have done well."

Tears welled in the nuckta's eyes.

"Fear not for me," Caleb said. "You must return to The Three; they will need your counsel."

Seeka nodded and disappeared again.

Caleb left to gather his men amidst the storm of hoofbeats.

Chapter 19

"Nice digs," Eve said. "These are the best accommodations we've had since we arrived." She walked around the room, touching the furnishings. "Can you believe it—real beds, with real covers, and separate rooms with real doors?"

"That's not all," Pete replied. "We have a private bathroom, and a table and chairs." He looked at the lavatory fixtures. "They're primitive, but I'm sure they'll do."

Ben peered into the bathroom. "If I could take you to the established place, I'd show you primitive." Ben motioned for Eve and Pete to join him at the table.

The three set themselves down.

"Even the chairs are comfortable," Eve said.

Pete nodded and then looked at Ben. "What's up?"

"Are you two comfortable with this?" Ben asked.

"Sure," Eve said, "in this day and age, we're living in the lap of luxury."

"That's not what he's talking about," Pete said, looking at Ben. "Go ahead," he urged, "What's on your mind?"

"You're right," Ben said. "It's not about this place."

"What do you mean?" Eve asked.

"What I mean," Ben said, "is Nilrem, Orac and the riders. Are you two feeling right about being here and with what's going on?"

"Ben," Eve said, "we're here because of your insistence."

"I know," Ben replied, "but I'm having second thoughts."

"Evidently you know more than we do," Pete said. "Maybe you should start by filling us in."

"You didn't hear what Nilrem said while we were still in the camp?" Ben said.

"No," Pete and Eve said in unison.

"Nilrem was talking to you," Pete said. "We want to respect any private transfer of information until you convey that information to us."

"I appreciate your loyalty," Ben said. He stood and walked around the table, "After Orac talked with one of the riders, the six aberrations left. I asked Nilrem where they were going. He said they would gather reconnaissance on enemies of Orac."

"And you didn't believe him?" Pete asked

"No," Ben said, "not at all."

"What did he say that made you doubt?" Eve asked.

"It wasn't just what he said; it was how he said it," Ben replied. "Aside from being condescending, he gave me the impression he had gotten us out of the way."

"Out of whose way?" Pete asked.

"Out of *his* way," Ben said, "Think about it. We're three less to contend with if we're on his side."

"Caleb?" Eve asked.

Ben nodded. "I remember Caleb telling us we were the only ones who could see the riders. With us out of the way, Caleb might as well be fighting the wind."

"Oh, no," Eve said. "What have we done?"

"Calm down;" Pete replied, "we're not sure that's where they've gone,"

"Pete's right," Ben said. "Until we find out, we play along."

"Ben," Eve said, "would learning anything new make a difference? Either we're with Caleb or we're with Nilrem."

Ben stood. "I need time alone; I'll be back." He kissed Eve's forehead and touched Pete's shoulder as he left the building.

Eve watched her husband depart. "Indecisiveness is something I've never seen in Ben."

"The burden of leadership," Pete said. "He takes everything personally."

"Would you have it any other way?" Eve asked.

"Not from someone I'm following," Pete said.

♦♦♦

Ben paced aimlessly along the dirt paths that ran around the buildings. The place was too small to call a village. It was more like an outpost, boasting four modest-sized buildings. At the moment, the streets and buildings, save for his, were both unoccupied.

"What's wrong with me?" Ben grumbled. "I've never experienced abandonment. Not even when I was alone in the *Orion*, expecting to die." He looked toward the heavens. "I don't suppose you're taking requests tonight." He chuckled, shaking his head. "Nah, I don't guess you are, and I can't say as I blame you."

"Your lack of trust is great," a strange voice said.

Ben whirled around. Two eyes hovering several feet off the ground stared back at him. "Who, or better yet, what are you?"

"Caleb sent me to provide counsel," the strange voice said.

"Caleb—" Ben squawked, "is he okay?"

A furry body materialized around the odd-shaped, yellow eyes. "Return to your group," the nuckta said. "The answer to your question will arrive soon."

"Seeka!" Ben exclaimed.

"That is all for now," Seeka said, and then faded from sight.

Ben could feel the ground rumble. "The riders," he whispered.

"I saw him," Ben stammered. "He spoke to me."

"Calm down and tell me who you're talking about," Eve said.

"That creature of Caleb's," Ben said. "I could understand what he was saying."

"Seeka?" she asked.

"Yes," Ben said.

Eve smiled. "Well, tell me all about it."

Ben glared at her. "You don't believe me."

Pete eyed Eve with a quizzical expression.

"Of course I do," Eve said, the sarcasm evident in her voice.

The room filled with a bright yellow light and faded back to normal. The nuckta appeared in the corner, shook his head and trotted toward The Three.

"Seeka," Eve said, "is that you?"

"No time," he replied, moving straight to Ben. "They have arrived; listen."

The riders lumbered past, coming to a halt at the structure farthest from The Three's quarters.

Eve hadn't noticed the hoofbeats. She was too busy gawking at the small creature talking to Ben.

"Let's go, people," Ben said.

"Where?" Pete asked.

"Re-con," Ben said. He disappeared out of the building.

Pete stopped at the door, turning to locate Eve. "You coming?"

She stood, unmoving, still enthralled by the talking nuckta.

"Eve," Pete shouted.

"Yeah," she replied, partially recovering from her entrancement.

"Are you coming?" he repeated.

"Oh, yeah, sure," she answered, robotically moving toward Pete.

The Three and Seeka gathered just outside their quarters.

"It's almost dark," Ben said. "Once the light is gone, we'll move to the last building and glean any bit of information we can."

"It's time," Ben said. "I think it best if we split up, surround the building and meet back in our room to discuss. Pete, work your way around front. I'll take the back, and Eve . . . " Seeka and Eve were deep in conversation. Ben grunted. "Could you break away for a moment to join us?"

"Sorry," Eve said. "He's so fascinating to—"

"Save it," Ben said

Seeka joined the group. "Forgive—"

"I expect more out of you," Ben chastised. He looked harshly at both and continued.

"Eve, station yourself at the end of the structure closest to us."

Eve nodded.

"Seeka," Ben said, "you can get into places that we wouldn't dare. Proceed as you see fit."

Seeka also nodded.

"Meet back here in half an hour," Ben said.

The group parted and made their way toward the target.

"It's been an hour or more, and he's not back," Eve said.

"He'll be here," Pete replied.

Ben nodded and sat quietly.

"I beg your forgiveness," Seeka said. He moved away from the diminishing yellow glow and joined The Three. "I required additional time. It was necessary to assess the situation."

"Okay," Ben said. "Eve, you first."

"Not much," Eve replied. "There were no windows on the end of the building you assigned me, but I detected voices, and think one of them may have been Caleb."

"Okay," Ben said. "Pete?"

"Not a lot more to tell," he said. "There were partitions that concealed the occupants from sight. Like Eve, I heard Caleb and at least three or four other voices that spoke in the same dialect."

"His men?" Ben asked.

"That's my guess," Pete replied.

Ben nodded. "I have nothing to add, but did either of you notice what we didn't hear?"

"I'm not following you," Pete said.

"Orac," Ben said. "Nilrem interrogated Caleb and his men; at least that's how I perceived it, but I didn't get the impression that Orac was there."

"Nilrem does all the talking anyway," Eve said. "Perhaps Orac was there and just silent as usual."

"I don't know;" Ben said. "it doesn't feel right."

"Since when did you rely on intuition?" Eve asked.

"Your Ben is correct," Seeka interrupted. "Orac was not there. Caleb and three of his men were detained by four of the riders. Nilrem asked the four; however, up to this point he has been unable to extract information." Seeka lowered his head. "I fear that Nilrem may resort to more drastic measures to obtain the information he seeks."

"What information?" Eve asked.

Seeka stared at her. "The Established Place," Seeka said.

"The Established Place!" Eve exclaimed. "What good could that possibly do him?"

"Nilrem has discovered the power of the krang," Seeka said.

"The krang!" Eve said. She turned toward Ben. "That's what Belac used to send Pete to help you."

"Well, this is the first I've heard of it," Ben said. "So why don't you explain."

Eve sat down. Following her cue, Ben and Pete joined her.

Seeka jumped to the top of the table. Now at eye level with The Three, he began to speak. "The krang is the power to move from one's present dimension to alternate dimensions."

"Do you mean time travel?" Ben inquired.

"In a sense;" Seeka replied, "though not physically. When one is in this state, he may move the essence of the mind to the desired realm and influence whomever he wishes."

"And The Established Place?" Eve asked.

"Nilrem will stop at nothing to ensure his rise to power," Seeka said. "He had hoped to avoid the fulfillment of the prophecy through The Three by turning you against Caleb." Seeka paced back and forth lengthwise on the table, alternating glances at The Three. "Nilrem fears that your betrayal to Caleb will not serve his purpose; therefore, he searches for the exact point in time in which The Established Place exists. With this information, he hopes to accomplish what Eleazor was not strong enough to do during that point in his evolution."

"And that would be?" Ben asked.

"To influence The Three, avoiding your entrance into this world, and therefore nullifying the prophecy."

"He can do that?" Eve asked.

"Yes;" Seeka said, "though I'm afraid Caleb would die rather than reveal the location of The Established Place."

"What about the curse?" Ben asked. "How can you explain that? I read it for myself in *The Book of the Chosen*."

"Nilrem used those words for his own end and to confuse The Three," Seeka said. "The curse pertains to Nilrem himself."

"Please explain," Ben said.

"The Three are to join with Orac," Seeka said. "This alliance will battle against Nilrem and his forces. *The Book of the Chosen* is a living book. It speaks to each of us in different ways, but always with the Great One's desire planted firmly in our being. Without this understanding, the words are open to evil interpretations outside of what the Great One plans for each of us. Had you opened yourself to this notion as you read the words, you would have known this. However, you were convinced that Nilrem was correct. To your detriment, that was the direction you took as you saw the words for yourself."

"That may be true," Ben said, "but Orac has allied himself with Nilrem."

"Yes;" Seeka said, "however, this was accomplished through misrepresentation as well. Orac's heart is not as dark as the one he calls Father."

"Is that why Orac was not present with Nilrem and the riders?" Ben asked.

"Again, yes," Seeka said. "Orac is being confined in the building adjacent to Caleb's holding place by the two remaining riders. Their beasts also reside there."

Ben sighed. "What's done is done," he said. "Our priority lies with Caleb, and then Orac."

"Yes," Seeka said. "If Nilrem does not get what he wants soon, he will resort to using the Kumult."

"Eleazor used that on Ben and me," Pete said. "It would have worked too, had Belac not gotten us away from him when he did."

"And if used for an extended period, or in sufficient quantities," Seeka said, "the effects become irreversible."

"We should not let on that we know this," Ben said. "The element of surprise might work to our advantage."

"We must not tarry," Seeka said. "Nilrem will engage torture to enhance the Kumult."

"What about the riders?" Pete asked. "Is there any way to destroy them?"

"No," Seeka said, "the destruction of the riders will be complete when the Living One returns the final time. Until then, they can only be dispatched to other areas."

"How do we accomplish that?" Ben asked.

Seeka jerked, his eyes rolling back into his head. The nuckta shook and then recovered.

"Seeka!" Eve screeched, standing and leaning over the creature.

"I fear it is too late," Seeka said, looking at Ben. "All may be lost."

"What is it?" Ben insisted. "What happened?"

"Caleb;" Seeka said, "he is free."

"That's great," Eve said.

"No," Seeka said, "you do not understand. Nilrem has extricated the information from Caleb and has invoked the power of the krang."

"Let's find Caleb," Pete said. "Maybe he can help."

"Caleb is under the influence of the Kumult," Seeka said, "and now deep within the control of Nilrem." He sat back on his haunches and sighed. "I have no doubt Caleb and his men will soon find us."

Ben didn't notice the parchment lying neatly on an unoccupied chair when the group left the building.

Chapter 20
Parallel Dimension II

(Parallel dimension aboard the *Morning Star* referenced from first book, *Rising Tide*)

"Mr. Davis," Evans barked, "prepare for departure."

"But, Captain," Stewart replied, "the new crew members have yet to arrive."

"Precisely," Evans said. "I received new orders, and the recruits are no longer necessary."

"What about the sealed envelopes?" Stewart asked. "I thought they were our new orders."

Evans glared at the helmsman. "I do not entertain commands from unseen persons who sneak aboard my vessel and deposit erroneous instructions in the hope that I will cooperate." He produced both envelopes and dropped them into the trash. "And remember this, Davis," he said, pointing a shaking finger, "I do not take orders from you." He turned his back on Stewart. "Prepare for departure," Evans hissed.

Stewart came to attention. "Yes, sir."

Evans winced as a voice inside his brain began to dole out instructions that he would soon have no choice but to follow. Lowering his head, he began to rub his eyes. "Mr. Davis, I'm not feeling well, I'll be in my cabin." Evans reached the wheelhouse door. "On second thought, wait for the two recruits; you may need help to operate the ship."

Stewart grinned smugly. "Of course, sir."

Evans stumbled into his cabin, made his way to his chair and grabbed a bottle of wine. As he turned the corkscrew, he winced in pain. He withdrew the cork, emptied the bottle and reached for another. "I know exactly how to clear this head," he said, turning the bottom of the second bottle skyward.

Chapter 21
Parallel Dimension I

(Return to *Deadly Reign*)

The Three pushed their mounts deeper into the forest. Seeka sat between Ben's legs, his foreclaws digging into the horse's mane. After an hour's ride, Ben slowed and then came to a halt.

"Seeka," he said, "tell us what you can."

"By now, Nilrem has entered the point in time in which The Established Place exists. The riders will surround him to keep their leader safe while he extends his mind into the distant realm, searching for one to control."

"Why does Nilrem need protection?" Eve inquired.

"Nilrem exists in a catatonic state as he displaces his essence to other regions," Seeka said. "It is during this time he is at his most vulnerable."

"Then we should use this time to attack," Pete said. "It's the weak spot we were looking for." He looked at Ben, his eyes fixated with determination. "Why have we been running?"

"If it were only so simple," Seeka said.

"It's seems cut and dried," Pete said, his irritation growing.

"No," Seeka said, "if Caleb had not succumbed to the Kumult, freedom would have eluded him, possibly to the point of death."

"How do you know that he was?" Eve asked. "Maybe all of this was unnecessary."

"I share a deep connection with Caleb;" Seeka said, "one that would be impossible to explain. I also hold an equally deep understanding of the krang." Seeka rose, placing his forepaws on top of Ben's shoulder. "Know that what I say is true. Nilrem is even now disrupting your presence in this world, and Caleb and his men are most certainly hunting our whereabouts. Caleb is bent on the destruction of anyone who stands in his way, even if he initiates first contact."

"You seem to understand the krang," Ben said. "Just how familiar with it are you?"

"Very," Seeka said. "I am the first to have called upon its power."

"Then you could follow Nilrem?"

"Yes," Seeka replied, "but I dare not do so until Nilrem has returned."

"Seeka," Ben insisted, "if Nilrem is successful, none of this will matter anyway."

"You must understand," Seeka began, "my transformation into alternate dimensions is physical and complete. Nilrem's and my presence in the same location would destabilize both worlds, possibly to the point of utter destruction."

"So we're damned if we do and damned if we don't," Ben moaned.

"Nilrem's venture will not be instantaneous," Seeka said. "He will set events in motion intended to lead to your demise; however, these events will require time to develop."

"So there is time?" Ben asked.

"Yes," Seeka said, "though how much, we cannot be sure."

"Ben," Pete yelled, "they're coming."

"Caleb," Seeka said. He lowered his frame down to Ben's lap.

"That would seem to be our immediate problem," Ben said, looking at Seeka. "I'm open to any suggestions."

Seeka's eyes widened, "Move!"

♦♦♦

Nilrem moaned as his head bobbed up and down.

"The master returns," one rider gurgled.

Nilrem's eyes popped open, closed, and reopened. He gasped and then slumped over in the chair in which he sat. After several minutes, he rose to an upright position. "The end of The Three is set in motion," he said, waving a hand in the air. "Now take me to Orac."

"Father," Orac exclaimed, "why have you imprisoned me?"

Nilrem smiled. "Dear Orac, I tried my best to raise you in the correct manner, but you would not embrace the ways of the Dark One. Therefore, I take it upon myself to assume the role which I for so long have groomed you."

"I do not understand," Orac pleaded.

Nilrem moved closer. "Do not call me Father," he said, backhanding Orac across the mouth. A trickle of blood flowed down the giant's chin.

Orac's eyes burned as he struggled to free himself from the riders' grasp. "Old man," he screamed, "I will kill you myself once I am free."

Nilrem laughed. He grabbed his own beard and pulled, stretching his face into an elongated, grotesque mask.

Orac became still and stared in horror as the skin gave way, and a new creature pushed through the top of Nilrem's skull and continued to grow. Within moments, a huge skinless monster, larger than Orac, stood in place of the slight man. It was ripped from head to toe with massive crimson musculature, the fibers of which twitched and glistened.

"Nilrem!" Orac gasped.

"No longer," the creature roared. "I am Colossac." A mad laughter emanated from the former Nilrem. "Release the imp; he is of no use any longer." Colossac peered down at Orac. "I allow you to live to tell the story and prepare my way," the monster said. "The Three will soon be no more; I have seen to that, and there is no one with the power to stop me." His lips contorted into a kind, almost paternal smile. "We will meet again, dear Orac, and I will crush the life out of you with my own hands." He paused. "Now go!"

Chapter 22

Ben brought his mount to a halt fifty yards from their previous position.

"Why are we . . ." Eve began.

"Shh," Ben warned.

The three waited silently as Caleb and his men thundered by.

"Sorry," Eve said.

"Will you ever learn not to question my actions?" Ben asked.

"Not as long as we're married," Eve replied.

"Hmm," Ben grunted. "Listen up everyone. We're going to double back to the outpost; that'll be the safest place for now."

"Are you sure?" Eve asked.

"Anyone who thinks otherwise can stay here," Ben said, glaring at Eve.

"Ben," Seeka said, "a stream ran close to the outpost. It should be no more than a few hundred feet to the west. Perhaps it would be prudent to follow it back."

"Good boy," Ben said, rubbing the animal's head. "The water it is."

"We must be getting close by now," Pete said.

"Indeed, we are," Seeka replied.

"Stop," Ben said. The group came to a halt. "Listen."

The sound of splashing could be heard, growing closer with each swish of water.

"Everybody out of the pool," Ben instructed. The three moved up onto the bank and waited.

A yellow glow centered over the stream came into view, growing brighter as it neared The Three.

"Look," Eve said, "there's someone in the water, and an orb is moving along with him."

"Wait until they get closer," Ben said. "Maybe we can tell who it is."

"No need," Seeka said. "It is Orac."

"Orac," Pete echoed, removing his bow from his shoulder. Eve did the same.

Ben looked at both. "I don't think that's going to be necessary,"

"Intuition again?" Eve asked.

Ben nodded.

"I'll hold onto it just the same," she said. "Forgive me if I don't trust you like you seem to trust you."

Ben chuckled. "Suit yourself."

Orac reached a point parallel to The Three. The orb began to drift to his right, moving toward Ben's position.

Orac stopped and watched the sphere retreat. "Do you wish that I would follow, is that it?" He paused as if waiting for an answer. "Well, you have led me thus far; I suppose that I will continue to follow." He climbed the embankment, took several steps and then froze. The orb illuminated the area, hovering over three mounted figures.

"I beg your forgiveness, travelers;" the perplexed Orac said, "I did not wish to disturb your gathering."

"Orac," Ben said, "it is The Three, and we beg your council."

"Ben, is it truly you?"

"Yes, it's me."

Orac made haste to The Three. "You should not be here; you and your companions are in jeopardy."

"I appreciate your concern," Ben said, "but—"

"We should not speak in this place," Seeka cautioned, peering around. "I fear that the very air we breathe may betray us."

"Where else is there?" Pete asked.

"Come," Orac said, "I will take you to a place where even my father—" he paused, shaking his head, "even the monster does not know of."

"Can we trust him?" Pete asked.

"What choice do we—"

"Yes," Ben interrupted. "Orac, we follow you."

"There's your answer," Eve mumbled.

"I spent much of my childhood and even more of my later times here," Orac said, as the party stopped in front of a large stone formation.

"Hanging around a rock?" Pete asked.

"No," Orac said, "follow me, and I will show you." He headed to the right side of the outcrop and disappeared into an opening. The others hesitated. Orac pushed his head outside of the entrance. "Please come and bring your mounts; there is room for all." He ducked back into the cave.

"Well," Pete said, "what's the call?"

"We go in," Ben said.

"Of course," Eve replied. "Why not?" She moved her horse forward and entered the cave first.

Pete looked at Ben, nodded, and the remaining two of The Three entered the cave.

Chapter 23

Colossac stomped into the midst of the gathering. "Are the riders ready?" he demanded, looking for a leader to emerge.

A single translucent figure stepped forward. "Yes, Your Lordship," it gurgled, "we are at your disposal."

"What are you called?" Colossac asked.

"Cahotic," the rider replied.

"Your resolution is progressing nicely." Colossac scanned the figure standing before him. "What once was featureless is now more discernable."

"Yes, Your Lordship," Cahotic said, subtly bowing. "Soon I will be visible to those who would see me."

"I will be the only one," Colossac said.

"What of The Three?" Cahotic asked.

"A mere memory, and soon to be even less."

"I follow the true one," Cahotic said, with another slight bow.

"You will be my second," Colossac said, placing a hand on the aberration's shoulder. "All others will answer to you."

"Thank you," Cahotic said, dropping to one knee. "What does my master wish?"

"Assemble your subordinates. You are to construct an air-fed fire pit, and with your knowledge of weaponry, you will forge six swords. With these, we will litter our trail of destruction with all who would stand in our way."

Cahotic darkened, becoming more visible, as did the riders.

Chapter 24

Pinning the dead mammal down with its talons, the bird's hooked beak ripped a small piece of flesh from the carcass. It turned its head upward and swallowed. The esophageal muscles rippled, causing the neck feathers to flutter until the piece of meat plopped into the acid-filled stomach and disintegrated. Moving through the digestive tract and breaking down into minute particles, it entered the circulatory system to fuel the metabolic functions. The flesh of the devoured contained a large percentage of toxicity. By design, the bird's digestive processes further concentrated these toxins in elastic membranes located in the wings. The liquid entered and was altered, absorbing compounds from the lining of these holding sacs and forming a flammable, unstable solution. Once this organic fuel mixed with air in two bone-lined exit ports, a bioluminescent charge would produce a spark. This ignited the fuel and produced thrust capable of pushing the host to near supersonic speeds.

The process of tearing and swallowing continued until nothing but bone and the tendor's eyeballs (being indigestible) remained. After consuming the tendor, the karron eyed the small group of large figures below, most of whom were visible. He used his wings in a conventional fashion to lift off the branch. As soon as he was out of the ground dwellers' sight, two lights pushed him deep into the night.

Chapter 25

The cave opened into a large area lit by the fire Orac had just kindled. Eve dismounted and was now kneeling beside Orac. He fed the flames, turning the meager fire into a blaze.

Ben and Pete joined the now standing giant. Eve remained in a kneeling position, staring at the fire.

"Nice," Pete commented, admiring his surroundings. "You say no one knows about this place?"

"No one," Orac replied.

"You said something about a monster earlier," Ben said. "What was that about?"

Orac lowered his head. "The one I once called father is now the monster."

"Tell us," Ben said.

Orac stood for several minutes and then sat down on the dirt floor. "Very well," he said.

Ben and Pete both lowered themselves to a squat position, facing Orac. Upon hearing the giant, Eve left the fire and joined her companions.

"I called him father for as long as I can remember," Orac said. He paused, wiping a tear from his eye.

"Please continue when you're ready," Ben said.

Orac nodded, and moments later spoke. "I protested when Nilrem instructed the riders to invade Caleb's village. I told him it was unnecessary to kill all who resisted, but to take prisoners for questioning. He instructed two of the riders to detain me. The other four left without further instruction," Orac smiled. "Thankfully so. The riders brought Caleb and three of his followers back. As far as I know, no one suffered any injuries."

"What about Nilrem?" Pete asked.

"The one I called father moved me to a separate location while he questioned the prisoners. I had no way of knowing what transpired during the interrogation, but I sensed he possessed a quantity of the Kumult and thought he might use it."

"It turns out you were right," Ben said.

Orac nodded and smiled grimly. "When Nilrem came to me, he was not the same man I had known as my father. I can only assume that he was exhibiting his true self and not the persona he had used to deceive me for so long."

Seeka now moved in and settled close to Ben.

"Ah," Orac said, smiling, "I see that the myth lives."

"What do you mean?" Ben asked.

"Even as a yearling," Orac said, "I was regaled with tales of the mythical nuckta. I never considered these stories to be factual; however, in recent days, Nilrem seems to have developed an obsession for these small creatures."

"In what way?" Ben asked.

"That if any existed, they must be destroyed at all costs." He reached out and rubbed Seeka's head. "If the stories are true, and I now know they are, I understand why the monster wanted you out of the way."

"Orac," Ben said, "please finish your original story."

"Of course," Orac said. "After a brief encounter, Nilrem emerged from his skin, growing into a raw being even larger than myself. He called himself Colossac."

"Raw?" Pete inquired.

"Yes," Orac said, "a form without skin."

Eve cringed at the thought.

"What can you tell us of the riders?" Seeka asked. "Are there any weaknesses we may exploit to defeat them? I would also ask you the same concerning Colossac."

Orac wrinkled his forehead and rubbed his chin in deep thought. "There may be," he said after some consideration, "though I am not sure. Nilrem was concerned that they may get caught in the water that falls from the sky before they first arrived in our settlement. Once the riders had reached our destination, they would avoid the river that ran in back. It was forbidden to store water in any place they occupied. That is why I followed the stream when I departed. I could not be sure if it would offer any protection, though, I hoped that it might."

"Water?" Ben asked, pondering its viability as a weapon.

"Yes," Orac replied, "however, I do not know what effect it will have, or even the quantity it will require."

"I will ask once again," Seeka said. "What of Colossac?"

"I can speculate," Orac said. "The colossac is also a mythical creature that lived in my stories as a yearling. According to the tales, the body is impervious to injury. Its head is the most vulnerable, and it can be completely destroyed through decapitation."

"Are you sorry you asked?" Ben inquired.

"Hmm," Seeka replied.

"Colossac also said that The Three would soon be no more," Orac added, "and that they would even be erased from memory."

"The krang?" Ben asked, looking at Seeka.

"Yes," the nuckta replied, "Colossac has returned and has implemented his plan."

"Does that mean what I think it means?" Ben asked.

Seeka looked at Ben. "You will need to enlist Caleb's help. Once this is done, turn your attention toward the riders and Colossac. I will attempt to retrace Colossac's path and undo the wrongs he has done."

"When will we know?" Ben asked.

"Either way," Seeka said, "you will know."

Ben nodded.

"I must now take my leave," Seeka said. "I will contact you." The nuckta backed away as the yellow orb waned.

The three watched as he faded.

"Take heart, dear ones," Seeka said. "Look to the Great One."

Chapter 26

"The trail has been lost," Caleb said, his normally calm demeanor now influenced by the Kumult. "Menday," he shouted, "to me!"

A man maneuvered his horse beside Caleb's. "Yes, Caleb."

"Menday," Caleb said, "the trail is now cold. Please explain."

"I cannot."

Caleb looked away and then back, grabbing Menday by the throat. "I will no longer tolerate your arrogance," he snarled. "If you cannot perform in the capacity of leader to which I have so graciously appointed you, then let me know now." He pulled Menday closer and glared into his eyes. "Take care in your answer, for I will kill you as you sit." Caleb continued his gaze. "My words are a promise," he said. "However, you may regard them as you will."

"Yes," Menday said hoarsely, "I will."

"You will what?" Caleb pressed.

"Make you proud of the trust you have placed in me." Menday strained, his face discoloring from the restricted airflow.

"Most excellent reply," Caleb stated, releasing his grip and allowing Menday to slump over, gasping for breath. "If you are done lounging, lead me to The Three, or I shall fulfill my promise." He kicked his horse and left Menday to ponder his words.

Menday raised his head from the tangle of his horse's mane. True sorrow filled his heart as he watched his friend retreat.

Chapter 27

"The small furry one is gone," Orac said, "but what and where is the Great One?"

Ben patted the still sitting giant on the shoulder. "You and I require more time to learn just the basics of this world. Let's unpack the horses and get something to eat."

Orac stood. "I possess necessities here. Perhaps we should use the provisions I have stored and leave your packs as they are."

Ben considered Orac's comment. "Yes," he said, and then looked at Pete.

Pete nodded. "We'll need supplies down the line, and if they're already packed—"

Ben nodded in agreement.

"Good," Orac said, "I am not such a bad cook." He moved toward another doorway leading from the main area. Stopping, he turned to look at The Three. "I will return soon and take care of you as you have done for me."

Eve turned to Ben. "I thought he was supposed to be our great enemy?"

"Not according to Seeka," Ben said, scratching his head. "And right now, he's got my vote."

"This is delicious," Eve said.

"Many thanks," Orac replied. "It is a dish of my own devising."

"What is it?" Pete asked.

"A crustacean that lives on the beachfront."

"Did you say beach?" Pete asked.

"The sea is but a short walk from here," Orac said, looking down at his legs and then up again smiling, "at least for one such as I. There are many creatures that remain in the sand after the water leaves them stranded twice each day."

"The tide," Ben said.

"I suppose," Orac said, looking puzzled.

"Please continue," Ben said.

Orac nodded. "I look for signs on the surface and then dig until I find my quarry." He smiled and resumed eating.

Ben looked at Eve and then at Pete, shrugging his shoulders. "Can you tell us about your quarry?"

"Of course," Orac replied. "You must be careful to interpret the surface details correctly." He held up his left hand. The tip of his index finger was missing. "For a normal-sized man, this injury would have equated to a severed hand, or possibly an arm."

Eve gasped. "What happened?"

"The creature I search for, and the one you are dining on, is known as a scoth. What I found was the lankier. You see the sand signature of the scoth is three bubbles in a triangular configuration, with the bubble slightly offset to the right. The lankier's pattern is essentially the same, but with the bubble slightly offset to the left. It developed this similar characteristic to hunt for its food."

"How dangerous is this lankier?" Pete asked.

"Once again, my size saved me." Orac smiled grimly. "Had I been a normal-sized yearling, I would not be here talking with you now." He scratched his head, and raising his eyebrows, thought a moment. "It has been said that the lankier can grow large enough to swallow a man whole, but I have never seen such a thing."

"How big was the one that attacked you?" Eve asked.

Orac wrinkled his forehead and pondered the notion. "Nearly as long as I am tall," he said.

"How do you determine the size, if it's underneath the sand?" Pete asked.

"You cannot," Orac said, "As the lankier attacks, it emerges from the sand, grabs its prey and begins to feed. In the case of the female, she will take her prey unharmed back to her den to insure the young have fresh meat when they hatch."

"Enough talk of sea monsters," Ben interrupted. "There are more important issues at hand."

"Certainly," Orac said. "Has everyone had enough to eat?"

The three nodded in unison.

"We must make plans to enlist Caleb," Ben said, hesitating, "or eliminate him."

"Eliminate him?" Eve exclaimed. "You mean kill him."

A sullen expression spread across Ben's face. "If the power of the Kumult in Caleb is irreversible, we will have no other choice."

"Any ideas?" Pete asked.

"Well, the big guy here will certainly be an asset," Ben replied.

A solitary figure slipped into the cave and then stepped into the light of the fire.

"They've found us," Pete shouted.

The Three stood, loading and aiming their weapons as they did so.

Chapter 28

Colossac carried a plain leather-bound case. He entered the smallest stone structure at a remote corner of the compound where Cahotic awaited his arrival. He set the two-foot-square box on the table.

"Pay attention," Colossac said. "I will not demonstrate this again."

Cahotic moved closer. "As you say, Lord."

"You must have the box in this position with the circle facing you," Colossac said. He took a massive finger and pointed to a one-inch diameter circle imprinted on the center of what was the front of the box.

Cahotic nodded.

Colossac placed his right thumb in an indentation on top of the box. He then placed the middle finger of his left hand on a crease on the left side of the box and pressed the imperfection flat. He rotated his right thumb a quarter turn, and a split appeared, dividing the box in two. Air hissed as if a vacuum seal had broken, releasing a mist that dissipated as it meandered upward. The box continued to open; a red sphere hovered in the center of the container. Colossac placed a fingertip underneath the orb, and it began to rotate. He brought the sphere out of the box and into the center of the room. Removing his finger, the globe remained in that position.

"The sphere is neutrally buoyant in the air," Colossac said. "It can neither rise nor fall on its own."

Cahotic surveyed the rotating sphere and then commented, "In what way does this concern me, Your Lordship?"

"One moment," Colossac said, turning his full attention toward the sphere. Colossac moved the orb back into its protective case. "This unimpressive object controls our very existence."

Cahotic nodded, his expression unchanging.

"Are you certain you understand the implication of this falling into the wrong hands?" Colossac slammed both hands on the table and moved his face within inches of Cahotic. "For at the moment, you seem less than concerned."

"It is my way of instilling confidence in the one who instructs me," Cahotic said, bowing.

"Very well," Colossac said, clutching the box to his chest. "You will follow these instructions to the letter."

What Colossac failed to tell his general was that the sphere he would soon acquire was the essence of the krang. This power would permit one to send his consciousness to alternate dimensions. Colossac also held a marble-sized replica allowing the one possessing it to travel within this present dimension, and with the aid of cryptic symbols, send his essence to alternate dimensions as well. However, Colossac was unaware that the essence of the Krang possessed intelligence and a penchant for good.

Cahotic once again nodded, and the two schemed, their plans destined for different ends.

Chapter 29
Parallel Dimension II

(Aboard the *Morning Star*)

Seeka crept down the narrow corridor moving closer to the voices, the faint yellow glow of his eyes visible. The nuckta neared the space where the chatter emanated, closed his eyes and pushed through the wall, ending up in the room.

"Makes little sense, Stew," Vinny said. "We pick up this Ben guy in the middle of nowhere. Now our nut-job captain has a ship packed with explosives, which, I might add, is headed to a place that doesn't exist according to our charts."

"Look," Stewart said, "if he wants to sail around blowing imaginary islands off the map, that's his business." He looked at Vinny. "At least we're getting paid, and he'll soon turn his attention to something we can sink our teeth into."

"Don't seem right," Vinny said, scratching at a sore on his cheek. "I signed on to this ship for a bigger piece of the pie than that. You said he had something big going."

"He did, but something changed his mind."

"What?" Vinny asked.

"Don't know," Stewart replied. "Evans had sealed envelopes he said were our orders, and then threw them away, stating that he had received new orders. Maybe the envelopes hold a clue."

"What about the warheads and launchers he's loaded on the ship," Vinny asked. "Where did they come from?"

"He had them loaded at the last minute, just before you came aboard."

Vinny nodded. "What about it, Skull, what do you think?"

Skull stared into oblivion, hearing nothing. *It should not have gone this way,* he thought. *I fear it may be over before it begins.*

Chapter 30
Parallel Dimension I

(Return to *Deadly Reign*)

"Kill me if you must," the figure said. "I will not raise a hand against you."

"Drop your weapon," Ben ordered.

The man complied, dropping his crossbow to the ground.

"You're one of Caleb's men," Ben said. "Where is he?"

"I am alone."

"What is your name?" Ben asked.

"I am called Menday," he said, bringing his gaze to focus on Ben. "It is of the utmost urgency I talk with you."

Ben lowered his bow. "Come closer."

Menday hastened his way toward Ben. His speed startled Orac, causing him to take a defensive stance as the newcomer neared.

"I have no quarrel with you," Menday said, as he passed by the giant.

"Speak your peace," Ben said.

Menday covered his chest and bowed. "Caleb remains under the influence of the Kumult. I fear he may not recover."

"Why doesn't the Kumult still affect you?" Ben asked.

"Caleb ingested thrice what my colleagues and I received, a concerted effort placed on extracting information from Caleb and Caleb alone. We were there to reinforce his conversion. Although our part appears temporary, I cannot say the same for my friend."

"You said, 'our' part," Ben inquired. "Have your associates also recovered from the Kumult?"

"Yes, Caleb believes I left the party to scout for signs of your whereabouts, while the others feign loyalty and lead him astray until I return."

"Were you expecting help?" Ben paused, furrowing his eyebrows. "That is, if you were successful in finding us."

"It is what I had hoped for. If I were unsuccessful in locating your whereabouts, our only option would have been to overcome Caleb ourselves."

"Why didn't you do that and then locate The Three?"

"Caleb is a formidable opponent and a dear friend." Menday slumped, sighing as he did so. "I fear the only way to subdue such a man would require force that may injure or even kill."

"I understand," Ben said, nodding. "You know Caleb better than anyone here. You must have something in mind to take him captive with the least amount of danger to all."

"Yes, there is a plan."

Ben gathered everyone close. "Let's hear it."

Chapter 31

"How do you know he's not leading us into a trap?" Eve whispered.

"I don't," Ben said, "but we're getting to the point where we're going to have to trust someone. We need Caleb, and this seems the most logical way to accomplish that."

"Okay," Eve said.

The three stayed back, watching Menday make his way into the camp. Orac circled around, positioning himself behind Caleb.

"Caleb," Menday said, "I have located The Three; however, we must hurry lest they leave the place they have chosen for shelter."

"Sit," Caleb replied, his words coming in slurs. "Drink; there will be time for the hunt later."

"Of course," Menday said. He looked at his two comrades, nodding ever so slightly. They acknowledged his signal and moved to either side of Caleb, who remained on the ground with his back against a small tree.

"Come;" Caleb insisted, "sit and drink with me."

Menday moved closer and squatted down in front of Caleb.

"You know," Caleb said, leaning forward and tenderly pulling Menday close, "if you go through with this, I will kill you before anyone can touch me."

Menday looked down. Caleb had a crossbow dart in his hand, poised to pierce Menday's chest.

Caleb smiled. "Call them off, and I may let you live until—"

A large pair of hands grabbed Caleb's shoulders, jerking him backwards and pinning him to the tree. Caleb let out a mind-numbing cry, pressing his hands to the ground and bringing his legs up and around the tree. He locked them about Orac's neck and pulled his head into the tree, causing Orac to release his grip. The two men on either side moved in, grabbing Caleb's arms. Caleb brought his arms together, knocking his would-be combatants into each other and to the ground. Orac regained his composure and lunged for Caleb, missing as his target somersaulted backward to avoid the giant's grasp. Caleb picked up the fallen dart, plunging it into Menday, as his friend leapt, ending up on top of him.

The three made their way into the thick of the commotion.

Caleb pushed Menday off and stood defiantly, waving his hands in an inviting motion. "Come to me if you wish to die," he beckoned.

Pete released a well-aimed shot, which would have killed Caleb, had Menday not recovered enough to pull Caleb's feet from underneath him. The arrow grazed Caleb's shoulder and then ended its short flight, quivering in the tree beside Orac.

Orac fell on the surprised Caleb, pinning him to the ground, while the others subdued the downed warrior. The giant lifted his great weight off the prostrate Caleb as the men finished binding his hands and feet. Caleb struggled to break free. The two men lifted him to his feet. "I brought one of you down," Caleb snarled, "and soon the rest will follow."

Menday rolled to his back, crimson fluid oozing from his wound. "Dear friend," he pleaded, "it must not be so."

Caleb looked down at Menday, his eyes afire. He opened his mouth to speak and then stopped. His demeanor suddenly softened.

"No," he whispered, "not Menday." He dropped to his knees over the top of his fallen friend. He cupped Menday's face in his bound hands and then looked up at Ben. "What have I done," he moaned, turning his attention back to his comrade.

Menday raised a hand and placed it on Caleb's wrist. "You're back," he whispered, "and that is enough." Menday's grip slipped from Caleb's wrist. He smiled and then closed his eyes.

Chapter 32
Parallel Dimension II

(Aboard the *Morning Star*)

Seeka slipped through a narrow gap in the partially opened door. Ben lay asleep on his bunk as Skull leaned over him, whispering in his ear. Yellow and green flashes bounced off the sleeping man's face. Skull rose, grabbed his jacket and turned to leave. A series of clicking sounds caused him to pause. At his feet, a never-before-seen creature seemed to be attempting to communicate. Skull smiled, knelt down and began to click in response. After a brief conversation, Skull patted Seeka on the head, spoke to Ben one last time and then left in search of Eve.

Seeka crawled underneath Ben's bunk and waited for him to awaken. Before long, he too was breathing in a long slow rhythm.

A woman's voice stirred Seeka from his slumber. He sat patiently, listening until she left. He made his way from underneath the bed, brushing Ben's leg as he did so.

"What!" Ben yelped. Seeka turned and sat down facing the startled man. Ben jumped up and grabbed a chair, raising it over his head. "You're the weirdest rat I've ever seen, but I'll soon take care of that."

"I hope you will change your mind," Seeka said. "I suspect that a blow with the object you hold over your head would be most uncomfortable."

Ben froze and stared at Seeka. He blinked several times. "What did you say?"

"If you place that chair back into its original position, I would be much more apt to engage in conversation."

"Uh, yeah," Ben said, as he lowered the chair.

"Please sit," Seeka implored. "There is much to discuss."

Ben took a seat on his bunk. "Since you're familiar with what you're talking about, and I don't have a clue, maybe you'd better start." Ben shook his head and placed his forehead into his hand. "I don't believe this; I'm talking to an animal."

"Indeed, you are," Seeka replied; "however, 'animal' is a bit awkward. Please call me Seeka."

Ben smiled. "I don't know why this should surprise me," he said. "Everything that's happened on this ship so far is only slightly less weird." He lowered his head and rubbed his hair vigorously. "I guess I'll eventually wake up," he said, rising to face Seeka. "Lay it on me."

"If by 'lay it on me' you mean for me to tell you why I am here, and I presume you do, I accept. I come to make right, what was turned to wrong."

"Come from where?"

"From where you will soon be."

Ben thought a moment. "The future?" he shouted.

"I do not understand your excitement," Seeka replied. "It is as I said."

"Just go on;" Ben said, "tell me why you have come from where I'm soon to be."

Seeka described the events of the past days in the alternate world.

"Whoa," Ben said, pushing his hands toward the newcomer. "Hold on."

Seeka donned a look of concern. "Have I offended in some way?"

"No, but when you started this story, you mentioned that time was of the essence. If you keep telling the tale in the same fashion, I'll have a gray beard by the time you get to the point."

"Forgiveness, please," Seeka implored. "I do tend to extend my words. It comes from my days as a young— "

"Seeka," Ben barked, "you're doing it again!"

Seeka shook his head. "Once again, forgive me. A scourge has entered this world to change its natural course of events."

"And I guess these events concern me."

"If they did not, I would not be here. An evil presence," Seeka began, "has come from my world—"

"Which will be my world," Ben interrupted.

"Yes, he has come to circumvent your passage from this place into the next."

Ben shook his head. "How is any of this possible?"

Seeka sat up straight. "Through the power of the krang."

"What is krang?"

"I will explain the krang another time; right now, simply know that we are here."

"So, you are not here alone?"

"I am the only one; however, stay your questions until I can make known to you the present danger."

Ben nodded.

"The one who entered this world before I has set his plan in motion. If successful, it will disrupt this realm and prevent you from coming into his world so that he may take control."

"I'm one guy," Ben complained, laying his hands on his chest. "I don't know this other dude. What's he got against me?"

"It is true you are but one, however, soon you will become the greater part of three."

"Maybe I shouldn't have asked you to leave out the details." Ben leaned closer. "Tell me what you know, but just hit the highlights."

Seeka nodded. "I will condense as much as possible." He relayed the story of Ben's life, as it should proceed from that point. Seeka left out specifics so that Ben's knowledge of these happenings would not interfere with future events. He finished with his departure from Orac's cave to rendezvous with the Ben standing before him.

Ben sat staring at Seeka. "Suppose that I buy your story. What do you expect me to do about your little problem?"

"First we must determine how Nilrem plans to disrupt the path this world should follow. What can you tell me of this ship's mission?"

"Not much; just that we're going to blow up an island."

"An island!" Seeka exclaimed.

"Yeah," Ben said, "an island."

Seeka stopped and glared at Ben. "A location until now unheard of by you . . . The Established Place."

Chapter 33
Parallel Dimension I

(Return to *Deadly Reign*)

"It is time," Colossac said. "Gather the riders unto you. We will embark on our trail of dread, beginning by honing our force on The Three." He laughed, massaging a protective gel into his skinless flesh. "This depends on their still remaining in existence." He chuckled once again. "No doubt that fool Orac has informed them of our intentions, although Caleb and his men may have already taken care of that menial task for us."

"No matter, Your Lordship;" Cahotic said, "whoever remains will soon cease to do so."

"Indeed," Colossac said. "Now ride, my servant! Bring honor to your lord!"

Cahotic bowed and then turned to face his subordinates. He was now completely visible. His stout body was covered in black leather, with sliver armor covering his chest, back, knees and elbows. A black half-length leather cape split several times along its span, draped down his back. His bulky, scale-covered, dark green hands and feet were the only visible body parts, save for his face, which was turtle-like. A thick, short beak served as his nose and mouth. A silver helmet festooned his head, covering the back of his neck, and a silver metal strip split his eyes, traveling partway down his nose.

"Mount, riders," Cahotic boomed. "We begin our journey of destruction."

A roar rose from the assembly as they clambered aboard their steeds. The beasts that bore the aberrations were built much like a rhinoceros—their forequarters and flanks covered in thick hardened skin. A black leather metal saddle draped over their sides, offering protection to the more vulnerable areas. The head was without horns, but boasted a set of short upper tusks that protruded down and out from their jaws. A horse-like mane hung over their short necks, covering each side in coarse flowing fur. Their feet were comprised of three toes, an appendage that doubled as a stabilizer, and an opposable thumb. This allowed them to climb steep rocks as well as large trees.

The assembly shook the ground as they departed. Colossac smiled as he finished applying the human-based gel.

"Yes," he hissed, "and so it now begins."

Chapter 34

Caleb sat, his face devoid of emotion. He rocked back and forth, mumbling a barely audible chant.

"What's he doing?" Eve asked.

"Mourning, I guess," Pete said. "I'm not certain they should cut him loose; he looks unstable."

"He'll be fine," Ben said. "This is probably something he has to go through." He looked at Pete. "It's like a funeral ceremony." He looked back at Caleb. "At least I think so."

"Hope would be a better word," Eve said.

Ben looked at her, raised his eyebrows, and nodded.

Caleb became silent and stood. "It is done." He walked toward Ben and knelt in front of him. "I have returned. Tell me what has transpired during my absence."

"Are you sure you're ready?" Ben asked.

"I killed one I loved," Caleb said. "He is with the Great One whom I petitioned, asking He grant me pardon for this unthinkable act. Now I must do what is most difficult and grant myself that same pardon."

"I'm sorry," Ben said. "I know it wasn't your fault."

"Regardless," Caleb replied, "it was by my hand. I now continue what I have been charged to do, and that is to guide The Three along their way."

Ben nodded. He told Caleb of his exit from Nilrem and the riders. Orac took over, relaying Nilrem's metamorphosis into Colossac, his flight from the riders, the meeting with The Three, and their time in the cave, including Seeka's exit. Ben joined in once again to help Orac finish the story of the fight to subdue Caleb and the ultimate demise of Menday.

Caleb nodded, retaining his stoic expression. "Is Colossac aware of Seeka's attempt to undo his devilry?"

"I don't think so," Ben said. "If he were, he'd be making a much more aggressive attempt to stop us than he has."

"Either way," Caleb said, "you may rest assured he will come for you."

"Then we take the fight to him," Ben said.

"Agreed," Caleb replied.

Ben looked at Eve and Pete. "We'll leave at first light."

"No," Caleb said, "with the evil that is now loosed, we will not see another rising of the Great Light until we stand in victory."

"Then we go now," Ben said.

"Which way?" Pete asked.

Ben thought for a moment. "Orac will lead us to the sea. If water is a viable weapon against the riders, we'll have our best chance there."

"Very well," Caleb said, standing. "We will pack provisions—" He paused, looking toward the sky as a north wind began to blow.

Eve shivered. "Caleb, how will you fight what you can't see?"

"Since my men and I were forced to ingest the Kumult, we've been given quarter with the riders. This relationship allows each of us to visualize the riders just as you."

"Our horses are laden with supplies," Ben said.

Caleb shook his head. "Not of the type we will need."

Chapter 35

The rider dismounted, and after a quick search, found what he was looking for. He removed the box containing the sphere and placed it on the ground. Assisted by his steed, he scooped great handfuls of earth, until a hole six-feet deep remained. The rider placed the box in the middle of the hole and cracked the seal. The box halves separated, leaving the sphere hovering. It began to rotate. As its speed increased, a red light emanated from the globe, growing in intensity and changing to a near blinding yellow. The rider and his beast stood back as the hole closed over. Within minutes, the ground bore no evidence it had been disturbed.

The rider pulled two shards of red crystal from his pouch. He took the first and pushed the sharpened end into his forearm. The flesh covered the wound and the object as if it had never existed. The rider did the same to his beast with an identical effect. Cahotic had instructed him in this procedure, with the assurance that these small shards would warn them in case anyone was to tamper with the buried object. His task complete, he left the area to rejoin his comrades.

Chapter 36

Snow began to fall when The Three, led by Caleb and Orac, began their journey.

"This wind is something," Eve said.

"Give me your reins," Ben said.

"Why?" Eve asked.

"Just do it."

"Okay," she replied, handing them to her husband.

He maneuvered his horse close to hers. "Jump over," he said. She looked into his eyes, and without hesitation, slid from her horse onto his, landing in front of him. Ben looped her reins around his wrist and then curled his body around hers.

"Well, hello," she said.

"Hello back," he replied.

Eve closed her eyes and nestled her body deeper into his. "This feels much better."

Ben kissed her on the cheek.

After several hours of travel, Caleb stopped. "We must shelter ourselves from the cold."

The four travelers dismounted. Caleb cut four pine boughs, handing one to each of The Three and keeping one for himself. "Assist me in clearing this area."

Within several minutes, an area sixty feet in diameter was free of snow and debris.

Caleb addressed the travelers. "I would ask that you would now gather wood for the fire, primarily dead, but also some green."

The Three and Orac commenced dragging wood into the center of the cleared area. Caleb gathered tinder and knelt down. He produced a piece of flint and a small steel bar. By the time The Three had filled the area with fuel;

Caleb had started a small fire and was pulling branches into the flames. Before long, a blaze illuminated the forest in all directions.

"Circle the horses around the perimeter to block the wind," Caleb said. "Stack the wood for the fire on the opposite side."

"Caleb," Ben said, "where are your men?"

"Thalyn and Korell will join us later. There are certain items that must be obtained by other means."

"My dear Eve," Caleb said, "would you prepare a meal? I believe you will find all you need among the items my brother packed for your journey."

Eve nodded. "Of course."

"Good job, sweetie," Ben said, wiping his mouth on his sleeve.

"A finer meal I have not eaten," Caleb confirmed.

"Indeed," Orac said.

Pete nodded, his mouth full of food.

"Orac," Ben said, "I'm sorry there's not a horse for you to ride."

"Think nothing of it," Orac replied. "There is not a mount that can carry my great weight."

"More wood must be gathered before we rest," Caleb said. "At that time, one will keep watch. We will rotate at regular intervals."

Eve moved closer to Ben. "If Orac's taking the first watch, then who's got the second?" she asked.

"Pete and then Caleb," Ben replied.

"What about you and me?"

"Near as I can tell, each will last about three hours. By that time, we'll all be up." He smiled and cleared his throat. "They wanted to give us a little time together."

"Are you crazy?" she said, swatting his arm. "Not here."

"We've got a lean-to covered with blankets." Ben looked around as if to remind her of their concealment. "They can't see us."

"Go to sleep," she warned.

Ben grunted and rolled over.

Eve smiled. "Thank you."

Ben sat upright. "Something's going on."

"What?" Eve said. "I was nearly asleep.

Ben didn't answer; he was already out of the shelter. Caleb and Orac were unloading two pack horses. Pete soon joined the party.

"I see your men are back," Ben said.

"Bearing gifts, no less," Orac added.

"What have we here?" Ben asked, moving closer to the provisions.

"Warmth," Caleb replied.

"Warmth?" Ben asked.

"What's all the fuss?" Eve asked, emerging from her sleeping quarters.

"That's what I'm trying to find out," Ben replied.

"Hides," Pete exclaimed, holding up a large pelt.

"Nice," Eve said, as she brushed her hand through the fur.

"I bet you don't use these very often," Ben said.

"This is the first time we have needed such things," Caleb replied.

"I'm glad you had the foresight to store the essentials," Ben said.

"We store nothing," Caleb said. "Thalyn and Korell hunted these creatures, removed the skins and then cured the hides for our use."

"That's impossible," Pete said. "You can't get fresh animal hides to this point in twenty-four hours."

"Thalyn," Ben said, "how did you accomplish the impossible?"

"Such things take time," Thalyn replied. "We have been away fifty-three risings of the Great Light."

Ben thought for a moment. "That's almost two months," he said, refusing to believe his own words.

"My brother and I have explained to you how time passes for each of us," Caleb said.

"Well, yeah," Ben said, "but how can it be different when we're together doing the same thing?"

"When we are in the presence of any of The Three," Caleb said, "time passes at the same rate. If we are apart from The Three, time moves at a different rate. So inversely, in fact, that soon after you leave this place we will cease to be."

"If we leave this place," Ben said.

"What's the point of the time difference?" Eve asked.

"To show that one must never look back, but stay the course, always facing forward," Caleb replied.

Eve opened her mouth to speak.

"Enough," Caleb said. "We must now rest; tomorrow will be a day of testing."

Chapter 37
Parallel Dimension II

(Aboard the *Morning Star*)

"Okay," Ben said, closing his cabin door, "I was able to get a look at our secret cargo."

"Can you tell me of the device that will destroy the island?" Seeka asked.

"A torpedo."

Seeka cocked his head to the side. "Please explain."

Ben thought for a moment. "Well, it's like a rocket that runs underwater."

"I do not understand torpedo or rocket."

"Imagine a cylinder this big around," Ben said, holding his arms in a circle, "and at least three times as long as I am tall." Ben watched the nuckta mull this information over. "This cylinder has a propulsion system that pushes it through the water. The opposite end contains a warhead."

Seeka squinted.

"It's the device that will destroy the island."

Seeka nodded. "Is this all?"

Ben rubbed his chin. "I'm not sure if the people on this boat know what they have. I was in the Navy, and we would only consider using the weapons on this ship as a last resort."

"How so?" Seeka asked.

"These torpedoes are among a new generation of weapons. They are meant to be fired from a submarine. Once launched, the sub can dive, avoiding any damage from the explosion. A surface running vessel, however, is a sitting duck."

"I will not ask that you explain the terms you have used. I can tell from your tone the dire circumstances in releasing the weapons from this ship."

Ben nodded. "Seeka," he said, "these weapons are of a hybrid nuclear variety. The shockwave will extend thirty miles from the center of the blast.

This vessel doesn't have a hi-tech guidance system; so to launch, it must be within sight of its target." Ben stared at Seeka, his expression conveying the concern wedged deep within. "We'd be toast milliseconds after detonation."

Chapter 38
Parallel Dimension I

(Return to *Deadly Reign*)

"How long before we reach the sea?" Ben asked.

"At this pace, nearly one rising of the Great Light," the giant said. "Since the Great Light no longer rises, we may never arrive."

"Ha, ha," Pete said, "a thousand demons clamoring for the job, and we had to end up with an overgrown, medieval comedian."

"I guess it's the same no matter where you go," Ben said, "even if it is another world."

Several orbs had joined the party to light their way.

"The trees seem to be closing in," Eve said, looking around. "It's almost claustrophobic."

"Just thick foliage," Ben said. "With the orbs lit above, it makes the canopy seem lower."

"I guess you're right," Eve replied.

One of the orbs blinked almost imperceptibly. Ben looked up in time to see a shadow pass over the sphere, momentarily blocking its light. He increased his pace, catching up with Caleb.

"Caleb," he said, "did you . . ."

"Speak not," Caleb whispered. "It has been with us for some time."

"What is it?" Ben whispered back.

"Stay close to Eve," Caleb said. "It must not know that we are aware of its presence. We must take it by surprise."

Ben opened his mouth to speak.

Caleb raised his hand. "To Eve now," he hissed. "You will know."

Ben slowed his mount, allowing Eve and Pete to catch up.

"Is something wrong?" she asked.

"No," Ben said, "I was asking when we were going to stop."

"Stop!" Eve exclaimed. "We just got started."

"Shh," Ben warned.

A dart flew inches above Eve's head, knocking a creature to the ground, several strands of her hair still clenched in its talons. Ben whirled to see Caleb and his men firing into the air as winged figures fell indiscriminately onto the forest floor. The Three loaded their bows and joined the carnage. With blow after blow, Orac sent bodies falling to earth with his massive fists. After thirty or more intruders were lying on the ground, the barrage ended.

Ben lowered his bow. "Not bad."

"Keep watch," Caleb said. "It is not over."

"They're gone," Ben replied. He turned to look at Eve, only to see her lifted from her horse and taken into the canopy.

Chapter 39

Colossac pored over the document he had seen Ben reading earlier that day. Hoping they would be of some strategic value, he was able to peruse the parchment Ben carelessly left in his haste.

"How very idealistic," he mused. "Unfortunately, I cannot adhere to these ten edicts," Colossac tossed the parchment across the room, "especially the decree forbidding the death of another." He stood and walked to the center of the room, a red aura surrounding him. It pulsated, growing brighter with each throb. Colossac was lost in the flood of crimson. As the aura faded, Colossac faded along with it.

Chapter 40

"To me," Cahotic ordered. "Riders, come to me." The five aberrations gathered around their leader. Cahotic looked at the group. "Raise your weapons," he demanded.

The five pushed their blood-covered swords into the air.

Cahotic contorted his face into a smile. "I command you to remember the color that covers your weapon."

The five lifted their voices in response. A red glow began to illuminate their meeting place. The group parted as the light deepened and then faded, leaving Colossac in their midst.

The riders moved as Cahotic approached his master. "It is good that you are here," Cahotic said, dropping to one knee. "Your wards have laid waste to this small province."

Colossac beamed at the devastation. "What of The Three?"

"Of The Three, there are no signs."

Colossac smiled. "Show me more of the evidence of your conquest."

Cahotic led his master though the dirt streets of the small settlement. The slaughter was complete: men, women, children and livestock.

"Excellent," Colossac exclaimed. "I see that I have chosen well." He laid a hand on the sergeant's shoulder.

"Thank you, Lord," Cahotic replied. "I left one young human alive to tell the tale of destruction and pave our way."

"How appropriate." Colossac laid a massive hand over the beginnings of a new flow of bodily fluid. "Do not tarry in rendering the appropriate parts down to formulate my protective gel."

"Right away," Cahotic said.

Colossac pushed his finger into a small leather bag. Removing a diminutive amount of its contents, he rubbed the salve on his forearm where the hole had developed. This stemmed the tide that had already formed a small puddle on the ground.

A flutter in the trees above caused a small avalanche of snow that cascaded down the tree and ended on the ground.

Colossac scanned the area. Blinded by arrogance, he continued to apply the soothing ointment.

◆◆◆

The boy made his way through the dense underbrush. The snow, not yet a hindrance, was beginning to intensify. Yoshi was eleven cycles old and already the last of his clan. With no concerns yesterday, save that of a carefree youth, his mission now turned to survival at any cost. He'd seen the ones who nurtured and protected him from infancy, slaughtered without mercy. If he had been allowed to escape or his flight was of his own doing didn't matter. His first thoughts were to live and preserve his nearly extinct tribe. His second concern intertwined with the first, as he would bring those responsible to justice. And this he most assuredly would do.

Chapter 41

"Eve," Ben screamed as another barrage of winged creatures attacked the group. Within a minute, the attack stopped as abruptly as it had begun.

Ben turned to Caleb. "They've got Eve!"

"We must move quickly," Caleb said. "They will try to confuse our search."

"What are they?" Pete asked.

"Narify," Caleb replied.

Pete looked at one of the dead creatures. It was about the size of a large cat and a deep leaf green in color. The wings were formed similar to bats, except the back of the wings bore a thick covering of green fur. Its head resembled a baboon, save for the protruding forehead and tufts of fur much like the wings. Their feet were three-toed and shaped like that of a raptor.

Pete felt an uncustomary shiver go through him and then turned his attention back to Ben. "What do we do?" he asked.

"First, you must remain calm," Caleb said. "These creatures will use any indecision, anxiety or apprehension on your part against you, leading you away from what you hope to find."

Ben took a deep breath and sighed. "Tell me what to do."

"You must hold yourself as if nothing has happened," Caleb said. "We will move slowly in the same direction. They will not understand our actions, and their natural curiosity will cause them to stop and observe."

"What good will that do Eve?" Ben asked.

Caleb stared at Ben. "If they stop moving, Eve stops moving."

Ben nodded. "Where are they taking her?"

The men resumed their original trek.

"The narify we killed are considered expendable," Caleb said. "They are bred to protect the colony by sacrificial means, allowing the others to escape and diverting attention from the main colony. That is where they are taking Eve."

"These things lying around on the ground aren't big enough to lift a human," Pete said. "Any ideas?"

"The narify parents," Caleb said, "are much larger and stronger; however, they are also much more vulnerable to attack."

"In what way?" Pete asked.

"Their flesh is very soft," Caleb said. "They molt every thirty risings of the Great Light, remaining impervious to injury for one rising and then returning to their normal selves."

Ben looked at Pete. "The tamar?" he asked.

"Makes sense, I guess," Pete said, "except in reverse. The tamar were vulnerable at birth and then hardened into near invulnerability."

"Caleb," Ben said, "how do we find Eve?"

"The narify themselves will lead us to their nest," Caleb said. "Through our lack of action, they are by now convinced that we have no interest in the one they have taken. As soon as the workers begin to swarm, we will follow them to their lair. We must also each gather one of the dead."

"Can't they hear us talking?" Pete asked.

"They have no need to hear," Caleb replied. "Their world is sensed through limited sight, smell and vibration."

The canopy began to vibrate as the narify workers set out for their dwelling.

Orac looked down, picking up two of the fallen.

Chapter 42
Parallel Dimension II

(Aboard the *Morning Star*)

"Are there ways to circumvent this destruction you have spoken of?" Seeka asked.

"None I know of," Ben replied.

"Then we must devise a way," Seeka said.

Ben glared at the nuckta. "Don't you think I . . ." Ben stopped. Seeka innocently stared back at him. Ben sighed. "I'm sorry."

Seeka cocked his head. "For what reason?"

"You're right. We have to find a way to either avert the launching or divert the torpedoes after they're launched."

"Superb," Seeka said. "Tell me how I may assist in this endeavor."

Ben smiled and knelt down, rubbing Seeka's head. "I don't know how; that's what we have to figure out."

Seeka nodded and then looked at Ben.

A knock at the door echoed through the cabin. Seeka scurried under Ben's bunk.

"Yes," Ben said.

"It's Stewart," came the reply.

Ben knelt down and looked under the bed. "Hang tight."

Ben opened the door. "Stewart, I wasn't expecting any visitors."

Stewart pushed a cart into the room. "I thought you may be getting hungry. The captain is dining in tonight. I think he's no longer concerned with impressing you."

"That's fine," Ben said. "I want nothing from him." Ben paused as a wave of deja vu passed over him.

"Anything wrong?" Stewart asked.

Ben came back to reality. "No, of course not. What's for dinner?"

"Not what you're used to, as far as dining with the captain, but it's better than nothing." He produced two bowls of beef stew and a plate of bread.

Forgetting about Seeka, Ben dove into the stew. "I didn't realize I was so hungry," he said amidst mouthfuls.

"Ben, I came here to ask you something."

Ben swallowed hard. "Me first; I think what I have to say may be a bit more urgent."

"Okay, go ahead."

"Tell me about the captain's intentions, as far as the weapons on board, and give it to me straight; our lives may depend on it."

Stewart's expression changed to one of concern. "Originally there were sealed orders, two envelopes the captain threw away in lieu of this new plan."

"Which is to destroy the island," Ben replied.

"You got it. He wouldn't divulge the source of the new orders, but I get the feeling that he doesn't have a clue. I retrieved the envelopes from the trash. By then, some external force was in control, taking the ship where it willed. I opened the first envelope. All it contained was a compass heading, and signed the 'Keeper.' Those coordinates led us to you."

Another unsettling wave of recognition passed over Ben, causing him to shudder.

"The funny thing is," Stewart continued, "after I'd opened the second envelope, our current coordinates were identical to the compass heading laid out for us to follow."

"We'll have to stop the launch," Ben said.

"What's the harm? We're on the intended heading. So what if we take a brief detour to blow up an errant piece of real estate, which according to our charts, doesn't even exist."

"To launch those torpedoes, we have to get to within eyeshot of the island."

"Good, if we're going to create fireworks, I want to see them."

Ben shook his head. "Not these, you don't. The warheads are nuclear; once detonated, they will instantaneously fry everything within a thirty-mile radius."

"Good reason," Stewart acknowledged. "But are you sure?"

"Yes, I had a chance to look at the cylinders. They're the same type we used in the Navy, although we never launched one. They were more of a deterrent than anything else."

"I assume that you didn't get close enough to touch them."

"No, not that close."

"Had you," Stewart said, "we wouldn't be having this conversation. The weapons are encased in a stacion field."

Ben raised his eyebrows in surprise. "Evans was able to acquire military hardware, but a stacion generator—we're talking top secret, state of the art technology. It's not something you can walk into your local drugstore and flop down on the counter."

"There's one more tiny problem," Stewart said.

"I don't like the sound of this."

"The captain has informed me that everything is taken care of. The launch is automatic; not even Evans can stop it. And if we try, you know what the stacion field does to any organic form that encroaches upon its boundaries."

"A puff of ozone and a few dust particles," Ben said.

Seeka crept out from underneath the bed.

Stewart jumped up. "What is that?"

"I felt it no longer prudent to remain hidden," Seeka said.

"It talks," Stewart said.

"Uh, Stewart, there's something we need to discuss."

Chapter 43
Parallel Dimension I

(Return to *Deadly Reign*)

"There is the entrance," Caleb said.

"It's hard to see," Ben replied. "The light's so dim."

"The orbs dare not move closer, lest they give our position away."

"When do we move in?"

"Now," Caleb replied. "You must remember to be careful within the nest. There are many dangers."

Pete moved in closer.

"The narify feed upon the nectar of the scook tree," Caleb said. "This nectar is toxic to all but the narify. Once they have processed the substance into food for their young, the toxicity level is tripled. Even to touch this thick black liquid will cause death."

"Any more good news?" Ben asked.

"There are many chambers and pitfalls leading to nowhere," Caleb replied. "A man could spend an entire lifetime searching for a way out and never find it."

"I've heard enough," Pete said.

"There is one more thing you must know," Caleb said. "We will gain entrance to the nest by wrapping ourselves with the bodies of the dead. Their sight is poor and their sense of smell keen, when in proximity."

"Then what's the problem?" Ben asked.

"There are sentries that patrol the inside of the chamber, looking for anything that may have slipped past the external guards. They possess an internal weapons system which uses the deadly black liquid as a projectile." Caleb paused. "Their accuracy is uncanny."

Ben swallowed. "You done?"

"Yes," Caleb responded.

"Can we go now?" Ben asked. "I imagine my wife has had enough monkey mania."

"We will leave the horses here," Caleb said, turning to Ben. "Use the crossbow we provided and leave the longbow here. You will soon see my reasoning behind this request, as space within the nest is at a premium. Throw the narify carcass over your shoulders. The sentries will sense their brother and allow us to enter. And do not forget to load your quivers and bring an extra bundle of darts."

"Ugh," Ben complained, as he threw the dead carcass around his neck, "this thing smells like somebody threw up on a dead dog."

"Get used to it," Pete warned. "I can imagine the aromas awaiting us."

"Do you wish to have a weapon?" Caleb asked Orac.

"No," Orac replied, raising his hands, "I have these."

Caleb nodded and moved toward the chamber entrance. Two sentries came into view.

"They look more like ants than monkeys," Ben whispered.

"Shh," Caleb warned.

Ben pointed to his ears, as if to ask, *I thought you said they couldn't hear.*

Caleb nodded as he mouthed the phrase: *vibrations, sound vibrations.*

Ben nodded back, feeling foolish.

The sentry clicked its mandibles together and then stood aside, allowing Caleb to pass. Ben was now close enough to see that the sentry stood about four feet tall. Its head was heart-shaped with a pair of antennae and an awkward looking set of thick mandibles. Tiny eye slits protruded on either side of its head. The creature's body consisted of two segments, with two pairs of extremities on each. Its uppermost pair served as arms and hands with six digits. The bottom pair were identical to its flying counterpart, ending in raptor-like talons. Green fur covered the back and chest. The smooth parts of its body bore a dull orange hue.

Orac, laying two of the narify along his shoulders, dropped to all fours. The sentry bade him enter.

Ben was the last to stand before the sentry. He bent over, exposing the head of the deceased narify lying along the back of his neck. The sentry pushed its nose close to its brother. The baboon's head draped across Ben's neck slipped off, causing the sentry to jerk back and click its mandibles in an erratic fashion. Ben raised his hand, tipping the dangling head back onto his neck. The sentry twisted his head from side to side and then moved closer. It ran its fingers along the fur-covered wings, which lay down each of Ben's shoulders. It sniffed the head and clicked several times, backing away to allow Ben passage.

Pete sighed as Ben joined the group. He looked at Ben and then threw the narify carcass off his back.

"No," Caleb hissed, "we will need them to move further into the chamber."

Pete nodded and slipped the corpse back onto his shoulders.

"After you," he whispered.

Ben smiled, placing his hand on Pete's head, rubbing his hair.

Caleb signaled for the group to follow and made his way deeper into the narify nest.

Chapter 44
Parallel Dimension II

(Aboard the *Morning Star*)

Stewart lowered his head and began to rub the back of his neck. He rose, looked at Ben and then at Seeka. "Pinch me so I can wake up."

"Look," Ben said, "it's hard to swallow, but I need to know if you're in."

Stewart looked at Ben. "I think I'm already in." He turned his attention once again to the nuckta. "I want to know what I'm in *to*!"

"Helping to put things right," Ben said.

Stewart remained fixed on Seeka. "Yeah, as long as you wake me up when it's over."

"It's a deal," Ben replied. He placed his hands on Stewart's shoulders. "We have to formulate a plan to disable the warheads."

"I wasn't lying when I told you that the launch can't be stopped," Stewart said.

"There is always a way," Seeka said. "One day soon you will learn to rely upon a greater power than yourselves."

"How about now," Ben said.

"The greater power I speak of," Seeka began, "will see you through, if you allow Him to do so, and sometimes, in spite of yourself."

"Again," Ben reiterated, "what's wrong with now?"

"Obedience will come in time," Seeka said. "Take comfort. He is always there awaiting your call, and what you do is not necessarily of your own making."

"That being said," Stewart replied, "I guess we need to get started."

"Yes," Seeka said, "it would seem so."

Ben shook his head along with an extended grunt.

Chapter 45
Parallel Dimension I

(Return to *Deadly Reign*)

The creature stood sniffing and rubbing the fur along the now decomposing body of the single narify. This sentry was a larger, walking version of the flying narify.

After the would-be rescuers were checked, they entered deeper into the nest, six pairs of yellow flashing eyes illuminating the way.

"Why is it I am able to see in the darkness?" A surprised Orac asked.

"It is a gift;" Caleb said, "one we will speak of later."

Orac nodded.

"We must rid ourselves of the corpses we carry," Caleb said. "The bodies are beginning to exude the stench of death. They soon will alarm our hosts."

"I didn't think it was possible for them to smell any worse," Pete mumbled to himself.

Caleb scratched into the soft wall at floor level. Once a large enough pocket was created, he crammed the carcass into the opening and packed as much dirt as possible on the corpse. The others did the same.

"Won't they be able to detect their dead?" Pete asked.

"The bodies will be too far away," Caleb said. "The narify's power of scent is limited, but keen when near the odor itself."

"What exactly are we looking for?" Ben asked.

"The birthing chamber," Caleb replied.

Ben looked at Pete. "Been there," he said.

"The narify will treat Eve as a new queen," Caleb said. "Once they discover her infertility, she will be dissected and used as food for the colony."

"How soon?" Ben demanded.

"There is no way to know," Caleb replied. "It is different in each—"

"I didn't ask you about every situation," Ben growled, slamming one fist into the other. "We're talking about my wife."

Caleb moved close to Ben. "I understand your frustration; however, the situation remains as it is and no amount of banter will change this." Caleb laid his hand on Ben's shoulder. "If you will listen to me, this will be your best chance to reunite with your wife."

Ben sighed. "Okay, I'm all yours."

"Time is of the essence," Caleb said. "We must not tarry." He turned to Orac. "The tunnel we are traversing seems to narrow ahead. Will this pose a problem for you?"

Orac dragged his forearm down the tunnel wall, removing a wide swath of material six inches deep.

"I see," Caleb said. "I wish for everyone to stay close." He motioned for all to follow as he inched forward.

After an hour of slow progress, Caleb came to an abrupt halt. He raised his index finger to his lips and pressed his back tight to the tunnel wall. The men did the same, except for Orac. His massive size nearly blocked the corridor, even with his back to the wall. He scraped his backside against the wall, gouging out a divot he could settle into.

From an adjacent tunnel, two creatures emerged. They moved toward the frozen men. These bore a resemblance to their winged counterparts but stood taller. Hollow tubes ran down each arm, starting at the neck and ending on the back of their hands. The tubes appeared to be a part of the things' anatomy. As they neared the men, they slowed, adopting a more defensive posture. Both creatures made a fist and raised a hand, parallel to the ground.

"They seem to be aiming that tube," Ben whispered.

Pete's eyes widened. "The toxic liquid," he said. "They're the shooters."

The creature closest to Pete shifted his head in that direction, upon sensing the vibration of Pete's voice. His arm also shifted to the side, placing Pete in his line of fire.

Pete watched as a spherical black object left the end of the tube in slow motion, propelled by what sounded like a release of compressed air. Pete instinctively gasped, waiting for the viscous mass to strike its target.

Chapter 46
Parallel Dimension II

(Aboard the *Morning Star*)

"What about the krang?" Ben said. "Could you use it to breech the stacion field and access the controls on the torpedoes?"

Seeka stood on hind legs, wiggling his front toes. "If you fit these with opposable digits, then perhaps I may be able to help."

"Think you're pretty funny, don't you?"

"I had hoped so," Seeka said, proudly. "It is my first attempt at what you call humor."

"Well, no," Ben replied, wiggling his fingers at the nuckta. "I can't do anything with your toes."

"What I have said is true. I can do no good as you asked; however, I may be able to take you with me."

Ben raised his eyebrows. "Explain."

"Although I have never before used the krang to transport anyone but myself, it may be possible to move both of us through the stacion field."

"Of course," Stewart said, looking at Ben, "you could disable the rocket motors."

"I don't know," Ben replied. "I'm not that familiar with the control system."

"You'll recognize more about them than any of us," Stewart said.

"Indeed," Seeka said, once again wiggling his toes in Ben's direction.

"Hmm," Ben grunted.

"Guess that means you'll do it," Stewart said, glancing at Ben, "or at least consider it."

Ben returned the glance. "Consider is a better word."

Chapter 47
Parallel Dimension I

(Return to *Deadly Reign*)

Colossac rubbed the newly rendered gel across his shoulder. "So good." He moaned with pleasure. "This batch is the best so far." He placed the crock of salve on the table and left the building, making his way across the settlement and entering the riders' stable.

"Cahotic," he barked, "come to me."

The second-in-command hastened to his master. "Yes, Your Lordship," he said, dropping to one knee.

"Ah, Cahotic," Colossac swooned, "you have done a great service unto me." He placed two massive hands on the rider's shoulders. "Now that The Three are no more, your mission is to conquer as many as you encounter in order to produce the gel that your lord needs."

"I will do as you have said."

"Good, very good indeed." Colossac left the stable, heading back to his quarters with a renewed sense of being. An aura of euphoria accompanied him, staying until he fell into a deep sleep.

Cahotic waved his arms, gathering the riders around him. "The master is becoming self-absorbed and weaker in his cause with each breath he takes." He raised his arms above his head. "We will soon be in control just as the Dark One has directed,"

A great roar rose from the assembly.

Cahotic lowered his arms and twisted his beak-like mouth into a smile. "Then all is as it should be."

Chapter 48

The winged creature dropped to the ground as the black mass struck it in the chest. It pulled the glob out of its fur and popped it into its mouth before continuing on. The tunnel filled with beating wings, blocking any chance for another shot.

Caleb motioned for the men to follow. They made a hasty retreat from the fray, stopping several hundred yards further into the nest.

"We will be safe here for a short time," Caleb said. "Pete, are you well?"

"Yes," Pete sighed, "although I don't know how."

"Be obliged to the Great One," Caleb said. "One can see His hand in the smallest of details."

Pete nodded.

"We are nearing the center of the nest," Caleb said. "Eve should be closer now."

"Let's go then," Ben said.

"Exactly," Caleb said, turning to leave.

"Caleb!" Thalyn screamed, tackling Caleb and pulling him to the ground.

Korell whirled around, placing himself between Caleb and the shooter. He fired twice, both darts piercing the first shooter's neck. The creature grabbed its throat and fell to the ground, quivering.

"Phoot, phoot," resounded through the chamber, barely audible, yet deafening in consequence. The two deadly blobs from the second shooter struck Korell in the chest. He stiffened and rocked forward before ending flat on his back, his life over before he hit the ground.

By the time Caleb had made it to his feet, the second shooter was lying beside the first, dispatched by Ben and Pete. Four darts protruded from its lifeless form.

"Dear Korell," Caleb said, kneeling beside his friend, "I have now caused the death of two of my closest."

Thalyn placed a hand on Caleb's shoulder. "Korell, as I, would gladly give our lives to further the Great One's purpose."

Caleb stood and then nodded. "We must bury our friend. Orac, will you assist, please?"

Orac nodded. "With much pleasure."

"In the same manner as the narify," Caleb said, "to avoid detection."

Orac scooped out an ample space for Korell. He then slid the body into the space and packed the loose dirt around the deceased, sealing him into the wall.

Caleb knelt in front of his entombed friend and offered a request to the Great One, for rest, additional strength and success in their journey.

Orac then began to dig another slot in the wall, this one much bigger than the first.

"Please explain your actions," Caleb said.

Orac struggled to his knees and opened his shirt. Several black splatters lay across his neck and chest. "I was closest to Korell when he was hit. I am now feeling its effect. My great size, along with the small amount of material, has postponed the inevitable."

"You dug your own grave?" Ben asked.

"You could not handle my bulk," Orac said, "and I fear my body would jeopardize your quest."

"Before I am unable to do so," Orac said, "I bid you farewell." He slid into his tomb. "Please do not cover me until you return this way, and Caleb, speak to the Great One on my behalf."

Caleb knelt down and spoke to the giant. Ben caught bits of the conversation about the Living One, acceptance and life for eternity.

When Caleb stood, Orac's face glowed with peace. It reminded Ben of his friend Stewart. *It seems so long ago*, he thought.

Ben and Pete stooped to speak to Orac for the last time. "Farewell," Ben said. "You have been a good friend for the short time I have known you."

"All is well," Orac said. "One day we shall meet—" He stopped in mid-sentence, his breathing now shallow.

Pete nodded at the dying giant and then both men stood.

Ben pushed back a tear. "I'd like to find my wife now."

Chapter 49
Parallel Dimension II

(Aboard the *Morning Star*)

"Where is my crew?" Evans' voice boomed over the COM, his words coming in thick slurs.

"The lion awakens," Stewart said. "Guess I'd better go."

"I'll go with you," Ben said. "Maybe in his present state we can glean information about the stacion field and the weapons themselves."

"Go," Seeka said. "I will await your return."

♦ ♦ ♦

Stewart snapped to attention with a sharp salute. "Davis and Adams reporting, sir."

Captain Evans ceased berating Vinny and Skull, his voice trailing off in an unintelligible array of garble. He slowly turned to face Stewart.

"Well," he said, extending his hand toward the console to keep from falling, "so nice of you to join us, Missster Davis."

"Yes, Captain," Stewart replied.

Evans looked confused. "What do you want?"

Stewart looked at Ben, and then at Evans. "Well, sir," Stewart said hesitantly, "we—"

"We thought you might like to have a drink," Ben interrupted.

Evans' eyes brightened. "But of course." His hand traced an inviting zigzag path toward the door. "Follow me." He took one step and would have fallen if not for Stewart. Ben grabbed his other arm and the two men all but carried the inebriated captain to his quarters.

♦ ♦ ♦

Seeka closed his eyes and began to concentrate. The yellow orb descended and then he was gone.

♦♦♦

"Let me help you with that, Captain," Stewart said.

"Of course;" Evans replied. "Make mine a double."

Stewart filled three wine glasses. "Here you go, sir," he said, handing a glass to Evans.

"Thank you," he slurred, sloshing wine from the glass until he managed to bring it to his lips.

"We should do this more often, Captain," Ben said.

"Yes," Evans mumbled, hardly able to open his eyes.

"Captain," Ben inquired, "about the weapons on board."

Evans sat upright, spilling his wine, all signs of drunkenness gone. "It is time for you both to leave."

"But, Captain," Stewart pleaded.

"Now!" Evans growled.

Ben and Stewart left Evans' cabin, closing the door behind them.

"Instant sobriety," Stewart said. "Something's got a hold of him."

"Yeah, and I'm afraid it's not from this world," Ben added.

Chapter 50
Parallel Dimension I

(Return to *Deadly Reign*)

"Here," Caleb said, cautioning everyone to stop. "She is here."

"Eve?" Ben inquired, his voice full of hope.

Caleb nodded. "Yes."

Ben nervously looked around at the stalled procession. "Then why are we stopping?"

Caleb made a calming motion with his hand. "If we storm into the chamber, Eve will be instantly killed."

"What do we do?" Ben asked, his movements becoming fidgety and erratic.

"We must move in slowly," Caleb warned. "In that way, the narify midwives will accept our presence."

Ben rubbed his cheek. "I hope you know that this goes against every instinct in my body."

Caleb opened his mouth to speak when a dim yellow glow began to illuminate the immediate area and then faded. All eyes turned to the source of the light. Caleb's face brightened. He knelt down, spreading his arms. An odd, furry creature lunged toward him, ending in his embrace.

"Seeka!" Caleb exclaimed as the nuckta nuzzled deep into his neck.

Ben smiled, momentarily pushing the predicament at hand aside. "It's good to see you," he said, reaching out to rub the animal's head.

Seeka turned. "It is good for me also, although you yourself are much furrier in this world than in the former."

Ben, for a moment, looked a bit perplexed and then recovered as Eve regained a firm hold in his thoughts. "You said that you would contact me if possible. Is that why you're here?"

"Partly," Seeka said. "It is also for reasons far removed from mere contact." He winced, lowering his head, and looked at Caleb. "I sense great loss in this place: one far removed, one very close, and another close, but fading."

Caleb nodded sadly. "Menday was first to fall, and by my own hand." He placed his hand on Seeka's back. "Korell and the giant, mere moments ago."

"I am sorry," Seeka said. "What of the girl?"

"She is close," Caleb said. "We are preparing to enter the birthing chamber."

"Allow me to precede your entrance," Seeka said.

Caleb nodded. "We will await your return."

Seeka once again disappeared in a yellow flash.

"What are you doing?" Ben protested. "We've got to get in there."

"We will wait," Caleb said sternly.

"You can wait," Ben said, moving toward the chamber. "I'm going in."

"Thalyn," Caleb commanded. The warrior stepped in front of Ben.

"So that's how it's gonna be," Ben said as he raised an arm and attempted to sidestep the blockade.

Thalyn placed his palm against the front of Ben's shoulder. He extended a leg behind Ben's ankles, taking him to the ground and pinning him there with a knee on his chest.

Pete moved to help his friend.

Caleb positioned himself to intercept. "Stand down!"

Pete froze, unsure if he should engage this formidable man.

"Ben Adams, you still do not understand. How long must I endure your insolence?"

Ben sighed and ceased his struggle.

"Release him," Caleb said.

Thalyn stood and helped Ben to his feet.

"What did you expect me to do?" Ben demanded.

"What I expect," Caleb said, "is for your self-absorbed attitude to cease."

"What do—"

"Do not speak until I am through," Caleb warned.

Ben nodded, taken aback by Caleb's demeanor.

"I have lost much on this journey," Caleb continued, "yet I have remained true to the cause, which is assisting The Three along their way." He pointed toward Ben. "You have displayed nothing but fulfilling your own selfish desires. To rush in would bring death to Eve, yourself and most probably what remains of this troop."

"I'm sorry, but I don't want to live without Eve."

"Then heed my instructions, and in this way you will not take your comrades with you when you go."

A yellow flash interrupted the dialogue, and Seeka returned. "Eve is well," he said. "However, make all haste; she will not remain so much longer." The yellow Orb returned and left, again carrying the nuckta with it.

"Scrape handfuls of soil out of the tunnel's sides, and rub it into all exposed parts of your body," Caleb ordered, "including your face and hair."

Chapter 51
Parallel Dimension II

(Aboard the *Morning Star*)

"I guess we're back to square one," Stewart said.

Ben nodded. "Where's Seeka?" he asked, dropping to his knees and looking under the bed. "I know we left him here."

Stewart shook his head and sat down on the chair adjacent to the bed.

Ben stood, looked around, shrugged, and then seated himself on his bunk. "Maybe we are dreaming."

Stewart smiled. "Which one of us is dreaming, and which one has invaded that dream?"

"Neither," a familiar voice added.

"Seeka," Ben exclaimed. He noticed the nuckta sitting in front of the bed, staring up at him. "It's good to see you." He hesitated "At least I think so."

A pleasant look crossed Seeka's face, dismissing the negative connotations in Ben's statement. "Might I add that it is good to be seen."

Ben nodded. "You may, and where have you been?"

"Exploring," Seeka replied.

"Find anything worth mentioning?"

"Perhaps; what do you recall of one named Eleazor?"

Ben contemplated the question. "I feel I should know that name intimately, but this is the first time I have heard that title."

"Same here," Stewart said. "In fact, it gives me a headache just considering it."

"The one I have mentioned may be the very solution to our problem," Seeka said.

"Where can we find this Eleazor?" Ben asked.

"He is much closer than you imagine," Seeka replied.

Chapter 52
Parallel Dimension I

(Return to *Deadly Reign*)

"There she is," Pete said.

"Where?" Ben asked, unable to contain his excitement.

"Remain calm," Caleb cautioned. "We will reach her momentarily."

"Why are these attendants allowing us to move through here unmolested?" Pete asked.

"We have the aroma of their surroundings," Caleb replied.

"The dirt we rubbed on ourselves," Pete said. "How did you know it would work?"

"I did not," Caleb replied. "It was what you would call a calculated risk."

Pete smiled. "Good move."

Ben reached Eve first. She was imprisoned in a rectangular shaped cell and bound with a sparse cocoon. He extended his hands to free his wife.

"Do not touch her," Caleb warned.

"Why?" Ben protested.

"To touch the queen will be interpreted as an act of aggression," Caleb said.

"So," Ben retorted, "what's that to me?"

"Instantaneous death," Caleb replied.

"Okay," Ben said, bringing his hands down to his side.

Caleb, Pete and Thalyn now stood beside Ben.

"Don't worry, sweetheart," Ben said. "We'll have you out of there soon."

"I hope so," Eve answered. "I'm getting uncomfortable in here."

"Eve," Caleb started, "what have they done to you up to this point?"

"Just poked and prodded," she said, shuddering.

"Good," Caleb said, "I can only hope they will not attempt to feed you until we gain your release."

"I can imagine how that would taste," Pete said, smiling.

"Like death," Caleb replied.

"The black liquid," Ben said, his face expressing near panic.

"What?" Eve asked. "What are you talking about?"

"Ben," Caleb reassured, "we are here now. Do not fret over such things."

"Wait a minute," Eve insisted. "Tell me what you're talking about!"

"Be calm, dear Eve," Caleb said. "There is no cause for worry."

"How about we switch places," she said, "and then you can tell me that."

An ant-faced midwife ambled toward Eve.

"Let her pass," Caleb said. The four men parted, allowing the attendant to come through. When she reached Eve, she extended an appendage full of black goo. She pried Eve's mouth open with the other and pushed the extremity, laden with the ebony death, toward her open orifice.

"No!" Ben screamed. He lunged, grabbing the midwife's arm. His forward momentum pushed the insect to the ground. Ben landed on top, sensing parts he could not comprehend give way under his weight. As he lifted his bulk off the creature, he heard the crackle of bodily elements in reverse. Ben stood over the dying figure. *Just stepped on another bug,* he thought.

As the fallen midwife twitched and clicked its mandibles together, Ben felt sorry for the one who would have brought certain death to his wife. He turned to see three sentries binding Caleb, Pete and Thalyn into separate cells adjacent to Eve's prison.

Ben moved to help his friends and found that he could not. He was the last to be pushed into an empty rectangle and encased in an unbreakable cocoon.

Chapter 53
Parallel Dimension II

(Aboard the *Morning Star*)

The yellow orb hovered above and then lowered over the nuckta and his companion. It pulsed several times and faded from sight, reappearing under a tarp on the foredeck of the *Morning Star*.

"Wow," Ben said. He wobbled and grabbed the metal object in front of him to keep from falling. "I feel like my head was pulled into bits and reassembled in the wrong order."

"Breathe deeply," Seeka said. "The sensation will soon pass."

Ben obliged, bending over, replenishing his oxygen reserves. He rose. "Where are we?"

"The weapons," Seeka said. "You must remember why we are here."

"Weapons?" Ben questioned, still dazed. He looked up at the covering above him, and raising a hand, he touched the canvas. "This wasn't here yesterday."

"Obviously a response to your last confrontation with Evans," Seeka said.

Ben took a step backwards.

"No!" Seeka shouted. "The stacion field does not extend more than a few feet from the torpedoes."

He rocked backward, expecting to disintegrate into a puff of nothing and then regained his footing.

"Are you finished?" Seeka asked.

"Give it a rest, fuzz ball," Ben retorted.

Seeka thought a moment and chuckled. "Touché."

Ben smiled at the nuckta and scrutinized the warhead. He removed a pen and paper from his pocket and wrote. When finished, he pocketed the pad. "Okay, got it."

Seeka nodded, and the brain-scrambling transportation process began once again.

"Did you get it?" Stewart asked.

"I think so," Ben replied, handing the list of tools to Stewart. "I'm pretty sure everything I need is on there."

Stewart studied the paper. "Shouldn't be a problem; I'll start getting these things together right away."

"What's our buddy up to?" Ben asked.

"Haven't seen him," Stewart replied. "I can only assume he's putting all his effort into his favorite pastime."

"Getting gassed?" Ben asked.

Stewart nodded.

"There are others on this vessel, are there not?" Seeka asked.

"Yes," Stewart said.

"I know of the one you call Skull and the girl," Seeka said. "Tell me of any additional personnel."

Ben looked at Seeka. "Are you holding back on me?"

"There are happenings I dare not tell you," Seeka said, "lest by knowing, you change the intended order of events yet to come."

"And the plot thickens," Ben said.

"There's one other," Stewart said, "Vinny,"

"Ah," Seeka said, "perhaps you should arrange a meeting for all to attend."

"When?" Stewart asked.

"At what time is your captain most likely not to interrupt?" Seeka asked.

"After dark;" Stewart said, "that's when he does his heaviest drinking."

"Then tonight it shall be," Seeka said.

Chapter 54
Parallel Dimension I

(Return to *Deadly Reign*)

"Here is the latest and last of your gel, My Lord," Cahotic said, handing a crock full of an amber colored salve to Colossac.

"Thank you," Colossac said, accepting the container.

"We go once again to disrupt another township," Cahotic said.

"Yes, yes," Colossac replied, now engrossed in spreading the gel across his chest.

Cahotic nodded, mounted his animal and roared out of the settlement with the riders in tow.

"Ah," Colossac moaned. He finished massaging the salve into his face, and then settled back, giddy with ecstasy. Closing his eyes, the giant one nearly fell asleep. His right shoulder twitched, causing him to sit up and scratch. The twitch turned into a sting and soon elevated to an excruciating inferno, which moved over his entire body. Colossac screamed and clawed at his skinless tissue. Every place he touched exuded a pinkish fluid that oozed in a thick stringy stream.

"Get it off!" he shouted, but there was no one to hear his cry. Colossac fell out of the building, writhing on the snow-covered dirt pavement. He removed the gel as he wriggled through the slurry of mud he had created, packing it in between the fibers of his musculature. He ceased rolling and pulled himself to his knees.

"I will destroy you, Cahotic," he growled through clenched teeth, the pain from the caked mud being marginally less than that of the toxic gel. Having turned the pain into rage, he focused his very being on the obliteration of Cahotic and the riders.

Chapter 55
Parallel Dimension II

(Aboard the *Morning Star*)

"So what's up, Stew?" Vinny asked.

"I'll let Ben take it from here," Stewart said.

Ben stood and faced the assembly. "I'm not sure how to begin, so I'm just going to jump in with all four feet."

Out of sight, Seeka imagined Ben with four legs and paws, catapulting off the ship and into the ocean.

Ben began by explaining the weapons onboard and the dire consequences of firing them at close proximity to the island.

"What can we do?" Eve asked.

"Yeah," Vinny echoed, rising from his chair, "what do we do?"

"Here goes," Ben mumbled. "Seeka!"

The nuckta, hearing his name, slinked out from underneath the bed and sat down before the gathering.

"What is that?" Vinny exclaimed.

Eve yelped and pulled her legs up onto her chair.

"Seeka," Ben said, "they're all yours." He sat down beside Eve and touched her leg. "It's okay."

Eve reluctantly placed her feet back on the floor.

The nuckta remained seated and cleared his throat. "I, like Ben, am not sure where to begin," he said.

"It talks!" Vinny exclaimed.

"Shh," Skull said, "let him speak."

Eve raised her legs once again. Ben pushed them back down.

"I apologize for such a disturbing appearance," Seeka said. "However, I wish to speak to you concerning a matter of the utmost urgency. Ben has told you of the danger. Now I will explain to you the reason."

Vinny wrinkled his forehead. Eve looked at Ben and then back to Seeka.

Seeka once again relayed the story of Nilrem, his plan to change the sequence of events, and Seeka's own attempt to right what had been wronged.

"So where's this dude now?" Vinny asked. "Let's go there and take him out."

"If it were only that simple," Seeka said. "He has gone, and the damage is done. It is now up to us to repair that damage."

"By stopping the launch?" Vinny asked.

"That's all we've been able to come up with so far," Ben said.

"What's this stacion generator you've been talking about?" Vinny asked.

"It projects a force field of sorts around the torpedoes," Stewart said. "It keeps anyone from tampering with the warheads."

"But that's a problem you've licked, right?" Vinny asked.

"As far as accessing the controls," Seeka said, "the answer is yes. Only Ben can resolve the rest of your question."

"Well?" Vinny inquired, looking at Ben.

Ben smiled grimly. "Getting there is not the problem. It's my limited knowledge of the control system."

"What does that mean?" Vinny insisted, rising from his seat once again.

"Calm down," Stewart said, urging Vinny to sit. "Ben is our best shot."

"Best shot at what;" Vinny retorted, "being blown into a thousand pieces?"

Ben stood to face Vinny. "You got a better idea?"

"Well, no," Vinny admitted.

"Then sit down and be part of the solution," Ben said, "not the problem."

"Sorry," Vinny said, reseating himself.

"Ben," Stewart said, "if the stacion field destroys anything it touches, would it be possible to use that to our advantage?"

Ben thought for a moment. "You might have something there." Ben paced and then turned to face Stewart. "Wouldn't a launch with the field in place destroy the ship as well?"

Stewart shook his head. "In theory, the warheads should vaporize instantaneously, not having time to detonate. If they do detonate, the field should contain the explosion; hypothetically speaking, of course."

"Were you able to fill my list of tools?" Ben asked.

"Yes," Stewart replied.

"Good, that'll be our failsafe," Ben said. "If we can disarm the warheads and then launch them through the stacion field, we'll have given ourselves the best chance for success."

"A most prudent conclusion," Seeka said.

"What about you, Skull?" Stewart asked. "You've said nothing."

"Sounds good to me."

Ben turned to Eve. "How about you?"

"You lost me at, 'It can talk.'"

Ben smiled. "Okay, Stewart, if you'll consolidate the tools so they're easy to carry, we'll get started on phase one."

Chapter 56
Parallel Dimension I

(Return to *Deadly Reign*)

"Etamay," Cahotic said, "you will be my second."

"You honor me," Etamay replied.

"Refer to me as General from here on."

Etamay bowed. "Of course, General."

"If Colossac does not perish, he will soon be in pursuit. We must prepare for this possibility."

"I will notify the others to be vigilant in keeping watch."

"Good. And the destruction here is complete?"

"Yes, General; no life remains."

"I wish you to oversee the gel production. We will require ongoing protection from the moisture contained within the white flakes that fall from the sky."

"It will be as you have requested."

"Good."

"Might I inquire as to how we will combat Colossac if the possibility you mentioned becomes reality?"

"Colossac could not know that he forged the very instruments of his own death," Cahotic said, smiling.

Etamay nodded, returning the grin.

Chapter 57

Ben found that he was unable to move anything but his facial muscles. "Looks like I've really done it this time."

"We were lucky to make it this far," Eve said, attempting to soothe her husband's ego.

"I'm sorry I got you into this."

"You didn't get me into anything that—"

"Hmm," Pete interrupted, "if you two are done massaging each other, we may have a matter that's just a tad more important."

"What is it?" Ben asked, obviously irritated.

"We have company," Pete replied.

A party of two midwives and two sentries stopped in front of Thalyn's cell.

"Pete," Ben said, "I can't see anything but shadows. What's happening?"

"Two bugs and two baboons just walked past me," Pete said. "I don't know what they're doing; I can't see much either."

"They have stopped in front of Thalyn," Caleb said. "I am also unable to discern their purpose."

The two simian narify moved in, holding Thalyn's head, forcing his lower jaw open. One of the insectoid midwives forced a palm full of the black goo into his mouth. Thalyn immediately began to gag. His head jerked backward, causing his silken bindings to dig into his flesh. Thin red lines developed across his face and neck, oozing life fluid in thin rivulets. He began to convulse, tightening against the restraints. His arms lifted to either side, straining his bindings. They gave way as the slender threads sliced through bone, depositing his hands and random portions of arm material on the ground.

Eve heard gurgling and a dull thud, not knowing that the sound was Thalyn's head making contact with the floor.

"They are attempting to feed us," Caleb said, his voice now taking on a solemn demeanor.

The narify watched as the dissected body crumbled before them. They looked at each other with disbelief, clicking and chattering, and then moved to the next cell, the cell that contained Ben.

"Thalyn," Pete exclaimed.

"He is no longer," Caleb replied.

"Where are they now?" Pete asked, struggling to move his head.

Ben produced a nervous chuckle. "Looks like it's feeding time at the Ben exhibit."

"No," Eve exclaimed, her face paralyzed in terror.

"Ben," Pete said, "I'm sorry."

"No regrets," Ben said.

"No regrets," Pete replied.

"Farewell, dear friend," Caleb said.

"Eve," Ben said, "I love you."

She didn't hear Ben's words but mumbled to herself. "Please, Great One, deliver us in our time of need."

The two narify moved toward Ben, stilling his head and forcing his mouth open. A midwife plunged a ball of black death toward his open mouth.

Chapter 58
Parallel Dimension II

(Aboard the *Morning Star*)

"Here are your tools," Stewart said, handing Ben a canvas bag.

"Thanks," he replied. "Are you ready, fuzz ball?"

Seeka grunted.

"We'll be back," Ben said, kissing Eve on the cheek. "It may be best if the four of you go to your cabins. It wouldn't look kosher for Mr. Paranoid to find you all together."

"He may think we're up to something," Stewart said with a chuckle.

Ben smiled and then disappeared in a yellow flash.

"I hate when he does that," Eve said. "It scares me."

"He'll be fine," Stewart said. "We should split up now."

Eve nodded, walked to the door and opened it. She gasped. "Captain Evans, how long have you been standing there?"

"Don't you mean Mr. Paranoid?" he answered, raising his hand. In it, he held a revolver.

Eve slowly backed away.

"Where is Adams?" Evans demanded. "I heard his voice."

"Captain, as you can see, he's not in here," Stewart said.

Evans stomped toward Stewart and placed the barrel under his chin. "Do not toy with me, Davis. The only regret I would have in dropping you right now is the waste of a good bullet."

"Captain," Eve pleaded, "Ben's not here."

Evans brought the gun down and backed away.

"No matter," he said, waving the pistol. "All of you move out of the door."

Stewart eyed Evans warily. "Where are you taking us?"

"Where you will cause no more trouble." Evans raised the revolver. "Now move!"

"Hand me the three-quarter box wrench, fuzz ball," Ben said.

Seeka looked in the bag, then at his front toes. He reared up on his hind legs, extended his front paws, grinned as best he could and twiddled his toes at Ben.

Ben lifted his head out of the control hatch and looked over his shoulder at Seeka.

"No can do, slick head," Seeka replied.

"Hmm," Ben grunted. He leaned over, nosed through the bag and found his desired tool. Rising, he looked at Seeka. "When are you gonna grow thumbs?"

"When nucktas fly," he responded.

"You learn too quickly," Ben said and went back to work.

"What is the timeline for disarming the warheads?" Seeka asked.

"Don't know; once I've figured this one out, I have to do the second." He rose to look at Seeka, "And since I don't know what I'm doing, it could be a while."

"I see," Seeka said. "Would it be possible to—"

"No," Ben interrupted, rising once again from the hatch. "I can't go any faster."

The barely audible hum that surrounded the pair began to die and then was gone.

"What was that?" Ben exclaimed, looking around and upward. "Did I touch the wrong thing?"

"I cannot be sure;" Seeka said, "however, I believe the stacion field has dissipated."

A slit in the canvas covering burst open. An armed Captain Evans stood in the opening, staring in disbelief at Ben and Seeka. A yellow aura surrounded the nuckta, and he began to fade. Evans pointed the gun at Ben's head. "Leave, and he dies."

Seeka faded to a point and reappeared, the light disappearing without him.

"So," Evans said, "the saboteurs." He stepped in, allowing the canvas to fall behind him. A small orb continued to bathe the area in a faint yellow light.

"Strange," he said, lifting his pistol and firing several shots. The orb flickered and continued its luminescence. Evans backed up, opening the canvas flap once again. "You two, move, now!" he barked.

Chapter 59
Parallel Dimension I

(Return to *Deadly Reign*)

The insectoid hand paused less than an inch from Ben's lips and began to quiver. It jerked violently upward, snapping at the elbow. The second midwife took to the air, ending her flight buried headfirst in the soft chamber wall. Ben felt his cheeks extend. The pair of simian narify holding his jaw were pulled from his side and slammed together. The collision sent a spray of green fluid in all directions. Ben's benefactor lumbered toward him and removed his bindings.

"Greetings, small one," Orac said.

"Orac," Ben exclaimed, "I thought you were—"

"As did I;" Orac said, "but as you can see, that is not the case."

"Ben!" Eve cried. "What's happening?"

"I'm okay," he answered. "Just hold tight."

Orac continued to tug and strip the silk-like threads from around Ben. After fifteen minutes he was free.

"Thanks, big guy," Ben said. "But how?"

"In time," Orac said. "There is much to do."

Ben nodded, and the two worked together freeing Eve, Pete and Caleb, taking care not to cut themselves on the slender threads.

Caleb moved from his prison and paused, staring at the remains of his friend. The others gathered around him as he spoke. "Be in peace. You are now in the embrace of the Great One and with your fallen brothers Menday and Korell. I am indebted to you for your faithful service and anticipate our reunion."

"Caleb," Ben said, "do you want to bury Thalyn?"

"We must leave," Caleb replied. "To linger here would endanger the living. This is but an empty shell. Who Thalyn was is no longer in this place. He has gone home."

"Follow me," Orac said. "In my instance, the black death no longer has any effect."

Ben, Eve, Pete and Caleb moved through the labyrinth, with Orac running interference. Not a single shot was fired as Orac crushed any creature that had the misfortune of confronting their exodus. In under an hour, the party reached the surface.

"Look," Eve said, "our horses are still here."

"Let us make all haste," Caleb said.

"The further from here, the better," Pete echoed.

After several hours of travel, the forest began to thin.

"We are now safe from the reach of the narify," Caleb said. "Circle the mounts, and we will gather wood. A fire and meal will do much toward our well-being."

♦♦♦

"It's so good to be out in the open again," Eve said, sighing.

Ben pulled her close, saying nothing.

"Orac," Caleb said, "please relay how you came to be after your near entombment."

"Very well," Orac said, wiping his mouth. "As I lay waiting to die, I conversed with the Great One, through the Living One. I expressed my gratitude for acceptance, even though I had just come to know each. They bestowed upon me great comfort, the like of which I had never experienced."

Caleb smiled and nodded.

"The Living One conveyed I would return to health and assist The Three and Caleb," Orac said.

"How did you know you were immune to the narify food?" Pete asked.

"I did not," Orac said. "As soon as I stood, I was attacked by two sentries, suffering no ill effects. It was then I made my way into the birthing chamber."

"And not a second too soon," Ben said. "Except for Thalyn," he added.

Orac produced a grim smile and continued eating, enjoying his meal with less fervor as he considered Ben's remark.

"We will finish our meal, rest, and resume our trek to the sea," Caleb said. He stood, walked to his horse, and returned with a quart-size container he set on the ground. He knelt down and asked everyone to stare at him and not to move. "There seems to be someone among us who does not belong." He picked up a stick and stirred the fire, acting as if he were unaware. "I sensed this among the horses as I fetched this container."

Forgetting Caleb's warning, Eve turned to look toward the pack animals.

"Eve!" Caleb chastised in a loud whisper.

She jerked her head back, "Sorry," she mouthed.

Relaxing, Ben leaned back to his original position. "So what do we do now?"

"Under the guise of unloading the animals, Pete shall move to the left of the mount closest to our store of wood."

"Before this gets started, let's get something straight," Eve said, in a low voice. "You're not leaving me out of this because I'm a woman."

Ben raised his eyebrows, and with a slight smirk said, "She's all yours."

Caleb turned his attention toward Eve. "You will be with me."

Eve smiled with acceptance.

"And, Pete, you will move to the right."

Pete nodded.

"I feel as though we are in no danger," Caleb said. "Only this new one brings an air of mischief."

"What about our weapons?" Ben asked.

"They will not be necessary," Caleb said. "In fact, they may serve to warn our guests of our intentions."

"Okay," Pete said, "when do we go?"

Caleb stood. "Now, but move slowly, acting as if we've no other purpose than to unpack the animals."

The three stood along with Caleb and moved toward their quarry, Pete breaking formation to the left and Ben to the right.

"Just retrieve the blankets for now," Caleb said as he and Eve reached the first pack horse.

Ben and Pete both pretended to unlash the provisions from their respective horses. Caleb made his way to the opposite side of the horse Eve was tending when he noticed one pack had been ripped open. Upon closer examination, he saw dried fruit, salted meat, and a fur seemed to be the only missing items. He called The Three to join him. "It appears as though our thief has taken only necessities and has now gone with no other evident motive." Caleb pointed to two small sets of footprints in the snow, one leading in and one leading out into the dark. The Three and Caleb walked back to the campfire.

"Please sit and relax," Caleb said. He picked up the container he had retrieved minutes before, then, filling his cup, he passed it to Ben who did likewise. Once each had indulged in the drink, Caleb spoke. "Please enjoy," he said. "This will help you sleep."

"Shouldn't someone keep watch?" Ben asked.

"I will take the first," Caleb said, "and shall wake Orac when it is time."

Eve yawned. "Good night," she said.

Unsure of the ones from whom he had pilfered his meager supplies, Yoshi sat huddled in the fur, chewing on a piece of dried fruit. He felt they could be trusted, but lacked the confidence to show himself to the group.

Maybe they would help him, he thought, *or perhaps kill him*. Yoshi hoped for the former but feared the latter; however, not enough to keep him from following close enough to see the fire yet remain undetected. All these things would have to wait. Yoshi was exhausted from lack of sleep and the sheer hell of what he had lived through during the past two risings of the Great Light. Closing his eyes, he slept the fitful sleep of the haunted.

Chapter 60
Parallel Dimension II

(Aboard the *Morning Star*)

"There are cameras and sensors in this room that will advise me if any of the six of you leave," Evans said. "If that happens, all will die." He began a devilish laugh as he closed and bolted the door.

"Go figure," Vinny said. "A sot outsmarted five people and a—" He looked at Seeka. "What are you?" he asked.

"A fuzz ball," Seeka replied.

"Yeah, that," Vinny said.

"Regardless," Ben said, "if we leave we die, and if we stay, it's the same, although it may be a bit quicker."

"Since there's not much we can do here," Stewart said, "I guess that answers that."

"Seeka," Ben said, his excitement growing, "how many can you transport at one time?"

Seeka thought for a moment. "Only two that I can be sure of. Before using the krang to move both you and me, I would have answered one to your query."

"So for all you know," Ben said, "you could transport this entire ship and all aboard?"

"I can only suppose that what you say is true;" Seeka replied, "however, it could kill all who choose to participate."

"Why don't we just travel back to a time before Evans caught us and dragged us into this hole?" Vinny asked.

All eyes looked to the nuckta for an answer. "We may travel from place to place, or even world to world," Seeka said, "but in every instance, time remains constant."

"Then it's a numbers game again," Ben said.

"It would appear so," Seeka replied.

"Whoever is helping Evans," Stewart said, "seems to have been very thorough."

"Exactly," Ben agreed. "For every move we make there is a counter measure taken."

"Then we'll have to make our next move one that cannot be countered," Stewart said.

"Checkmate," Ben said.

"What?" Stewart inquired.

"Checkmate," Ben repeated. "We're playing a game. We've been able to put Evans in check, but now we'll close the net, and it's checkmate."

"I'm all ears," Stewart said.

"It's easy, Stew," Vinny said. "There are six of us—" He glanced at Seeka. "Well, five and a half. All we have to do is spread out. He can't take all of us."

"What if we allow Seeka to transport as many of us out as he can in one attempt?" Stewart said. "The ones who make it to the outside can hide themselves, but close to the entrance. When Evans comes to investigate, we pounce from all sides."

"That's it," Ben said.

"Are you forgetting that he has a gun?" Eve asked.

"No," Ben replied, "but at this point, it doesn't matter." He turned to look at Seeka. "Ready?"

"Gather closely together," Seeka said. He walked into the middle of the human assembly, and the familiar yellow orb descended on the mass. As the orb pulsed and began to fade, three figures remained.

Stewart, Vinny and Ben stared at each other.

"Oh, no," Ben whispered.

Chapter 61
Parallel Dimension I

(Return to *Deadly Reign*)

Orac stopped at the frozen stream. He bent down, and with several blows of his fist, opened a hole big enough to drink from.

"We will water the horses and rest for a short time," Caleb said.

Orac backed away from the opening and motioned for Caleb to go first.

"No," Caleb said, smiling, "what you have done would have taken many hours to accomplish otherwise. The right is yours to drink first."

Orac nodded, dropped to one knee and gorged himself on the pristine fluid.

Ben and Eve knelt together.

"This is so good," she said.

"Look," Ben said, "this ice must be at least a foot thick." He turned to Orac and back to Eve. "I can't imagine the power in his hands."

Eve slurped a last bit of water, and drawing a finger across her lips, she said, "Be glad he's on our side."

Ben nodded and stood with his wife.

Caleb and Pete took their turn, then watered all the horses.

"Pete," Caleb said, "there are skins on my mount. Would you fill them with water please?"

"Sure," Pete replied. He untied the containers and walked to the break in the ice. He stared at the hole that was once again frozen over. "Not going to get much water out of this," he said. Pete turned to locate Orac. "Hey, big man, would you come here."

"How may I assist?" Orac said, walking up to Pete. Several orbs followed, moving a short distance ahead, stopping, and growing brighter.

"I think we need another opening," Pete said.

Orac looked at the hole and then at Pete, smiling.

"Of course, small one," he said. He knelt down and pushed his fist through the ice. Standing, he looked at Pete.

"My turn," Pete exclaimed. He knelt and filled the water skins. Once three containers were full and he'd started to fill the fourth, the slushy water began to vibrate at regular intervals. He watched as the ripples moved across the partially frozen surface. Pete pulled his hand from the water. *Strange*, he thought. He continued to follow the pulsation until he felt it moving through his body, growing in intensity as it progressed. He looked up at Orac. "We have a problem," he said.

"Indeed," Orac replied, "and it now stands before us."

The orbs glowing as bright as ever before, cast their light upon six enormous figures.

"The riders," Orac whispered.

Chapter 62
Parallel Dimension II

(Aboard the *Morning Star*)

"Where are the men?" Eve exclaimed. She looked at Skull. "I didn't mean you weren't—"

"No problem," Skull said. "I was wondering the same thing."

"The paranoid one is coming," Seeka said. "Perhaps we should remove ourselves from sight."

Eve and Skull ducked behind a drum beside the door leading to the holding room.

"No," Eve whispered, "you need to find someplace else to hide."

"No," Skull insisted, "I want to stay with you." His face bore the expression of a frightened child. "Please."

Eve raised her head and pointed to a cabinet on the other side of the entrance. "There," she hissed. "We have to spread out so we can attack Evans from all directions."

Skull looked at her with terror in his eyes. "If you say so." He left Eve and made his way to her specified point, just as Evans came into view.

Seeka, now almost invisible, crouched near the hinge side of the door.

Evans stood at the entrance fumbling through his keys. The smell of stale wine and urine wafted through the air. Eve pinched her nose to keep from gagging. He found the correct key, inserted it in the lock, twisted, and slid the bolt back, allowing the door to open.

"I told you," Evans slurred, "that you all would die." He pointed the pistol at Ben and Stewart, his hand swaying from side to side, as he struggled to keep his balance.

Vinny remained poised behind the door, ready to pounce as soon as Evans entered far enough into the room.

"Captain," Stewart said.

"Don't waste your breath," Evans snarled. He cocked the pistol, closed one eye in an attempt to aim and squeezed the trigger.

Seeka moved with blinding speed. Lunging between Evans' legs, he twisted, inverting his body as he did so. Once he reached his target area, he clamped down hard on Evans' crotch, causing the first shot to miss by several feet.

"Ah!" Evans screamed. He brought the gun butt down on the nuckta's head, causing Seeka to release his grip and fall unconscious to the ground. Any evidence of inebriation was now far removed from the captain. He raised his foot to apply the deathblow to Seeka's quivering body.

Vinny pushed on the door, slamming it into the one-legged captain. Evans tipped onto the floor, the pistol flying from his hand.

Taking advantage of the prostrate Evans, Ben and Stewart piled on top. The three struggled to gain control. Evans was winning the skirmish.

"Vinny!" Stewart cried. "A little help, please." Vinny joined the fray, and the tide shifted.

Eve and Skull entered the room.

"Eve," Ben exclaimed, "grab the gun!"

Evans made one last effort to free himself, nearly succeeding until steel touched his forehead, followed by the unmistakable sound of the hammer cock. The drunkenness returned, and Evans fell back cursing, his thick-tongued words barely recognizable.

The three men eased their weight off Evans. He came to a sitting position and slid into the corner, still mumbling to himself.

Seeka had rolled onto his stomach, his tongue lolling out one side of his mouth. His eyes glazed, and his head swayed from side to side.

"Keep him covered," Ben said.

Eve nodded.

Ben knelt. "How you doing, fuzz ball?" he asked.

Seeka wove his head up to glance at Ben, used his extended tongue to emit a raspberry, then weaved his way back down, resting his head on his forepaws.

Ben chuckled and rubbed the nuckta's head.

Seeka winced. "Not the head," he whispered.

"Oops, sorry," Ben said. He stood and joined the others. "What gives?"

"Shh," Eve cautioned.

Skull was leaning over Evans; the captain's face expressionless. Tiny flashes of yellow and green bounced off his cheeks.

After several moments, Skull stood up and turned to face the group. "He will remain subdued for a short time. Use these moments to your advantage." Skull blinked. "Hey guys, whatcha lookin at?"

"Come on buddy," Vinny said, taking Skull's hand. "We could both use some air."

Stewart leaned over Evans and unhooked the ring of keys from his side. "You heard the man. Let's get to work."

Eve picked up Seeka, leaving Evans in the corner babbling. Ben closed and bolted the door.

Chapter 63
Parallel Dimension I

(Return to *Deadly Reign*)

"State your purpose," Orac demanded.

"I believe my purpose is known to all present," Cahotic replied.

Caleb, Ben and Eve joined Pete and Orac.

"Mount up," Caleb said, "and do not remove your eyes from them."

Pete complied and climbed onto his horse.

"Prepare your weapons," Caleb ordered.

"I need no other than these," Orac stated, holding up his fists.

"Now, Caleb," Cahotic chastised, "is that a proper welcome for old friends?"

"Orac," Caleb said, motioning to the giant.

Orac backed up to meet Caleb. "Yes?" he said.

Caleb leaned over and whispered into Orac's ear.

Orac smiled and then nodded, returning to his previous spot.

"Make ready," Cahotic said, "and separate the necessary parts. We must renew our supply of gel."

The riders pulled their swords and moved forward. The line was staggered in a stepped orientation, allowing each rider to shield the one behind. As the first aberration moved onto the snow-covered ice, an inaudible cracking ensued. Caleb sensed the ice give under the great weight, as the second rider followed his predecessor.

"Now, Orac," Caleb ordered.

Orac bent over, slamming his mammoth fists into the ice. Cracks developed in the crust, spreading from the epicenter in spider-like fashion. Orac continued his barrage, crawling further onto the ice as he decimated the concrete water. He felt two points of pressure along his back. A small figure wrapped in fur vaulted from his flank and onto the rear of the first rider's beast. He wielded a spear with a fine bronze tip attached to a smooth brown shaft. The newcomer plunged the spear with no ill effects, hitting pieces of armor and plated green scales. The first rider and his steed dipped to the left and then to the right. An ear-splitting crack echoed through the forest, and the rider sank. As the creatures continued their descent, the small figure jumped from the rider. With uncanny agility, the strange fur-covered form bounced along small chunks of ice, floating in the stream until he reached the bank. Astonishment enveloped The Three, uttering not a sound as they watched this acrobat.

The second rider attempted to turn and make it back to solid ground, reaching the bank as the ice collapsed beneath him. The animal sank to its midsection before it could gain a hold with its forelimbs. The aberration it bore slid off its back. Steam drifted upward from the pair as the water permeated their bodies.

"Orac!" Caleb yelled. "Enough."

Orac ceased his assault and circled around to return to his comrades.

Caleb turned to Ben. "Gather wood for a fire."

"What about the riders?" Ben asked.

"Wood," Caleb barked, "and quickly."

Ben, Pete and Eve dropped from their horses as the ice gave way, plunging Orac into the frozen slush.

The first rider was now chest deep in the center of the stream. Huge bubbles from underneath exploded as the beast that bore him disintegrated. The rider himself silently melted into the stream, his head exploding in small puffs as if boiling in a cauldron.

The second rider's mount, using its front claws, inched itself onto the bank. Its rider plunged his sword deep into the beast, allowing it to pull him along. The pair breeched the water's surface, both formless from the midsection down, their remaining torsos dissolving in a mass of tiny gurgling eruptions.

"Give ground," Cahotic commanded. The four remaining riders turned. "We will meet again, Caleb," Cahotic's voice trailed as they thundered into the perpetual darkness.

Caleb had the fire tendered. Ben and Pete helped the frozen giant out of the stream. They sat him in front of the meager source of heat. He was shivering violently and unable to speak. Caleb and Eve fueled the flames, bringing it to a roaring blaze.

"Two down and four to go," Ben said, "not counting our new friend over there." He threw a thumb in the boy's direction.

"Five," Caleb corrected, "and that is depending on where his alliance rests." Caleb thought a moment. "Although I do not believe it to be with our enemies."

The small one stood several yards away, bent in a defensive posture, pointing his spear at Caleb and The Three.

"Could he be the one that relieved us of the missing supplies?" Pete asked.

"I'd say so," Ben replied. "Just look at the fur."

"How ya doing, big man?" Pete asked.

"Much better now, thank you," Orac said, a lingering shiver causing his teeth to chatter.

"We will stay here for a short time," Caleb said. "The water will offer protection while Orac recovers."

"What about short stuff over there?" Ben asked.

"Time will also allow us to decide concerning the small one," Caleb said.

"If you ask me," Eve said, "he needs a woman's touch." She smiled. "Look at him; he's just a terrified little boy."

"Maybe not as little as you would suppose," Ben said, remembering the boy's abilities. Having seen these for a few seconds, he wondered what else this young one was capable of.

"If you wouldn't mind, dear Eve," Caleb said, "see if you can influence the yearling."

Eve stood, and extending a hand, moved slowly toward the boy.

♦♦♦

Deep below the surface of the earth, a dormant beast shuddered each time a rider was dispatched. Buried in this subterranean lair eons ago, the time for the marcovian was soon at hand. The creature was something akin to a cross between a large crab and a scorpion. Standing around twelve feet tall, the width of its carapace was narrow, more like that of a scorpion. Its tail stretched fifteen feet from the back of its shell, ending with four sharp barbed spikes, which, unlike its cousin, contained no poison. Two sets of claws, one in front underneath the head and the second protruding from the base of the tail, also housed a set of rudimentary eyes. These ocular appendages could distinguish shapes, giving the marcovian a simple form of rear vision. Down each side of the body projected a set of four legs, each with three joints and pinchers at their tips. The head contained two sets of eyes, allowing a one hundred-eighty-degree field of vision. The mouth held a set of pinchers to grab its prey and grinding pads to complete the pulverization of the contents before it entered the stomach. For now, the marcovian would rest in its partial state of hibernation until called into service if that time ever came.

Chapter 64
Parallel Dimension II

(Aboard the *Morning Star*)

"How could Evans become so strong?" Eve asked.

"He's got someone else working with him," Ben replied.

"The one Seeka spoke of?" Stewart asked.

"Yes," Seeka said.

"Seeka," Eve exclaimed, "you're all right!" She leaned over and caressed the nuckta.

"Far from it," Seeka said. "However, I am coherent." He bobbed up and down several times, and then weaving his way up, focused on Eve.

Ben knelt down. "How you doing, fuzz ball?"

Seeka slowly turned his head and looked at Ben. "Not as well as you might think," he replied. "However, in partial answer to Eve's question, the one I named as Nilrem I sense has undergone a distinct change."

"What do you mean 'sense,' and what kind of change?" Ben asked.

"I am still connected to my rightful world," Seeka said, "and through this connection, I am able to discern changes within that world."

"Explain the change," Stewart said.

"The one I speak of has taken the place of the one we thought to be our original enemy," Seeka said. "This one has grown in stature as well as power; however, I feel that turmoil has invaded his plan."

"How so?" Ben asked.

"I do not know," Seeka replied. He lowered his head, gingerly shaking it as he did so. "At least I do not think that I know." He looked at Skull as if asking for confirmation.

Skull smiled, seemingly oblivious to anything of importance going on around him.

"No matter," Seeka said. "The troubles I speak of have no bearing on our present situation. We must turn our attention to the weapons."

"Agreed," Ben said. "Stewart, take everyone and search for the stacion generator. Seeka and I will resume our attempt to disarm the warheads."

Stewart nodded. "Skull, go check on Evans; then we'll get started."

"Okay, fuzz ball," Ben said, "we left the tools there, so take us back."

Seeka nodded, wobbled and then began to concentrate.

After several moments, Ben glared at the nuckta. "Well?" he said.

"I do not understand," Seeka replied. "Perhaps it was the blow to my head."

"What's wrong?" Stewart asked.

"Ah, fuzz ball's not working," Ben said. "He seems to have closed his travel agency."

"You mean he can't transport?" Eve asked.

"Unfortunately, you are correct," Seeka said. "It appears that the krang has chosen to depart for a time."

"Then you'll get the power back?" Eve asked.

"I do not know," Seeka replied. "I was speaking out of hope."

"We can't disarm the warheads with hope," Ben said.

Seeka cocked his head sideways, looking at Ben. "I beg to differ," he said. "Without hope, what do we have?"

"I know what we don't have," Ben fumed, "and that's a way to get to those two ticking time-bombs on the deck of this vessel. And without that, there is no hope."

Skull burst into the room, bringing the debate to a halt. "Evans," he gasped. "He's gone!"

Chapter 65
Parallel Dimension I

(Return to Deadly Reign)

Yoshi retreated, making short jabs with his spear as Eve neared. He dressed in light colored leather pants, pulled tight with a drawstring. He wore a short-sleeved, V-neck cotton shirt that appeared to have been bleached at one time, but now bore a menagerie of stains. He had the fur draped over his shoulders and tied with a string where the upper edges of the garment met his neck. On his feet were leather shoes.

"No one will hurt you," Eve said in a voice she hoped expressed her most soothing characteristics.

Yoshi looked at her, stopped moving and shook his head.

Eve knelt down. "Do you have a name?"

His eyes moved from her to Caleb, Orac and The Three; then, as if expecting a surprise attack, looked right and then left. His eyes met Eve's once again. "Yoshi," he muttered.

"Yoshi," she repeated.

The boy cautiously nodded.

Eve smiled and once again extended her hand. "My name is Eve, and I assure you that no one will bring you any harm."

Yoshi clenched his teeth and snarled. "Tell that to my mother and father!" the boy screamed. He burst forward, his spear leveled at Eve, and was on her in an instant. Unable to rise from her kneeling position, she moved sideways, extending her leg outward. Eve caught the spear in the upper part of her left shoulder as Yoshi tripped over her.

Caleb and The Three pounced on the youngster. Orac, the last one to arrive at the disturbance, climbed over the boy, pinning his arms and legs but being careful not to injure with his great weight.

"You were told no harm would come to you," Caleb said.

Yoshi made no comment, continuing his futile attempts to escape.

Ben attended to Eve, first removing the spear from her shoulder.

"How is it?" Pete asked.

"Not too bad," Ben replied, "Do you have any more of that spongy material we got from Belac?"

"Coming right up," Pete said. He unlashed the material from his bow, pinching off a small amount and handing it to Ben.

"This should do it, sweetheart," Ben said. "The discomfort will subside quickly."

"Good," she said, wincing at the pain coursing through her shoulder.

Ben rolled the material between his fingers forming a plug the size of Eve's wound. He pushed the plug into the hole in Eve's shoulder. As he forced the plug in, a greenish-brown fluid oozed out. Ben held the plug in place, and disturbed by the familiarity of the exiting fluid, thought a moment. *That's it; the slime that the riders and their beasts turned into when touched by the water.* He panicked for a moment, and then, remembering the healing powers of the moss, forced himself to calm down.

"How does it feel?" Ben asked.

"Much better," Eve replied. "It still stings, but it's more manageable now."

Ben nodded but thought it best to keep his worries to himself, lest he cause undue concern.

Caleb instructed Orac to release Yoshi. The young man sat up, brushed off his pant legs and looked at Caleb. "Now that you have me, what are you going to do?"

"As soon as you apologize to the fair one you have injured," Caleb said, "you shall be given a meal and a chance to tell your story."

"You would pardon my offense?" Yoshi asked.

"It is not mine to pardon," Caleb said, nodding at Eve as she sat down beside the boy.

Yoshi looked at Eve. A tear ran down his cheek. "Please forgive me," he said. "I did not know what else to do."

Eve's first instinct was to wrap her arms around him and pull him close, but she thought it best not to push this budding relationship. "That's okay," she said. "I know you were scared." She reached out and touched his shoulder. He flinched, then relaxed, realizing she meant him no harm.

Caleb had Ben and Pete prepare a meal and then gathered everyone around.

After eating, Eve commented, "That wasn't too bad, darling; that is, if you consider dirt a culinary experience."

"I'll ignore that comment, considering the source," Ben said.

"I think it best," Pete agreed.

"Now that we are done," Caleb said, "we shall give Yoshi a chance to tell his story."

♦♦♦

Yoshi swished a mouthful of water and then swallowed. He looked at each one in the circle, unsure of how to begin.

"You are among friends," Caleb said. "Please, speak as you will."

Eve smiled and nodded her approval.

Yoshi sighed. "I am of the Sonyetti Nation, from Clan Clator. Our numbers were few, but our strength is well known among our brethren."

Caleb nodded. "Your reputation precedes you, and a formidable reputation it is."

"I am obliged," Yoshi said, looking as if he bore the weight of a thousand restless souls. "Before the Great Light ceased to rise, an unseen malevolence weighed heavily upon our village. It would leave and return at random. Once the Great Light was enveloped in darkness, the scourge took the form of dark riders." Yoshi paused. At that moment, even as he held a man's weapon, Yoshi couldn't have looked more childlike. He fixed his eyes on the fire. Yoshi's face was emotionless as he continued to speak. "My people are known for their speed and agility."

"This is true," Caleb said. "Much has been told of your prowess."

Yoshi acknowledged Caleb's comment. "But it was this that was their undoing. The riders and their beasts numbered twelve strong," Yoshi continued. "They were twelve, and we were over sixty, but our opponents formed a circle and closed in."

Caleb looked at Yoshi and raised an eyebrow. "I do not understand your disadvantage," Caleb said. "Every warrior knows the importance of mobility in battle."

Yoshi nodded. "These were not conventional warriors." He stared deep into Caleb's eyes. "Agility means nothing when your enemy can split you in twain with a flick of the wrist."

Caleb nodded.

"The slaughter was complete," Yoshi whispered, "and they left me alive to tell the tale."

He caught a tear rolling down his cheek with the back of his hand. "I left my home and the spirits of those who bore and nurtured me. At first, I could feel the fires on my back. The sight of the blaze would follow me for hours."

A deafening silence followed as the gathering came to an end.

"How ya feeling, big guy?" Pete asked, kneeling down beside Orac. "Ready to trash more goons?"

"If you mean dissolve the remaining riders, then yes," Orac replied.

Eve moved toward Yoshi. The boy rose as she approached. He stood staring at the ground, kicking up small clouds of white dust. She placed her open hand under his chin and raised his head until their eyes met.

He opened his mouth to speak.

"No," she said, "I know what you're going to say." Eve smiled. Yoshi mimicked her expression and the two embraced.

"It's time to go and lots to do," she said.

Yoshi nodded.

Caleb joined Orac and Pete. "I trust you are ready to travel?" he asked.

"Yes," Orac replied, standing, "I am now ready to trash the additional goons."

Caleb stared at the giant and then at Pete. "Good," he said, breaking into a smile. "Then we make ready our departure. The ice has frozen once again, large one. Would you make sure the remaining skins are filled before we leave?"

"With pleasure," Orac replied. "I will rehearse on the ice as I anticipate the goon reunion."

"We must work on your delivery," Pete said, taking Orac's arm. "C'mon; I'll help you fill the skins."

The group trekked across the frozen stream, stopping to look at the black puddle of viscous material that was the riders' remains.

Caleb dismounted and freed the sword from its gooey entombment. He rubbed it in the snow, removing most of the gunk, and finished the cleaning with the coarse material used to construct each storage pack. He handed the sword to Orac.

The giant held the weapon, slicing it through the air. "May be useful," he concluded. Orac pushed the blade inside his belt and led the way. Ben and

Caleb rode abreast. Pete followed the pair with Eve behind him. Yoshi sat in front of Eve, fingers entwined in the horse's mane.

"You doing okay?" Eve asked.

"Yes," Yoshi replied.

Eve sensed a twinge where Yoshi's sword had penetrated her shoulder. It turned to a dull ache, which climbed up her neck and curled around her brain. A notion entered her mind at that moment. "Say nothing," she whispered to Yoshi. He turned toward her, afraid to ask why. Her eyes told him to obey. Eve dropped back from the rest of the party. When she determined the distance was great enough, she eased off the trail and into the woods.

Caleb yawned.

"Am I keeping you up?" Ben asked.

"There is no escape from weariness, my friend. It will find us all eventually."

"Sorry, I can't help you with that," Ben said.

"Orac," Caleb said, "tell us more of your childhood."

"Gladly," Orac replied. "Remember my youngest years, I cannot; however, I will begin at my earliest recollection. As the light that cuts the darkness, it was practically thirty complete cycles ago."

"So, you're thirty years old?" Ben asked.

"I do not know years," Orac replied. "If a cycle is the same as a year, then yes; the preceding time I do not remember. I was familiar with Nilrem at this young age. He was my constant companion and caregiver."

Orac cleared his throat and shared his story—

"So, small one," Nilrem said, "I see that it is not to your liking."

"No, Father," Orac replied, pushing the bowl away, "I wish to grow strong, but I do not believe I can eat this."

Nilrem slid the bowl closer to his adopted son. "You will grow accustomed. You shall eat a small portion each day, and soon it will be as a delicacy to you."

"I will do as you say," Orac replied, taking a small portion and pushing it into his mouth.

"Very good," Nilrem said, patting the youngster on the head. "It is time to tend to your work."

"Yes, Father," Orac said. He reluctantly swallowed, smiled and left.

Nilrem watched the young one leave and then moved to a set of double doors. He opened them and then dropped to one knee, lowering his head. A glowing red sphere appeared, hovering above a silver cylindrical object. The piece measured three-feet-tall with a six-inch diameter base. It tapered to a point at the top. The sphere began to rotate and pulse with a snake-like, azure light curling within.

"Why have you summoned me?" a deep voice boomed.

"Forgive me, Dark One," Nilrem said shakily. "I seek your council concerning the boy."

"Proceed," the Dark One said.

"The yearling is not an acceptable specimen," Nilrem said. "He possesses no evil tendencies."

"Your ward is as he should be," the Dark One replied. "Only by corrupting the pure of heart will our purpose be realized."

"May I employ the Kumult?" Nilrem asked.

"No," the Dark One answered. "In one such as he, the Kumult will do nothing to turn his center; however, calling upon such a power may bring dire consequences."

"Is there no other way?"

"Were you not told of this from the start?"

"Yes; however, I did not perceive the difficulty—"

"Silence," the Dark One bellowed.

Nilrem dropped to both knees and laid his head on the floor. "Forgive me, Master."

"Then take charge of your ward and bother me no longer, lest I crush you like the worm you are."

"Yes, Your Lordship, I will do as you have asked."

"Make no mistake;" the Dark One hissed, "what I have decreed is not a request."

The sphere slowed, faded, and disappeared, filling the room with a deafening silence.

Nilrem remained with his head to the ground for several minutes, only rising when he was sure the threat of retribution had passed. He stood and walked to a small cupboard adjacent to the altar. Pulling a small crock from the cabinet, he grinned. "We shall see."

"So Nilrem used the Kumult despite the warning?" Pete asked.

"Yes, it would appear so," Orac said, as his voice trailed off. He grew silent, withdrawing inward.

"I hate to bring this up," Pete began, "but how could you know what transpired after leaving Nilrem?"

Orac continued to walk in silence, shaking his head.

"What's wrong with him?" Pete whispered.

Ben shook his head.

Orac stopped. The group instinctively came to a halt.

"I can remember everything I did after I left my father," he said. "However, I cannot understand how I discerned the events that took place after my departure." He looked at Ben, his eyes pleading for help to understand.

"Perhaps I can help you remember," Caleb said.

Orac turned to face Caleb. Instead, he looked past him to the last one in their group. It was Pete.

"Eve and the boy," Orac's eyes now fixed on Caleb's, "they are gone!"

Chapter 66
Parallel Dimension II

(Aboard the *Morning Star*)

"Gone?" Ben exclaimed. "How?"

Skull stood, arms spread, shaking his head. "The door was open."

"Obviously, the captain still has help," Stewart said.

"This certainly changes things," Ben said. "Do you still have the pistol?"

Eve nodded, producing the weapon.

"Good," Ben said. "Is that the only gun we own?"

Stewart nodded at Vinny. Vinny reluctantly pulled a thirty-eight caliber snub-nosed pistol out of his pocket.

Stewart took the piece in hand. "We thought this was the only gun onboard until Evans started waving his around."

"Why didn't you use it when Evans threatened to shoot us?" Ben asked.

Not wanting Ben to know of his original plan to take over the ship, Stewart interrupted Vinny as he began to speak. "Ah, we didn't think there'd ever be a need to use it," Stewart lied, "so it stays unloaded in my cabin."

"You do have shells, don't you?" Ben asked.

"Since the Evans incident," Stewart said, "it stays loaded."

Ben nodded. "We need to split up," he said, "but we'll do it in groups so no one is unarmed."

"You're doing fine so far," Stewart said.

"Okay," Ben replied, "since Seeka and I will keep trying to move through the stacion field, we'll stay together." He looked at his four shipmates. "Skull, you come with me and bring Vinny's pistol. Stewart, you keep Evans' gun and take Eve and Vinny with you. No matter what, gentlemen, we meet back here in one hour."

Vinny handed Skull his weapon. Skull passed the revolver to Ben. The group nodded to one another and departed.

Chapter 67
Parallel Dimension I

(Return to *Deadly Reign*)

Ben spun his horse around and raced back to where Eve should have been. "Where is she?" Ben demanded.

Pete shook his head. "I didn't realize she was missing."

Caleb joined Ben and Pete. "There are one set of tracks, which we know belong to Pete."

Ben turned and lashed out at Pete. "How could you let her out of your sight?"

"Eve was traveling just behind me," Pete said, "so she was never in my sight."

"Calm must prevail," Caleb insisted. "This bickering will do nothing to aid in locating Eve."

"He's right," Pete said, glaring at Ben.

"I'm going back to see where she left the trail," Ben said.

The three men backtracked down the trail.

"There," Pete cried. "Tracks! A single set of horseshoe-shaped depressions, nearly covered with snow, leading into the woods.

"There is no sign of a struggle," Caleb said. "However, her disappearance raises much suspicion."

"Eve wouldn't willingly leave," Ben insisted.

"We could assume that she left of her own volition, according to the evidence;" Caleb said. "Although, I believe darker forces may be involved."

Ben sighed and then looked at Pete. "Sorry, big man, it wasn't your fault."

Pete smiled and nodded his affirmation.

"We should make all haste locating the fair one," Caleb said, "for we know not what lies ahead."

Ben heard none of Caleb's warning. He was already following Eve's trail.

◆◆◆

"Before you ask," Eve said, "we had to get away from them. They were plotting our death."

"Why?" Yoshi asked. "They fought against our common enemy."

"You will not speak in such a manner," Eve growled. "The enemies you refer to are our closest allies. In fact, that is where we go now."

"This cannot be; these are the ones who slaughtered my people."

A hand clamped around the boy's throat. "Stay your tongue or join your people."

Yoshi made not a sound, his heart sinking deeper into despair, until he caught a glimpse of a familiar object loosely lashed to the side of Eve's horse.

The snow intensified as the pair continued deeper into the gloom.

"The trail is becoming harder to follow," Ben said. "The hoof prints are filling up with snow."

"I fear we shall soon lose the prints we have followed up to this point," Caleb said.

Ben nodded, each of his movements accentuating his anxious behavior.

"Take heart;" Caleb said, "she cannot be far ahead." Caleb looked at Ben. "We will find her."

"I wish I had your confidence," Ben admitted.

"Progress will be slowed by the ice that falls from the sky," Caleb said.

Ben glanced up at the relentless snow and then back down to the fading footprints.

Caleb patted Ben's shoulder and then turned to Orac. "We should talk as we search. There are unknowns that must be uncovered."

"Of course," Orac replied.

"As I remember," Caleb said, "when we last talked of Nilrem and your childhood, questions of how you remembered events you had not experienced brought you great distress."

"Indeed," Orac replied, having forgotten the conversation. "It would seem an impossibility."

"Do not fret so," Caleb said. "What you have seen is a glimpse of the wrongs forced upon you as a boy, but through avenues of the Great One, these wrongs have been negated."

"Even so, it is painful," Orac replied.

"For complete healing, grief is often necessary," Caleb said. "In time, your endurance will earn great benefits."

"If it must be so," Orac said, "I will bear this burden."

"You will soon cease to bear anything but death," a memorable voice hissed.

"Father?" Orac asked suspiciously.

"I am not your father, you regretful excuse for a living being. You waste the very air I breathe."

Colossac stepped into the light of the glowing orbs. The mud-caked giant dripped pink fluid, giving him the appearance of a massive burnt pink candle.

"What business do you have with any of these before you?" Caleb demanded.

Colossac laughed. "Caleb," he said, "of all those here, you should know. At one time you embraced the same cause."

"Not by choice," Caleb growled, "but by your twisted coercion." He loosed his crossbow from his shoulder, pointing it at the man mountain.

Ben and Pete bore their weapons down on the same target.

"Do not insult me with your empty threats," Colossac said. "The toys you wield will only serve to annoy me."

Colossac eyed Caleb, Ben and Pete. "The girl," he said, surveying the scene, "where is the girl?"

"That is business other than your own," Caleb said.

A wide grin spread across Colossac's face. "You do not know." A great roar of laughter emanated from the skinless beast.

Caleb and the two stood silent.

"How humorous;" Colossac said, "the great Three reduced to the not so great Two."

Orac drew his newly acquired sword.

Colossac grinned, eyeing the weapon with recognition and distaste for the one who carried it. "The blade you carry will be the instrument of your destruction," he said.

"Not until the monster I used to call father and the aberrations under his charge lie cold on the ground," Orac warned, slicing the sword back and forth through the air.

Colossac's grin widened. "You would do well to consider a weapon with attributes to perform such a task." He inched backward from the light, growling as he ducked into the shadows.

"So," Ben said, "once again the plot thickens."
"It would seem so," Caleb replied.

Chapter 68
Parallel Dimension II

(Aboard the *Morning Star*)

"Where are they?" Eve asked. "He said to meet here in an hour." She took two paces, turned, and retraced her steps. "It's been more like two hours."

"They'll be here," Stewart said.

"Sorry," Ben said, walking up behind them.

Eve whirled and confronted Ben. "Where have you been?" she demanded.

"Slow down," Ben said, placing his hands on her arms and holding her fast. "We've been hiding from Evans."

Seeka galloped up behind Ben. "I believe your captain has followed." He turned to look behind him. "We should make all haste to conceal ourselves."

"Why?" Stewart asked. "We can put him out of his and our misery."

"No," Ben said. "No harm can come to Evans." He looked at Stewart's confused expression. "I'll explain later."

Ben, Eve, Stewart and Vinny hid among the various crates and barrels in the ship's hold. Choosing different vantage points, they waited for Evans to come into view. Ben and Eve were closest together. Seeka stayed near Ben.

Eve did a three-sixty, checking her surroundings. "Where's Skull?" she whispered.

"Don't know," Ben replied. "He was right behind me."

Evans stumbled into view. In his right hand he clenched Skull's shirt collar, dragging the scared young man along. Evans pushed him forward, then jerked him back, causing Skull to stagger like his drunken captor.

"There's your answer," Ben said.

"We have to do something," Eve replied.

"Hold tight," Ben said.

Evans came to a halt, forcing Skull to his knees. "Now," he announced, "I have something you want." He reached for a crate to steady himself. "If you want it back breathing, then show yourself. If not, it makes no difference to me." The captain peered around, using rapid, jerky motions. "Now!" he screamed. Evans knelt beside Skull, wrapping his hands around his throat.

"Captain," Ben said, stepping into the open.

Evans paid no attention as his grip tightened around Skull's neck.

Ben ran to Skull's side in an attempt to break the captain's death grip. Stewart soon joined him, pulled his pistol and cocked it, laying the barrel against Evans' head.

"No," Seeka barked, "such an act will destroy us all."

Stewart looked at the nuckta with disbelief. He sighed, shook his head, and raising the gun butt high into the air, drove it into the captain's head.

"How appropriate," Seeka said.

Chapter 69
Parallel Dimension I

(Return to *Deadly Reign*)

"Cahotic, I propose a truce."

"Then show yourself and remove all doubt," Cahotic replied.

The man mountain stepped into the dim firelight.

"Colossac," Cahotic said, keeping his surprise at bay.

Three riders drew their weapons and moved toward the intruder.

"Stand down," Cahotic ordered. "We will hear this one."

The riders came to a halt but remained at the ready.

"Do not tarry with your proposal," Cahotic warned. "I grow weary of your presence even now."

"I see only four of you remain," Colossac said. "I have been before your adversaries and determined they possess one of the forged blades. Even a fool could deduce that a severe blow has been dealt by the hand of The Three."

"Continue," Cahotic urged. "You have said nothing that is not known." He waved a finger at his subordinates, and they began their slow advance once again. "Speak your offer, and quickly; else you die where you stand."

"Your weakness has been discovered," Colossac said. "It is with that weakness I can be of service. In this way, we will both achieve our goal."

Cahotic raised what appeared to be an eyebrow. "How?" he inquired, halting the riders a second time.

"It is this that you and I will determine," Colossac said.

Cahotic nodded. "Disperse, riders. Leave us until I send for you."

Chapter 70

Yoshi and Eve rode for over an hour without a word spoken between the two. He felt her head bob up as if she were dozing off and then catching herself. He measured the length of time it would take for her head to drop, waking her again. Yoshi waited until it was time for her head to fall, taking advantage of Eve being at her groggiest. He threw his head back, catching Eve in the chin on its expected trip downward. Jerking back and nearly falling from her horse, Eve shook her head and caught the boy by the hair to keep from tumbling backwards into the snow.

Yoshi turned and brought his fist down across Eve's wrist, causing her to lose her grip, but still coming away with a handful of hair. He dropped both legs over the edge of the horse and slid down. Eve made one last attempt at grabbing him, as he dropped but came up empty. Yoshi caught his spear as he fell, holding on until he could untie the weapon and drop to the ground.

Arrows flew around him as he fled. One grazed his arm, while most impaled trees or fell to the ground. Eve screamed with a primeval rage as Yoshi disappeared from sight.

Chapter 71
Parallel Dimension II

(Aboard the *Morning Star*)

"He can't be," Eve pleaded.

"When Evans comes to, I'm gonna put him down for good," Vinny said. "I'd do it now, but I want him to know it's coming."

Ben moved closer to Stewart. "Talk to him," he said.

Stewart looked at Ben, incensed. "Why?" He then turned to face Ben full on. "Skull lies dead, and you want me to defend his killer. I'm seriously considering helping Vinny."

"Not you too," Ben said. "To harm Evans will jeopardize all of our futures."

"Tell that one to Skull," Stewart said. "I'm sure he'd like to weigh his future options." He walked to where Skull lay, kneeling beside the covered body. "Sorry I got you into this," he whispered. Standing, he turned toward Vinny. "Put Evans back in the lockup and chain him this time. Take Ben's pistol in case he comes to."

"I don't think so," Ben said.

"We can't send him with no means of protection," Stewart said.

"I can't trust either one of you in your present state," Ben said.

Stewart looked at Ben, shook his head, and then looked back at Vinny. "Don't hurt him;" he said, turning to glare at Ben, "at least not now."

Vinny nodded. "Not until you give the word."

Ben reluctantly handed the weapon to Vinny.

Vinny grabbed one of Evans' legs and dragged him toward the room.

"Vinny," Stewart said, "if he comes to and gives you any trouble . . ." Stewart paused, "kill him," he finished, without looking at Ben. "We'll take Skull topside and get him ready."

Vinny nodded and resumed pulling Evans. *Please wake up*, he thought.

"Give me a hand," Stewart said. "In this climate, decomposition takes over quickly."

Chapter 72
Parallel Dimension I

(Return to *Deadly Reign*)

The fur-covered creature moved slowly through the deepening snow. It carried a long, slender object.

"What do you make of that?" Ben said, drawing an arrow from his quiver and loading his bow.

"Stay your weapon," Caleb replied. "I think force may be unnecessary."

The object was no more than a hundred yards away. Caleb, Ben, and Pete moved in and surrounded the creature. A corner of the fur lifted, exposing the face of a young boy.

Caleb smiled. "The young one has returned." He breathed a sigh of relief.

"What about Eve?" Ben pressed. "Where is she?"

"Yes," Caleb said, "time is of the essence."

"Now!" Ben demanded.

Yoshi told the three men of his abduction and escape from Eve.

"What could have happened to make her do such things?" Caleb asked.

Ben shook his head.

"I don't care why she did what she did. We need to find her."

"I attacked one of the riders and turned my weapon on Eve," Yoshi said, frowning. "I think the residue on my blade may have poisoned her." He looked at Ben and then at Pete.

"Remember?" he asked.

"You don't know how lucky you are being only eleven years old," Ben snarled.

"Yes," Pete said, ignoring Ben's comment, "when I tended to Eve's shoulder, I noticed the same thick fluid inside her wound."

Ben stood abruptly, clenching his bow.

"I'll go alone if I have to."

"No," Caleb said, standing as well, "we will go."

♦♦♦

Eve groaned as she made her way into a thicket somewhat sheltered from the snow. She slid off her horse and would have fallen, had it not been for the animal to lean against. The pain in her shoulder had grown to the point of being unbearable. Eve was compelled to search for something but had no inkling of what that something might be.

"It's got to be here," she said. "I can sense it." She thought for a moment. *How silly is this? I've identified something I can't identify. I swear it's here and claim to myself that I can actually feel it.*

Eve laughed until the pain in her shoulder seemed to slam into her, almost as if coming from an outside source. This time there was nothing between her and the ground. She pushed herself to her knees and rolled over onto her buttocks. Her jaw went slack, and her mouth fell wide open. Eve made it to her feet and ran her sleeve across her mouth to remove the ice-laden dirt.

"What?" was the only word she could muster. Before her stood an obelisk; it looked as though it was made from pure quartz. It stood thirty-two-feet tall and projected from a base that was an additional eighteen feet in height, making the entire structure a total of fifty feet. The base was twenty-four feet square with a one-foot-wide and six-inch-deep overhang at its top.

The entire structure was smooth as glass and transparent, with no distortion when viewing objects on the other side.

Eve blinked several times and raised her eyebrows. "Well, I guess I've found it." She began to walk around the structure. "Now, what do I do with it?"

As she turned the third corner, she noticed a square indentation just wide enough to slide into sideways. Eve suspiciously eyed the opening and shook her head. "Why I'm getting ready to do this, I don't have a clue."

She took a deep breath. "But, it's now or never." Eve slid into the crevice and moved toward the center of the obelisk. The clear material closed in, conforming to her shape, but did not impede her progress. After several moments of moving through the crystal, she emerged into an inner chamber.

A white-cloaked figure stood, head bowed, in the center of the room. The figure moved toward her. "Eve," said a familiar voice.

Chapter 73
Parallel Dimension II

(Aboard the *Morning Star*)

Vinny stepped onto the deck. Ben and Stewart were standing by the shrouded figure of Skull. Eve stood by the rail, peering into a never-ending expanse of water. Seeka lay at her feet, his head resting on his front paws.

Vinny joined Stewart. "Guess this is it," he said.

"Guess so," Stewart replied. He motioned to Ben. "Let's get this over with."

The two men knelt down and lifted the board that bore Skull's lifeless body. They placed the foot end of the board on the rail.

"Don't know what to say," Stewart began.

Vinny shrugged and shook his head. "I don't think it matters."

"Do it," Stewart snarled.

The board tilted upward, depositing its contents into the sea. The water immediately began to boil with a yellow hue and then calmed to normal.

"Never seen that before," Stewart commented.

"Whatever," Vinny mumbled. "I say we bring Evans up here and make him the second burial at sea today."

Seeka perked up at hearing this.

"Not yet," Stewart replied. "Ben and his fuzzy friend are going to give me one good reason to spare Evans, and then we'll bring him up here." Stewart moved away from the rail and closer to Ben. "Give me a reason;" he growled, "it doesn't even have to be a good one." He whirled and glared at Seeka. "You tell me that this nut job is necessary. Here's your chance to convince me."

"It is simply this," Seeka began. "If Evans dies, we all die."

Chapter 74
Parallel Dimension I

(Return to *Deadly Reign*)

"I've all but lost her trail," Ben said. "There's one, maybe two more visible hoof prints, and I'm not sure of those."

"We've been traveling in a mostly northerly direction," Pete said. "Guess our best bet would be to continue heading north."

"How can you tell north from south?" Ben said.

"Don't know the exact terminology," Pete said, "or an accurate way to describe it, but men are equipped with a magnetic particle in their heads. This magnetic field is stronger in some than in others." Pete shrugged. "I guess I got a good dose, because I've always been able to sense a northerly direction."

"Yeah, right," Ben said. "Why don't you tell me another one?"

"He is correct," Caleb said. "Unfortunately, I myself do not possess this gift in ample measure to make it of any use, but rest assured your friend has spoken true."

"Then north it is," Ben said, extending his palm, inviting Pete to lead.

Ben jerked back on the reins, causing his horse to stumble. "Did you see that light?"

"No," Pete said, "but it must have been pretty potent to almost take you to the ground."

"A flash," Ben said. "A flash of light, but not from a direct source; more like a reflection." Ben scanned an area in a hundred-eighty-degree radius. He pointed in the general direction from where he thought the flash had originated. Moments later, a second flash occurred. "There it is again," Ben said.

"I saw it that time," Pete confirmed.

"Gentle sirs, it appears we have reached our destination," Caleb announced.

◆◆◆

"Sarith!" Eve exclaimed. Her first thought was to wrap her arms around him, but somehow she knew better than to do such a thing.

"It pleases me to see you again," Sarith said. "However, the conditions I wish could be different."

"Please explain all this," Eve pleaded. "I am so confused."

"I had to bring you here to get a small piece of the evil that is attempting to take over this world. This crystal structure in which we now stand is a fortress of sorts to prevent the darkness from interfering with our meeting."

"I don't understand," Eve said. "Something overtook me and led me to this place. Once I entered, I became my normal self again."

"I have enlisted the one known as Yoshi, the sole survivor of his people. During your confrontation with the riders, Yoshi retained a small portion of their dissolved essence on the tip of his spear. When he attacked you, this material was driven into the wound on your shoulder and captured in the moss plug used to treat the puncture."

"You're still not making any sense," Eve said.

"I had to procure this essence to bond with this leather-wrapped wooden handle, which by itself could not survive outside of this crystal structure."

"But, why?" Eve asked.

"The handle in its purity must be conditioned to withstand the dark forces it will face when you leave. Please remove the plug from your wound."

Eve pulled the plug from the puncture, wincing as she did so, and handed the slime-covered moss to Sarith.

"No," Sarith said, taking a step backward. "This material I cannot touch." He extended the wooden handle to Eve. "Merely bring the two together, and the union will be complete."

Taking the handle, Eve touched it with the contaminated moss. A bright flash of light instantaneously transformed the wooden leather-bound handle. It became a beautiful silver concave-shaped rod. It was covered with intricate carvings and an oval indention on one of the two flat ends.

"Time is short," Sarith said. "I must ready myself for travel beyond this realm. What I am about to share with you, you shall remember, though you shall retain nothing more from this meeting. Protect this piece with your life, for your very existence depends upon its power."

"But what do I do with it?" Eve implored.

"You will know when the time comes; however, its energy is not limitless, so use it wisely."

Sarith, along with the crystal structure, faded, leaving Eve alone, stunned and clueless as to what to do.

"Eve!" a comforting voice called from afar.

Her eyes widened, finally a glimmer of hope.

"Where did you come from?" Eve asked as she crawled all over Ben.

"Slow down," Ben said, in a muffled voice. She smothered his face in kisses. "I could ask you the same thing. Where have you been?"

Eve loosened her legs from around Ben's waist and slid to the ground. She stared into the darkness in silence.

"I don't know," she said, looking into Ben's eyes. "I can't remember anything after my confrontation with Yoshi." Eve furrowed her forehead and squinted. "Something is there, something that makes all this necessary." She shook her head. "But I have no clear idea what it could be."

Yoshi walked up and faced Eve. "I am so sorry that I hurt you," he said. "I never would have done such—"

"Stop," Eve said. "You have no reason to apologize." She knelt to face him. "We will not speak of this again."

Yoshi smiled and nodded.

"These are things we will discuss at a later time," Caleb said. "As for our time, it must be used for more important affairs."

Eve gave the boy a quick hug and then stood again.

"Nice stick," Ben said. "What's it do?"

Eve looked at the ornate metal piece she carried in her hand and shrugged her shoulders. "Not a clue," she said.

"We must continue our journey toward the sea without delay," Caleb said. "Any further setbacks could prove disastrous."

Yoshi once again traveled, seated with Eve.

"How long will it take to reach the sea, moving as we are?" Caleb asked.

Orac thought for a moment. "One rising, perhaps two," he replied.

"If this is true, we should hasten our pace," Caleb said. He further reinforced his statement by increasing his horse's gait. "Is this stride acceptable to you, large one?"

"It is agreeable," Orac said. "You may move faster if you wish."

"This will do for now," Caleb replied. "Any faster and I fear we would be unable to match your pace."

Orac smiled. "As a yearling," he said, "I outran all the horses of my day."

"Outran?" Pete said, with disbelief.

Orac nodded. "In the days of my youth, the race was the mark by which the prowess of a young one was measured. I can remember my first challenge as vividly as the day it came to pass. My closest comrade, Rilec, suggested I run with the beasts of the field."

Orac's mind drifted back to the memories of that time.

"No," Rilec said, "and you will not find another in the entire village, nay, the entire area to run with you."

"Then how shall I train?" Orac replied.

"The only ones you have not defeated are the beasts of the field," Rilec said. "Perhaps it would do you well to choose a four-legged opponent."

"Ah," Orac said, waving his friend off, "I look for solutions, and you regale me with jest."

"It may not be as daft as you now reckon," Rilec said. "Give the idea consideration, and it may bring surprise."

Orac smiled sarcastically. Unseen was the subtle notion that had begun to grow. By the time he reached home, the impression had grown to a near obsession.

"Father," Orac said, "I have grown to such size and strength that I can find no one who will accept my challenge."

"Orac," Nilrem said, "you manage to find defeat in victory. Having bested everyone, young and old, it is now time to seek out those who would challenge you."

"How?" Orac questioned.

"The answer to this, even now, burns within you," Nilrem said.

"The horses?" he answered, cautiously.

Nilrem nodded.

A wide grin crossed Orac's face. He glanced momentarily at Nilrem and then ran from the building.

Nilrem smiled as he watched his protégé leave. "And still deeper we go," he whispered.

The animals bolted as the abnormally large figure rushed into their midst, waving his arms and screaming. Orac paused, admiring their prowess as they ran, and with a great grin, took off after them. Catching up with the panicked quadrupeds, he matched their speed and erratic turning patterns precisely. After several minutes, he stopped as the herd thundered away.

"The equine are not as fast as I had expected," Orac said, "but I am to think that they are the best that I can hope for."

Nilrem looked on as the boy bested the herd. He made his way back home and then retired to his closet shrine.

"Orac grows strong," Nilrem said. "His size increases daily."

"At last the potion has realized its potential in this one," the Dark One replied.

"Yes," Nilrem said.

"Remember the Kumult?" the Dark One said. "Its use is forbidden."

"Of course, master," Nilrem replied. He watched as the sphere faded from sight, a sardonic smile crossing his face.

"What allowed you to move so quickly?" Eve asked.

Orac's attention returned to the present. "The potion I was given is the reason for my great size and the strength I possess," Orac replied.

"And what of the Kumult?" Caleb asked. "What were the detrimental consequences surrounding its use?"

"None I can recall;" Orac said, "at least none as yet."

"Curious," Caleb replied. "It seems as though it would have shown itself, with so much time having passed."

"Perhaps it may be so," Orac said.

"*May be so?*" Caleb asked. "I do not understand." He noticed a worried look on the giant's face. "Do not allow fear to be your guide. Tell me what you know to be the truth."

"I do, however, recall periods in my life;" he looked at Caleb, "times of great anger concealed within an almost impenetrable fog."

"Is this all?" Caleb asked.

"No," Orac replied, an expression of horror staring back at Caleb, "but thankfully, I have no recollection of this, other than that it exists."

Caleb nodded, and the group continued on, each carrying within themselves memories of virtue and those of dire consequences.

Chapter 75
Parallel Dimension II

(Aboard the *Morning Star*)

"You want to explain why Evans' demise would have anything to do with us?" Stewart demanded. "He'd just be one more dirt bag out of the way."

"No, knowing of future events," Seeka said, "you could destroy the course which has already been put into motion."

"Sorry;" Stewart said, "not good enough." He turned and headed for the door leading below deck.

"No!" Ben said, grabbing Stewart's arm, whirling him around.

Stewart faced Ben, brandishing a revolver. "Don't do that again," he warned. "I'll take you out, too. Vinny, get down to the lock up; I'll be right behind you." Vinny complied, leaving the deck.

Stewart backed away, not taking his eyes off Ben until he reached the doorway. Turning, he disappeared down the corridor.

Ben, Eve and Seeka moved cautiously down the last corridor leading to the room holding Evans.

"At least we haven't heard a gunshot," Eve commented.

"Yeah," Ben replied, "maybe they're just beating him to death."

"I do not believe that to be the case," Seeka said as he rushed past his comrades, stopping in front of the now opened lock-up door.

A faint, yellow, pulsating light emanated from within the room, casting its luminescence into the corridor. Ben and Eve joined the nuckta and peered into the room. An orb hovered above Evans, still chained and sitting on the floor. Vinny and Stewart stood facing Evans, their hands at their sides, half-heartedly holding their revolvers. The voice of Skull radiated from the sphere, timed with the pulsations. As the entity began to speak, Vinny's gun dropped to the ground.

"You will do nothing to harm the Evans," it said. "Your self-indulgent irrational behavior has no place here. Seek council from the one known as Ben Adams and the small furry creature. In this way, you will move along your destined path."

Ben stepped into the room.

"I will stay a short time longer," the entity continued. "Do what you must; however, do not tarry." The glow diminished slightly, and the orb became silent.

Vinny stooped to retrieve his weapon and then joined Stewart in turning toward Ben.

"I'm sorry," Stewart said "I didn't know."

Vinny nodded his apology, his face still devoid of emotion.

"What's done is done," Ben said. "Right now we have an island, not to mention a ship, to save."

Chapter 76
Parallel Dimension I

(Return to *Deadly Reign*)

"Then let it be so," Cahotic said. "It would be beneficial to engage The Three united."

Colossac grinned and then nodded. "Indeed, you have much potential under the proper guidance."

Cahotic glared at the giant. "I fear you have not reconciled this situation." He leaned closer. "You were allowed to live because I chose to make it so."

Colossac waved a huge hand. "Do not misinterpret my comment. I only meant to say that your resolve is admirable." Colossac placed a hand on Cahotic's shoulder and grinned pretentiously.

Cahotic eyed him with caution. "Of course."

Colossac accepted his comment as an avenue to gain control. "Gather your men, if it is agreeable to you, and we will devise a plan to eliminate those who would stand in our way."

"It is agreeable;" Cahotic said, "however, from this point on, it will be understood that you will remember your place."

Colossac symbolically dropped to one knee. "It will be as you say, Lord Cahotic," he replied, lowering his head.

"Good." Cahotic walked to where the remaining riders stood. "We will meet with Colossac to talk of our next confrontation with The Three." He glanced back to make sure the giant had not moved closer. "Once we have accomplished our initiative, you are to destroy him."

Chapter 77

Ben turned his head and smiled at Yoshi. "Since we've been sharing stories, is there anything you'd like to add to what you told us earlier?"

Water welled in Yoshi's eyes as he remembered his slain kin. Wiping away tears, he began to speak. "As I have said before, we were a member of the Sonyetti Nation. I belonged to Clan Clator." He drew his sleeve across his eyes and then continued. "My direct lineage included my father, my mother, a brother two years my elder and my younger sister." His eyes glazed over as he spoke his next words. "She had just learned how to walk."

Ben and Pete both ground their teeth in an attempt to hold back their tears. The salty water on Caleb's face was beginning to freeze, even though his expression remained stoic.

Eve openly sobbed, wiping tear after tear as they cascaded down her cheeks.

"My father was a tiller of soil," Yoshi said. "It's not that we didn't hunt; we did, but most of our sustenance came from the produce we grew ourselves. We were fortunate as we had natural caves that could house about a third of our population and all of our livestock. The rest of my people built homes from the large trees close by our cave dwellings."

"How about your mother?" Eve asked.

Yoshi smiled. "She would tend crops, prepare meals and gather the living produce provided by our livestock."

"Living produce?" Ben remarked.

"Indeed," Yoshi said. "Spands from the cormaron, eggs from the toleco, . . ."

"Hold on," Ben said. "Did you say toleco?"

"Yes," Yoshi replied, "the Clator are the only people throughout history who have been able to domesticate the toleco." A wide smile spread across his face. "It is a source of great pride for my people." His smile disappeared. "At least it was."

Ben gave the youth a few moments to compose himself before he spoke. "How about the spands; what are they?"

"An edible parasite we gather every other rising," Yoshi said.

"Tell us about your siblings," Ben said.

Yoshi's eyes brightened. "Even though he was my elder, Cirtic and I were well matched in our abilities. As you know, my people are known for their speed and agility." Once again, Yoshi paused, remembering he was the last of his race. Gathering strength within, he resolved that he would not dwell upon the past, but look to vindicate his slain people. "We were also very competitive," Yoshi continued. "Either one of us could conceive a game out of the most mundane task."

"And your sister?" Eve asked.

"A precious addition to our family," Yoshi said. This time his smile did not leave his face. "Adalia was just beginning to toddle about." His smile turned into a chuckle that infected the entire group.

"What's so funny?" Ben asked.

Yoshi wiped his eyes, this time removing tears of joyful remembrance. "We included Adalia in one game my brother and I used to enjoy. We would swing from treetop to treetop, challenging one another according to speed and distance, before returning to our starting point. The first to arrive would signify the winner."

"Certainly not your sister," Eve protested.

Yoshi held up his hand, shaking it emphatically. "Of course not," he said. "We gathered tree boughs, and laying them on the ground, would have her jump between the branches. Each time she would leap, Cirtic and I would wager whether she could complete her attempted distance in a standing position, or fall short of her mark." Yoshi shook his head several times.

"What is it?" Pete asked.

"Our mother caught us during one such escapade, and when father found out, our workload increased sevenfold for thirty risings."

"So your father was strict?" Ben asked.

"Not so much strict," Yoshi replied, "as he was fair." Yoshi lifted his spear. "My father taught us in the ways of hunting, fishing, self-defense and battle. Even my mother was experienced in these tactics."

"It sounds as though your early years, even though cut short, were a delight," Caleb said. "You would do well to remember the days of your youth, even though they are painful. These times will strengthen you as you grow."

Yoshi nodded.

Chapter 78
Parallel Dimension II

(Aboard the *Morning Star*)

"Ben!" Stewart exclaimed.

Ben turned to see Stewart running toward him. "What?" he answered, as Stewart reached him.

"The generator," Stewart said, leaning over to catch his breath.

"What generator?"

Stewart looked up at Ben and then stood upright. "The stacion generator; I found it."

"And?" Ben said.

"Think!" Stewart implored. "It doesn't matter that Seeka can't transport. We can turn the generator off, and you can get to the warheads."

Ben smiled. "Of course," he said, patting Stewart on the shoulder. "Sorry for being so dense."

"That's okay," Stewart replied, "but—"

Ben didn't hear him. "Come on," he said to Seeka. "Let's get back to work."

"Hmm," Stewart said, "maybe we should figure out how to turn it off before you get fried walking into the stacion field."

Ben stopped and turned toward Stewart. "That knowledge would be beneficial," he said. "You mean you don't know how to turn it off?"

"Well, no, I wanted to let you know that I had found it first."

"All right," Ben said. "Show me."

They made their way below deck to the front of the ship.

Ben climbed a ladder to examine the device mounted to the underside of the forward deck. It was rectangular, gray and about the size of a handheld toolbox. A small circular port, with a half-inch high rim, had been drilled in the center down one of the long sides. It was situated in the apparatus, facing the torpedoes, which lay overhead. The lens-like object appeared to pierce the skin of the box, extending into its interior. Along the opposite side were two toggle switches and two LED lights underneath a panel secured by a single screw.

"So, this is it," Ben said, as he ran his hands around the casing.

"Yes," Stewart said. "Just go no further."

"Why?"

"If you touch the projection port you'll turn into a puff of smoke."

Ben abruptly pulled his hand back from the lens. "Oh," he said, dropping his hands to his side. He looked down at Stewart. "Hand me a Phillips screwdriver. I'll remove the bottom panel and take a gander inside."

Stewart complied.

Ben backed the screw out, lowered the hinged cover and peered in at the works.

"What do you see?" Stewart inquired.

"Looks pretty straightforward. All we need to . . ." He paused, noticing two hair-thin wires leading from the canister. They ended, attached to a white block of material mounted on the end of the box, hidden from view by a fan.

"Well?" Stewart insisted.

Ben waved him off. "C-4," he whispered. He descended the ladder and stood facing Stewart. "It's straightforward, just like I said."

"Then why didn't you turn it off?"

"It's wired to explode if tampered with."

"Are you sure?"

"There's enough C-4 inside that unit to take out the entire front of this ship."

Stewart sighed. "What now?"

"Don't know," Ben said, looking up at the device. "I'm going back up for another look."

Chapter 79
Parallel Dimension I

(Return to *Deadly Reign*)

Orac sniffed the air. "The sea grows much nearer; the scent of salt fills the air."

"Great," Ben replied.no "I haven't seen a wave in quite a while."

"I don't smell anything," Eve protested.

"It'll come," Ben assured.

"We should stay close to the river until we reach our destination," Caleb cautioned.

"We are but a few steps from the water," Orac said. "I know that the cover of ice makes it hard to see from where you sit, but easier for me to determine whence I trod."

"What's the worry?" Ben said. "As close as we are to the sea, the riders wouldn't dare mess with us."

"Ben Adams," Caleb replied, "once we reach the sea, the riders will have no choice but to confront us. Although prudent thought leads me to trust that an attempt to thwart our mission will be made before that comes to fruition."

"What is our mission?" Pete inquired. "We seem to move forward just to survive."

"Survival," Caleb replied, "is our mission." He turned toward Pete. "That is in as exact terms as I can relay to you."

Pete nodded.

Caleb's horse whinnied and came to a halt. A single yellow orb moved ahead, stopping a hundred yards from the group. It pulsated, illuminating a single rider. The rider ambled toward the group.

"Orac," Caleb said, "two of the water skins, to me."

Yoshi's hand tightened around his spear.

Orac removed two skins from one packhorse as Caleb had requested. He pulled them from deep within the animal skins, where they had been placed to keep the water from freezing. He handed one to Caleb.

"There are two skins left," Orac said. "I fear that the ice has become too thick for even me to crack when refilling the skins becomes necessary."

Caleb nodded. "Keep the other and move three paces to my right," he said.

Orac took his position as Caleb had instructed.

"Remove the cord which secures the skin and await my signal," Caleb said.

Orac nodded and untied the knot.

The rider moved closer, not drawing his weapon or uttering a word.

"Now!" Caleb cried once the creature was within three feet. He squeezed hard on the water skin. The narrow neck turned the water into a stream that washed over the rider. As the aberration dissolved, the trickles of fluid flowing from its body onto its mount etched channels into the beast's hide.

Orac's aim proved faulty as the stream from his water skin washed over the left side of the steed's face before coming to bear on the rider itself. The rider's beast bucked, reached around and took the rider by the foot, throwing the blob of goo from its back. Pieces of the rider clung to the animal's hide, burning deeper into its flesh. The steed turned and lumbered off, now blind and dripping from the left side of its face.

"Yes!" Eve exclaimed.

"I don't believe what I saw," Ben said.

Pete unloaded and shouldered his weapon. "It was too easy," he said.

"Yes," Caleb replied, "very much so."

"But, why?" Orac asked. He turned to look at his comrades, arms spread wide, a childlike demeanor radiating from the giant.

Caleb deliberated for several minutes. "Sacrifice," he said.

"Sacrifice?" Ben asked.

"Yes," Caleb replied, "we must assume that Colossac and the remaining riders have teamed in order to defeat us. By sacrificing one rider at a time, they will deplete our meager supply of water, leaving us much more vulnerable to attack."

A rumbling deep in the ground caused the horses to stumble sideways, knocking an unsuspecting Orac to the ground.

"Whoa," Ben said. "Earthquake?"

Caleb steadied his mount and looked off into the distance. "Perhaps;" he said, "unfortunately, I think not."

Orac jumped to his feet. "Whatever the source of the shaking," he said, "I wish for it not to occur again."

"Gentlemen," Pete interrupted, "you may want to continue this conversation at a later date."

"What is it?" Ben barked, whirling to glare at Pete.

"We have another visitor," Pete replied.

Ben turned to see another rider taking the place of the one they had just eliminated.

"You are indeed willing to sacrifice your own," Colossac said.

"I do not consider myself expendable;" Cahotic replied, "therefore, it does not matter."

The remaining rider stirred uneasily on his mount.

Colossac smiled and nodded. "I see." He paused to look at Cahotic. "I see," he repeated, his voice trailing off into a barely audible hiss.

Chapter 80
Parallel Dimension II

(Aboard the *Morning Star*)

"Did it make any difference?" Stewart asked sarcastically.

"No," Ben retorted, "but I think we can cut it off with the toggle switches."

"Ya think?!" Stewart exclaimed. "I hope you can do more than think before you haphazardly flip a switch."

Ben glared at Stewart, pointing upward at the generator. "You want to give me your knowledgeable opinion?" Ben's hands clenched into fists. "Maybe you're better suited to determine what we should do."

Stewart sighed. "Sorry, I wouldn't know the difference between that and a washing machine. You're the expert."

Ben dropped his defensive demeanor. "Such as it is, it's about all we can do."

"Can you disarm it?"

"If there's time," Ben looked up at the generator. "But don't forget, I still have to disarm the warheads."

An alarm began to sound throughout the ship.

"What now?" Ben growled.

Chapter 81
Parallel Dimension I

(Return to *Deadly Reign*)

"What choice do we have but to eliminate this one too?" Pete asked.

"None, I am afraid," Caleb replied. "At the very least, it will leave but two riders and Colossac to contend with; however, it will deplete our one source of defense."

The rider drew his sword and began to move forward.

"Looks like this one wants a fight," Ben commented.

"And get a fight he shall," Orac replied. The giant retrieved the two remaining water skins and turned to confront the aberration.

"Hold on," Pete said, joining Orac. "You can't have all the fun." He extended his hands. Orac smiled, releasing one of the skins to the smaller man.

"Follow my lead, big guy." Pete smirked. The two men separated, flanking the rider to the left and right.

The rider looked to his right as his mount canvassed the left.

"They're watching us from both sides," Pete said, as he crouched and moved, trying to avoid the rider's gaze. "Their only blind spot is from behind."

"Follow my lead, small one," Orac said. "I make my own blind side."

Pete observed as Orac confronted the rider. The rider raised his sword. Orac grabbed the wrist wielding the weapon. The rider's mount swiped its foreleg, taking Orac to the ground. A puff of powdered snow, displaced by the giant's great bulk, formed a cloud before settling back to the ground. The rider raised his sword once again to plunge it into Orac, as his mount pinned the fallen one to the ground. Pete moved closer, emptying his water skin onto the rider as Orac did the same, dousing the beast. The mount reared, releasing Orac from underneath its forelimbs. Orac slid to safety, dodging globs of dripping flesh.

Pete helped Orac to his feet. Caleb, Ben, Eve and Yoshi joined the two as the rider and the front half of his mount bubbled in a steaming mass.

Caleb grabbed the aberration's sword, wiping it against the heel of his boot. Ben walked to the first rider's corpse and picked up its weapon.

Ben said, "We should keep moving before any more show up."

Yoshi scrutinized the bubbling mass, now indiscernible whether rider or beast as he passed by.

Chapter 82
Parallel Dimension II

(Aboard the *Morning Star*)

Eve was the last one to arrive on the bridge. "What is it?" she asked.

Ben looked at Seeka. "You tell her; I still don't believe what I'm seeing."

"Dear Eve," Seeka began, "the island we have discussed in great detail—"

Eve peered out of the bridge windows. "I don't see anything," she said.

"It's too far away to observe. The curvature of the earth sets the horizon at ten miles. We have a ways to go before we reach that distance," Stewart said. "The alarm sounded when the ship's instrumentation detected the landmass."

"It'll be several hours before the island comes into view," Ben said. He sighed and looked out of the window. "That should give us enough time to disarm the generator and the warheads."

"Not if we stay up here gabbing about it," Stewart said.

"Hand me the dikes," Ben said, peering into the generator housing.

"The what?" Stewart asked.

"The small side-cutting pliers." Ben fumed.

"Sorry, I've never heard them called that before." Stewart rifled through the toolbox and handed Ben the implement.

Ben took the tool, hesitated, pushed the pliers into the box, withdrew them, hesitated again, and then positioned the pliers to surround one of the wires.

"You don't look too sure of yourself," Stewart said.

Ben looked down at Stewart, his face full of doubt. "I'm not. If I cut the wrong wire, we're all outta here, and in a big hurry, if you know what I mean."

Stewart nodded and smiled grimly. "Yeah, I do. I'm sweating right along with you." He wiped a sleeve across his brow.

Ben began to apply pressure to the handle of the pliers and then stopped, looking down once again at Stewart. "I'm not sure!"

"I kinda figured that," Stewart said. "So what are you going to do?"

"Don't know," Ben said, dropping his hands from the box. "I wish there was someone more knowledgeable to ask."

"You're it," Stewart said. He paused, considering his comment. After several moments, he looked earnestly at Ben. "There's no one else to ask. It's up to you."

Ben nodded and turned his attention back into the generator housing. Without hesitation, he slid the pliers into the box and clipped the bare wire.

Chapter 83 Parallel Dimension I

(Return to *Deadly Reign*)

"What will we do for water?" Eve asked. "If it's our only defense, aren't we lost without it?"

"That's why we're making our way to the sea," Ben answered.

"But won't it be frozen too?" Eve asked.

"No," Orac said, "at least not solid. The higher salt content in the water lowers the freezing point considerably."

"That being said," Pete interrupted, "we have to get there first."

Caleb raised a finger causing everyone to grow silent. The faint sound of advancing and receding water lapping against the shore could be heard in the distance.

"It seems our arrival is at hand."

Colossac watched from a distance as the mounted party continued its trek toward the sea. He paused, listening to the distant waves, and then turned to inspect the remaining riders.

Things have surely changed, he thought, *but do not worry my friends. I will see that you are used to your absolute fullest.*

The waves washed onto the shore, heavily laden with the frozen slush they carried along.

"We will make camp as close to the water as possible," Caleb said, "taking into consideration the amount of ice that will liquefy due to the fire."

Within an hour, a spot was chosen, wood gathered and the group sat eating around the fire.

"Future arrangements must be our next order of discussion," Caleb said. "It will be necessary for two to depart."

"I wish to go," Yoshi said. "My heart burns to bring to justice those responsible for my people's demise."

Caleb placed a hand on Yoshi's shoulder and knelt to face him. "I understand your desire for retaliation;" Caleb said, "however, such a task is too great for one so young." He stared into Yoshi's eyes. "Take all care you do not let this need for what you refer to as justice, turn into vengeance. This would bring greater damage to yourself than any deed you could enact against your enemy."

Yoshi turned without uttering a word, his thoughts drifting back to the last meal he shared with his family—

"Wonderful dinner, as usual," Yoshi's father, Demitri, said.

"Thank you," Reaha replied. She gave her husband a kiss on the cheek as she cleared the evening dishes.

"You three may be excused," Demitri said, addressing the children. This time of year, the Great Light would be visible for a bit longer in the sky. The children wasted no time in making their way outside to enjoy the waning light.

Demitri gave his wife a hug. "I'll be gathering firewood for the night."

"Well, then be gone with you," she said, smiling and patting him on the butt.

"Take care, woman," he replied. "Your man shall return soon enough."

Yoshi and Cirtic were busy scaling the tallest trees close to their dwelling when they heard a steady rumbling and screams echoing throughout the village.

"Shh," Cirtic said. "Listen, there is trouble afoot."

Adalia sat in a pile of sand in a world of her own, creating different figures and shapes from the loosely packed grains. The riders paid no attention to the child as they made their way toward the house, trampling Adalia as they did so. The two boys slid down the tree.

"Adalia!" Yoshi screamed as he ran to his sister.

Cirtic passed Yoshi and moved toward the house. He entered through the opened door. "Mother," he said in shocked horror. His mother lay in two pieces, torn apart at her midsection. There was no sign of his father. Cirtic had no time to mourn, as one of the riders' swords removed his head with a single swipe of the blade. The riders moved outside and grabbed Yoshi, pulling him away as he tried to bury the lifeless body of his sister.

"Let me go!" he screamed. His resistance was no match for the strength of the two riders.

Yoshi was taken before Cahotic, who bade him tell the story to all he met, concerning the fate of his people and the mercy shown to him. Before Yoshi left the village, he crept back to his home and procured his father's spear. The boy saw what used to be part of his father's hand. He bent over, emptying the contents of his stomach before he ran.

"Before Yoshi's story, you made the statement that two must go; please explain," Ben said over the rolling surf.

"There is an urgent matter to the south that requires immediate attention," Caleb said.

"Is it wise to separate with a confrontation looming?" Ben asked.

"It is for that reason," Caleb replied. "Something was placed that will assist our endeavor."

"What?" Ben asked. "And by whom?"

"I have no answer other than an entity who has taken part in these worlds, past and future. In this way, these events will be recorded in *The Book of the Chosen*," Caleb replied.

Ben sighed. "Okay, I've learned better than to fight this world's logic."

Caleb nodded. "I will stay; Orac and Pete will go."

"What are we looking for?" Pete asked.

"You will move south, paralleling the shoreline," Caleb said. "You will recognize your quarry once you find it."

"Is that all you can tell us?" Pete asked.

"Yes," Caleb replied, "the story is being written as it plays out, even though it has been recorded in our future and left in our present—"

"By someone from our past," Ben finished.

"Even though there is little I can tell you concerning your journey," Caleb said, "it will be fraught with danger and pitfalls, each designed to keep you from completing your undertaking."

"Sounds like fun," Pete said. "Come on, big guy; looks like it's you and me."

Chapter 84
Parallel Dimension II

(Aboard the *Morning Star*)

A small pop emanated from the stacion generator housing, followed by a puff of white smoke. Four heads slowly rose from behind a crate, their owners still crouching, poised to duck again if the need arose. They alternated their gaze between the smoking device and each other.

After several minutes, Ben broke the silence with a whisper. "Guess I cut the right one."

Several more minutes passed.

"Guess so," Stewart whispered back.

Eve stood. "Why are you whispering?"

Ben looked at Stewart, and Stewart at Ben. They both stood along with Vinny.

Ben shrugged, trying to ignore her comment. "Let's shut the generator down." He climbed the ladder and flipped the power switch. A high frequency hum began to sound, growing lower in pitch until it ceased.

Ben looked at Seeka. "Time to get to work, fuzz ball."

Chapter 85
Parallel Dimension I

(Return to *Deadly Reign*)

"Need help?" Pete asked.

"No," Orac replied. He pushed back from his kneeling position in front of the kindled fire, coming to rest beside Pete. "However, thank you for offering your assistance."

The pair sat quietly, gazing into the growing fire. Miniature rivers of melted snow began to spread in all directions as the flames intensified. Once the water traveled far enough to escape the heat generated by the fire, it began to freeze, crystallizing into a new form.

Pete was the first to break the silence. "What do you think we'll find?"

Orac slowly shook his head, his eyes still fixed on the dancing flames. "I am unsure and very anxious to learn."

An ice spear grazed Orac's ear, cutting a one-inch slit through his earlobe and shattering against a tree twenty feet away. The pair turned to see four large ice creatures reflected by the light of their fire.

"Which one do you reckon this is," Pete said, drawing and loading his bow, "danger or pitfall?"

"It matters not;" Orac replied, "either will do."

The creatures stood sixteen feet tall and appeared nearly identical to human skeletons. They carried an arsenal of different weapons, seemingly made in any shape desired, using the runoff from the fire and molding the ice into weapons.

Pete jumped sideways as an ice hammer slammed into the ground beside him. Orac countered with a blow to the ice creature's arm, his sword cracking and then severing the appendage just below the elbow.

"That's one way to fight them," Pete said. "Let's see what this will do." He let five arrows fly in quick succession, each contacting one of the creatures' necks, cutting a line more than halfway across. Pete held his breath as the creature stood upright with its arms by its side. Its head began to tip, finally falling to the ground and shattering into several large pieces.

Orac was busy chopping one of the ice beings to pieces as it attempted to reach one of its weapons. *How ironic*, he thought. The creature wrapped its hand around a weapon resembling a scythe shortly before Orac hacked the hand and the weapon to crystals.

"Watch this," Pete said. He cut the head off the last of the ice creatures in the same fashion as the first. The two men began to chuckle. Their amusement soon turned to hysterical laughter as the beheaded ice monsters stumbled about, tripping, falling and bumping into one another in a comedy of errors.

Pete tapped Orac on the back. "Look," he said between breaths, "at the ones you slashed to bits." The pieces of the decimated creatures vibrated violently, packing the snow into a tight layer as they moved closer together. The two headless forms began to close in around their fallen brethren. Pete and Orac continued to laugh until they realized, and nearly too late that the creatures were reassembling themselves.

In less than thirty seconds, the four ice creatures reassembled and resumed their attack.

"What are they doing?" Pete asked.

"It appears as though they have changed tactics," Orac replied.

The four creatures stood close enough to the fire to melt the ends of their arms. As the ice turned to water, they withdrew their heated appendages and formed sword-like extensions where their hands would be.

"Perhaps we have underestimated their resourcefulness," Orac said.

Pete looked at Orac, rolled his eyes and remained silent.

The four creatures closed in on the outnumbered duo. As soon as Pete or Orac severed the ice weapons, the afflicted creature would immediately renew the limb.

"This may be it," Pete stated.

"It has been my honor," Orac replied.

"Mine as well," Pete said.

A frigid blade ripped Orac's shirt, scratching his chest and starting a modest flow of blood. Before the creature could plunge his deadly weapon deep into Orac's chest, a small white-hot explosion removed the ice creature's entire arm.

"Looks like the cavalry has arrived," Pete said. He finished chopping through the femur of one creature, causing it to fall sideways as its head exploded, turning to liquid from the intense heat.

"I know nothing of this cavalry;" Orac said, "however, it has my complete approval."

Multiple projectiles were now raining from the sky, destroying the ice creatures even as they tried to reanimate.

After the deluge, a single entity hovered over Pete and Orac. The light faded, and a white and blue-feathered creature lit onto Pete's shoulder.

Orac stared at Pete.

Pete stared back and shrugged his shoulders. "Nothing surprises me around here anymore." He eyed the new addition perched on his shoulder. "I don't want to seem ungrateful, but what do you want?"

The bird looked at Pete, cocking its head from side to side, then let out a haunting cry that was something akin to whales communicating, except in a higher pitch. Pete squinted in concentration. He wasn't sure, but he would almost swear he picked up a human voice mingled within the bird's cry.

He turned his attention back to Orac. "We should develop a plan; but how can you plan for something when you don't have a clue what that something is?" At that instant, Pete's friend left his shoulder, circled three times, then proceeded in a northerly direction.

Orac's gaze shifted from the circling creature and then back to Pete. "It would seem that our course has been laid for us."

"It does," Pete said, "and I guess there's no time like the present."

"Agreed," Orac confirmed. He looked upward. "I fear the white that falls from the sky will soon intensify."

Pete nodded.

"Even though it matters not," Orac concluded.

Pete pulled his ermine collar closer together and lowered his head against the blowing precipitation.

Orac was now dragging his feet through calf-deep snow.

"If this keeps up it'll be hard to see anything," Pete said, "especially since we don't know what we're looking for." The yellow orb hovering above them began to pulsate and move forward.

"Perhaps not," Orac replied, as the sphere moved ahead of the pair, blinking in what Pete perceived to be recognition.

Chapter 86
Parallel Dimension II

(Aboard the *Morning Star*)

"This is as bad as trying to diffuse the stacion generator," Ben grumbled.

"Is there a problem?" Seeka asked.

Ben looked down at the questioning animal. "I don't know which wire to cut."

"Use your instinct as before," Seeka said.

"Make yourself useful and go get Stewart," Ben said, his annoyance now evident. "He's on the bridge."

Seeka nodded and then scurried away, quickly reaching the wheelhouse. As he stepped onto the bridge, an alarm sounded. He hurried toward Stewart and leapt onto the console, questions pouring from his eyes as he peered at Stewart.

Stewart looked at the wondering nuckta. "The island; it's now close enough to see."

"Oh dear," Seeka said.

"*Oh dear* is right," Stewart echoed. "Look at this."

The nuckta peered at the flashing console. A small set of LED lights blinked in rapid succession.

Seeka's gaze left the console and fixed on Stewart. "I do not understand."

Stewart returned the stare, expressing great concern. "The launch sequence is preset, and I can't stop it."

"This is hopeless," Ben said. Throwing his wrench to the ground, he leaned back against the warhead. A whining noise began, originating from his right. He turned toward the sound as it built in intensity and then surrounded him.

Ben looked around in wonderment, his skin tingling. "It's back on," he whispered. "The stacion field is back on."

Chapter 87
Parallel Dimension I

(Return to *Deadly Reign*)

"I cannot be sure of the exact total," Maskore said. "Many were sacrificed, even in such a small skirmish."

"The cost is too much to bear," Phlagran replied, "but the choice is not ours to make."

"Where is Elgin?" Maskore asked.

"He was with the brethren during the first phase of the attack." Phlagran preened several feathers back into place. "There has been no word since then. Elgin's original plan was to stay behind and guide the humans. Whether he made it through the battle, I cannot say." Phlagran paused. "If he did not, then another would take over directing the humans."

"Let us hope by the divine grace of the Great One," Maskore said, "that all is as well as can be."

"We must make sure that all is in order," Phlagran said. "I will need you to check our store of tendor. It is imperative we retain a sufficient amount of food to provide enough fuel to sustain us when in combat."

"I will do as you have asked," Maskore said. "Please notify me of any news from the battlefield."

"I will, old friend."

Chapter 88

A karron circled slowly, its white light shining as a beacon, guiding Pete and Orac unto itself. An orb had stopped and brightened. The unlikely pair continued to move toward the increasing brilliance. As they neared, they noticed a depression in the snow six feet in diameter under the pulsating sphere. Within this circle, the ground appeared as if on fire. Orac and Pete, fascinated by the sight, stepped to the edge of the burning ring.

"How beautiful," Orac whispered.

Pete nodded.

In the center of the circle lay a chain, each link the size of a normal man's fist. Orac knelt down and cleared snow-laden debris from the circle. When done, he grasped the chain and pulled with no results. Without a word or prompt, Pete grabbed the chain and lent his meager strength to the tug of war. The chain gave way, pulling a six-inch plug of material from the earth. The burning circle extinguished, as did the overhead orb. Orac and Pete sat on their knees, in awe of the gusher of green and yellow light streaming upward from the narrow outlet. The light rose to a height of fifty feet, then parted and curled back onto itself, forming a large, pale, yellow sphere. Within this entity, the figure of a young man appeared. He smiled, winked, and then was gone, along with all traces of the pyrotechnic light show. All that remained was the single orb, glowing above the snow-covered terrain.

Pete turned to look at Orac. "Do you suppose that was what we were looking for?"

Orac returned the gaze. "If not, I wish to find nothing further."

"Yeah," Pete replied.

"I do not understand this," Orac said.

"Understand what?" Pete asked.

"If this was what we were to find, how could it have any bearing on our victory over Colossac and the riders?"

"I don't know," Pete replied, rising to his feet and facing Orac. "But if we're—" Before the warning screech of the karron could alert the two men, a massive force slammed into Pete's shoulder, sending him sprawling through the air. The beast then turned toward Orac. Orac jumped to his feet, removing the sword from his belt.

"So, beast," he snarled, "you have returned without your demon rider to die alone."

The beast snorted, reared and circled the giant, fluid still dripping from the open wound on its face. Slug after slug of exploding bird flesh peppered the animal with no appreciable effect. A barrage of arrows bounced off the animal's front quarter, producing a light show each time the projectile tip glanced off the impenetrable hide. The huge head turned to see Pete emerge from the darkness and into the light of the orb, steadily firing. Orac swung his sword across the beast's neck, producing a shower of sparks, but a mere nick in the thick hide. The aberration retreated and positioned itself between Orac and the flying arrows.

The immediate area remained drowned in such light as to appear midday, sourced by a pyrotechnic show of avian explosives and sparking swords and arrows. Pete stopped his assault and moved closer.

Orac held his weapon with both hands, swinging it from side to side. Pete joined his companion, his weapon at the ready. A horde of karron attacked the injured side of the beast's head, causing the oozing fluid to burn until the wound was cauterized.

"What are these explosive lights that seem to attack the beast?" Pete asked.

"I cannot be sure;" Orac replied, "however, given their relentless trajectory, I would wager they are friends."

"Let's hope so," Pete said. He fired another arrow and watched it glance off the armored hide. "And as I guess you can see, my arrows have no effect."

"Penetration can be achieved if we attack the beast from underneath," Orac said.

"How do we accomplish that?" Pete asked. "I don't think he's gonna let us flip him over."

"We wait for an opportunity," Orac replied, "and if possible, create our own."

The beast leapt with astonishing agility, landing at the base of a tree. It scaled the trunk until its great weight brought the timber to the ground with an ear-splitting crack. With its belly momentarily exposed, Orac yelled, "Now!"

Pete released his arrow. The projectile bounced off the creature's side as it quickly righted itself, rendering the lethal shot harmless.

"It's too fast," Pete growled.

"Patience, small one."

Pete managed a brief smile.

The beast sidestepped, aligning itself for a charge. It lunged forward, stopped, looked left and then right. The creature reached a decision and snorted as it backed into the shadows.

"Back to back," Orac ordered.

"What?" Pete stammered.

"Place your back against mine; the beast is devising an ambush."

Pete hesitated and then complied. The two men circled, anticipating the attack.

After an hour, they relaxed their stance. The karron had long since ceased their assault, their losses too high for the little damage done.

Elgin perched in a tree, watching for any opportunity to provide assistance.

"Are you sure it didn't just leave?" Pete asked.

"I am no longer sure," Orac said.

Both men looked upward as the snow came to an abrupt halt, and the clouds thinned, allowing the moon to shine through. The clouds then closed in, and the snow fell once again with an increased vigor and an almost menacing intelligence.

"At least we know it's nighttime," Pete said.

Orac crouched. "Look at the orb."

Pete turned his attention upward. The sphere circled in an ever-widening pattern, exuding a pulsating urgency.

"It knows," Orac whispered.

"Knows what?" Pete insisted.

Elgin sent one of his own to its death to warn the two men.

A hail of huge tree limbs plummeted from above, as so much bird flesh splattered in a ball of fire. Orac wrapped his arms around Pete and tumbled to the side, just in time to avoid the full weight of the beast as it plowed into the ground. Orac rolled over Pete and jumped to his feet. Pete lay, unable to move, with the wind knocked out of him.

The creature charged. Orac grabbed Pete's collar, adding to his breathing difficulties, and jerked him out of the way. The beast whirled, catching Pete under his right arm. It flipped its massive head backward. Orac could hear joints separate, as Pete flew end-over-end, landing on one of the downed tree limbs.

Orac rushed to help his friend. Pete's arm was bent in a grotesque fashion to one side, blood dripping from his nose and ears. His eyes were open, revealing two white marbles. Orac knelt to lift the battered body and move him to safety.

A blast of foul, exhaled breath flashed across the back of his neck. The giant turned to see the beast hovering directly overhead. "So, fetid one," Orac said, "it has come to this."

A maniacal, animal-like chuckle emanated from the creature's mouth, as it reared on its hind legs to crush the two combatants.

"Please pardon my manners," Orac said, "but I think not." He rolled onto his back, grabbed his sword by the pommel, placed his feet on the cross-guard, and plunged it deep into the soft underbelly of the descending beast.

A deafening high-pitched scream erupted from the creature as a vortex developed around the wailing beast. Orac lay over Pete to shield him from the flying debris. As the whirlwind spun faster, the creature began to disintegrate, and the pieces absorbed into the funnel. Orac could feel himself being lifted from the ground. After several minutes, with the beast's destruction complete, the vortex dissipated and the giant returned to earth.

Orac rolled off Pete. "So that is their fate if not dissolved with water," he mumbled and then turned his attention to Pete.

Chapter 89

"I think it's getting colder," Eve said, "as if that were possible." She shivered and pulled her fur covering tighter to her chin.

Ben nodded. "And the snow sure seems to be picking up." He inched closer to the fire.

"The menace continues to spread," Caleb said. "It becomes stronger with each passing moment."

"I assume by your tone, we would rather that not happen," Ben replied.

"The stronger the iniquity grows, the more difficult it becomes to eradicate," Caleb answered.

Ben brushed the hair back from Eve's forehead. "You up to making something to eat?"

"I guess," Eve replied. "Maybe if I move around, it'll warm me up." She rose, shaking the accumulated snow from her shoulders. For whatever reason she could not explain, she felt it necessary to carry the mysterious metal stick she had acquired earlier. Eve walked to the heaviest laden packhorse.

"So," Ben said, "isn't there something we can do besides wait for their return?"

"No," Caleb replied, "it is essential they perform their task before we confront the enemy."

Ben nodded. "All right, I don't like doing nothing when there's so much to be done."

Caleb smiled. "It does you well."

"I guess." Ben looked toward the packhorse. "You need any help, sweetheart?"

There was no answer.

"Yoshi," Ben said, "see if Eve needs anything."

The boy traced Eve's path to where the horses gathered. "Ben," he yelled.

Ben frowned at Caleb. "Probably can't find a frying pan," he said.

Caleb smiled.

Ben walked toward the horse. Upon reaching Yoshi, the boy's face was pale white.

"What's wrong?" Ben asked.

Yoshi moved his mouth, but nothing came out.

"Answer me," Ben demanded.

"Ben," Yoshi blurted, "she's gone!"

As Yoshi searched for Eve, he squatted and walked underneath one of the pack horses. He didn't notice a rider slip behind Ben, encircling him in an unbreakable embrace.

Yoshi opened his mouth to yell for Eve, and would have given away his position, had he not heard Colossac. The rider didn't see the boy, but Ben made eye contact before Yoshi ducked and made his way into the woods. He stayed far enough away to remain undetected, yet close enough to see everything that transpired. Yoshi couldn't shake the feeling of guilt, believing himself too young to be of any assistance . . . or was he?

Rock-solid arms clamped around Ben. He tried to move, but his imprisonment was complete. Whatever had him, moved into the light of the fire.

"Caleb!" Ben exclaimed, but Caleb was unable to respond. The skin-bare mountain held him fast, his legs dangling off the ground, a sword pressed hard against his throat.

"Where is the boy?" Colossac barked.

"If you can't keep up with him, that's your problem."

Colossac sneered. "No matter, the yearling is of little concern."

"What have you done with Eve?" Ben demanded.

"You ask for much, for one in such a position as yours," Colossac warned. "However, it would please me greatly to impart this information." He dropped his hostage, placed his foot on his chest and pressed the point of his weapon deep enough into Caleb's throat to pierce skin and draw blood. "She is being held at another location," Colossac continued. "Cahotic is her keeper. He awaits a rendezvous."

Ben snarled, "Couldn't you have left her here just as well?"

A broad smile crossed Colossac's face. "This ensures," he said and hesitated, staring at Ben, "your being a bit more cooperative."

"What do you mean cooperative?" Ben's face grew stern once again. "Cooperation with what?"

"Again, you insist upon exacting information," Colossac said with a smirk. "Before you learn any more, you must learn to respect."

Ben began to ponder Colossac's comment as an unanticipated blow to the side of his head took him to delirium and then to unconsciousness.

"We must leave soon," Orac said. "It is imperative that we reach the others and tell them of our venture."

"Uh-huh," Pete groaned. He attempted to sit up and then fell back onto his side.

"Rest, small one; we shall stay a bit longer."

"No," Pete moaned, "go now."

"In time," Orac soothed, "in time."

Pete settled down, falling into a fitful sleep.

"Sleep and heal, my friend," Orac whispered.

Orac laid Pete on the makeshift sled.

"I can ride," Pete protested.

Orac chuckled. "Lay down, little man. There is a time for action and a time to be still and let others bear the load." He stood. "Now is the time for the latter."

Too weak to argue, Pete lay back and nodded almost imperceptibly.

A small white figure fluttered downward, its landing barely detectable by its host. Feeling the light touch on his shoulder, but sensing no malice, Orac turned his head slowly in order not to frighten the newcomer.

"Greetings, small one," Orac said. "What brings you out on such an unwholesome night?"

Through the song-like voice of the one called Elgin, he explained to Orac his intentions and attempts to help up to this point.

"I am sorry for your great loss," Orac said, "but rest assured the fallen will not have done so in vain."

"Thank you," Elgin said. "You may know that we will be ever vigilant and among you when necessary." Orac stroked Elgin's head just above the beak. Elgin closed his eyes. He reopened them and fluttered off Orac's shoulder.

Waiting until his organic jet motors would do no damage, he ignited both and disappeared into the darkness.

Orac watched until Elgin was out of sight. He then checked the ropes, lashing the sled to Pete's mount. Satisfied, he rubbed the horse's neck. "You bear your master. Bear him with all ease and take us home with all haste as you dare."

The horse blew air through his lips, nodded, and took off at a manageable gait.

Pete's thoughts drifted to Ben and his attempt to reach the surface in the decompression chamber, *Orion*. *Little man,* he thought. *I guess the soft leather shoe is on the other foot.* He quietly chuckled and then fell into unconsciousness.

Chapter 90

"So, this is it?" Eve complained.

"Explain your query," Cahotic said.

"Crappy accommodations, don't you agree?"

Cahotic thought for a moment. "It is not a prerequisite that you are pleased with your surroundings, only that you tolerate them with minimal discussion."

"Minimal discussion," Eve retorted. "Whether you've realized it or not, being the female of our species, I am not kept quiet just because an overgrown, armor-laden slug requests me to do so." She crossed her arms, staring defiantly at the puzzled rider.

Cahotic grunted, took a step toward Eve and grabbed her by the throat, lifting her off the ground.

"My previous statement has been misconstrued as a request," he hissed.

Eve pawed at Cahotic's hand, making gurgling noises.

"I know nothing of this female belonging to your species," he stated. "However, I will remove your throat in a most unpleasant fashion, if necessary, to stay your tongue." Cahotic paused. "Have we reached an understanding?"

Eve's eyes rolled over white, and her body went slack.

"I will regard that as an affirmative." Cahotic released his grip, dropping her in a heap onto the ground.

Eve gasped convulsively. She took several erratic breaths, shuddered and began to breathe at a near normal rate. She moaned and came to a sitting position, rubbing her throat. Trying to speak, she coughed, thought better of what she had planned to say and remained silent.

Cahotic rested the point of his sword on the ground, knelt, and wrapping his hands around the hilt, stared at Eve.

Chapter 91
Parallel Dimension II

(Aboard the *Morning Star*)

"Don't come any closer," Ben warned.

"Why?" Stewart asked, taking another step.

Seeka bit down on Stewart's ankle, causing him to whirl around, the cuff of his shirt grazing the stacion field.

"What are you doing?" he demanded and then froze. He raised his arm, pondering the bare skin from his wrist to his shoulder. "What happened to my sleeve?"

"Man, you just don't listen, do you?" Ben said.

Stewart's eyes widened. His gaze moved between his exposed arm and his bleeding ankle. He looked at Ben and took several steps backward. "It's back on, isn't it?"

"Duh," Ben mocked, dropping his lower jaw.

Stewart shook his head and knelt to pet Seeka. "Thanks, fuzz ball."

"You are welcome, I believe, would be the appropriate response."

"I'm over here," Ben said, "if you two can stop ogling over each other."

Stewart stood and turned to face Ben. "Sorry, but how did the field turn itself back on?"

"Perhaps it did not," Seeka said.

The vessel shook violently, throwing Ben and Stewart to the deck. Seeka squatted low, bracing against the quake. Once the tremor subsided, Seeka spoke. "I fear the presence has returned."

Once again, the vibration rattled the *Morning Star* and quickly dispersed.

Vinny burst on deck. "Evans—he's gone!"

Chapter 92
Parallel Dimension I

(Return to *Deadly Reign*)

Ben moaned and then rolled onto his knees. He slumped, cradling his head in both hands.

"Ah," Colossac said, "the arrogant one awakens."

Ben slowly rose to all fours, his head rocking from side to side. "What . . ." he mumbled.

"Take heart, friend," Caleb said, "we will—"

A hard kick to the ribs silenced Caleb. He coughed several times and then returned to his stoic character.

Ben's eyes began to clear, although, to him, everything still seemed to move in slow motion. As his body returned to the realm of normal, he saw Caleb lying on his back, his hands and feet bound with heavy cord.

"All right," Ben said, sitting up on his haunches, "why do you need my cooperation? You might just as well beat whatever you want out of me."

Colossac grinned. "That would certainly be the preferred method; however, in this instance not the most prudent."

Ben stared at him. "Well, are you going to ask me?"

Colossac slowly nodded. "I require a small piece of information, a meaningless tidbit from your past."

"Tell him nothing," Caleb retorted.

Another kick to the ribs brought a second round of wheeze-filled coughing and a trickle of blood-speckled phlegm from the corner of Caleb's mouth.

Ben burned with rage, yet hid his fury from the man mountain. "You're not exactly cultivating goodwill among the ones from whom you desire information," he said.

Colossac scowled, pressing his face within inches of Ben's. "I care not about your goodwill," he seethed. "Give me what I want, or I will cultivate your blood."

Ben stared back, refusing to back down. "I'm still waiting on you."

Colossac regressed, adopting a condescending approach. He cocked his head to the side.

"Of course," he said softly, "there is that bothersome detail." He sat down beside Ben. "Your time on the *Morning Star* with Captain Evans," he began.

Ben jerked his head in the direction of Colossac. "How could you know of the *Morning Star* or Evans?"

"Worry not about such details;" Colossac said, "it is enough at this point that I know."

Ben shrugged. "There is one instance . . ."

Colossac began to chuckle. "I had hoped you would clarify." His amusement grew. "I am sure you remember the event."

Ben couldn't help but smile at the laughing man mountain. "Perhaps."

Colossac ceased his laughter. "Yes," he soothed, "I am certain that you do."

♦♦♦

"Must you sit there and ogle me?" Eve asked, her voice still raspy from the earlier confrontation with Cahotic.

The rider remained silent, not moving.

"Okay, I get it." She crossed her legs in a squat position and pulled her fur closer. "Can I at least sit by the fire?"

Cahotic hesitated and waved a finger in the direction of the flames.

Eve wasted no time in moving toward the radiating warmth. Cahotic moved along with her and resumed his previous position.

She ignored her jailor and then turned to face him. "What's for dinner?"

Cahotic squinted. "Perhaps you will eat again, perhaps you will not."

"That's comforting," Eve said, moving her attention back to the fire. "Thank you."

"You are wel . . ."

"Never mind," Eve interrupted.

Cahotic grunted.

"If it's not too much trouble," Eve said, "I need to relieve myself."

"Do as you wish," Cahotic replied.

Eve stood in defiance. "Not with you gawking at me."

"I know of no other way," Cahotic said.

Eve whirled to face him. "Well, you'd better think of a way!"

Her sharp tone surprised Cahotic, causing him to recoil from her. He eyed her with contempt. "Very well."

He grabbed her by the wrist and led her to a large oak tree. "You may necessitate your bodily function on that side." Cahotic pointed to the trunk. "I will wait on this side."

Eve began to move when Cahotic pulled her close. "Do anything other than relieve yourself," he hissed, "and I will dismember you where you stand."

She nodded and looked at his hand clamped around her wrist until he released his grip.

Eve positioned herself and began. A thought raced through her head as she listened to her urine melt the snow beneath her. She finished, covered herself and dipped her cupped hands into the tainted slush.

"Thank you so much, Cahotic," she said. "I feel much better now." She stepped around the tree and caught the faint image of the rider's face illuminated by the distant fire.

"Back to your place," he commanded.

"Of course." Her eyes widened and a great smile spread across her face. "But first, allow me to send you straight to hell!"

Cahotic didn't have enough time to experience surprise before the waste-soaked slush embedded itself deep into his ocular sockets. Wails of agony emanated from the rider as he pawed viciously at his face. The heavy salt and mineral content of the urine more than doubled the caustic effect over that of plain water.

Mesmerized by the moaning aberration, Eve barely ducked in time to miss a blind swipe from Cahotic. She moved to a safe distance and observed as the rider stumbled back into the makeshift camp and into the fire. His beast moved closer to his master and looked on. Cahotic stood and began to dig the dissolved flesh out of what once were his eyes. He swiped a hand across his face, removing the remaining piece of his nose and most of his upper lip. Eve saw nothing after Cahotic fell into the fire, her escape into the darkness made complete with his supposed demise.

Cahotic stood in the midst of the dying fire breathing heavily. "You will pay," he snarled, his speech unintelligible from the missing lip. "Make no mistake, soft one, you will pay."

◆◆◆

"Small sips," Orac said. "Too much at one time and it will not stay down."

Pete gagged and winced at the pain pounding in his head. "What is that?" he demanded. "I don't think I could keep even a small sip down."

"It will make you feel much better," Orac replied. "I was fortunate to find it with this white covering on the ground. Without the help of the orb, I fear it would have been impossible."

Pete looked at his benefactor. "Let me guess—you boiled your socks and gave me the broth."

Orac smiled. "Not so, small one."

A curious look crossed Pete's face as he cocked his head to the side. He raised his eyebrows and looked at Orac. "The cobwebs are clearing." He motioned with both hands, curling his fingers toward himself. "Give me more." He took another drink and contorted his face, waiting for the initial wave of nausea to pass. "Again," he said, letting out a deep sigh, "what is it?"

"The clavian tark," Orac replied. "It is a medicinal plant used for many ailments; however, its most remarkable healing properties are reserved for cranial injuries."

Pete nodded. "Well," he said, rising to his feet, "let's get a move . . ." He stopped in mid-sentence, held his head, wobbled and then fell forward.

Orac grabbed Pete before he could hit the ground and helped him back to a sitting position. "It will help you to feel better;" Orac said, "however, the process of healing still requires time."

Pete lowered his head between his legs until the vertigo subsided. "That's good to know," he groaned. "I wish you had shared that with me a little sooner." After several minutes, Pete raised his head. "So what do we do now?"

Orac handed him the cup. "Have a bit more of the clavian broth, and then we will depart." Pete took the cup and drank. He wiped his mouth and handed the cup back to Orac.

"Fill 'er up again there, big guy," Pete urged.

"That is enough for now; we must take our leave."

"Then lead on, Macduff," Pete said, extending his arm as if holding a sword.

The delirium begins, thought Orac as he helped Pete to the sled. "Do not hesitate to inform me of any discomfort as we travel," Orac said.

Pete nodded. "I'll be fine, big boy." He held out his hand. "Give me my crossbow, and let's get outta here."

"I think not," Orac said. "To trust you with such a deadly weapon in your condition would not be a wise thing to do."

"I think not," Pete mimicked. "With all the danger around us, it would be foolish for me to be unarmed."

Orac unloaded Pete's crossbow, thinking he would not have the strength to reload the weapon. Pete accepted the gift without comment. As soon as Orac turned his back and led the horse, Pete, using all of his remaining strength, pulled the crossbow string back and locked it in place. He pushed the notched end of the dart into the firing position.

Within thirty minutes of the pair's exodus, the orb lighting their way began an erratic dance. Orac stopped, bringing the horse to a halt. Pete, having dozed off in a sitting position, wove his way back to consciousness. "What's happening?" he asked, still heavily sheathed in a drug-induced stupor. He blinked several times and fumbled for his crossbow.

"There is something ahead," Orac replied.

"Stand down," Pete demanded, raising his weapon.

Orac turned to face Pete. He noticed that his friend's crossbow was loaded. "Lower your weapon, small one. There is nothing here to cause you harm."

"I said stand down," a delirious Pete insisted.

Orac moved toward the confused man. Through Pete's blurred vision, he saw an indistinguishable large mass lumbering toward him. He wrapped a finger around the crossbow's trigger and fired.

Chapter 93

"And that instance is . . . ?" said Ben.

"Ah," Colossac replied, "I see intrigue in your eyes."

"Perhaps," Ben said. He hesitated and then looked at Colossac. "Are you going to ask me?"

Colossac nodded. "You remember the other crew members on board the *Morning Star*?"

"Yes," Ben said.

Colossac sat down beside Ben. He leaned over, placing his elbow on his knee. He laid his chin in the palm of his hand and stared at Ben. "There was one in particular," he said, "different from the others. One with . . ." he paused, searching for the correct words, "shall we say, with special talents."

"What kind of talents do you mean?"

Colossac leaned closer. "Do not patronize me," he whispered with increasing menace. "I am considering your first suggestion of beating the information from you." He allowed Ben to mull his words over. "Now," Colossac continued, "what shall it be? And do not tarry, for my patience wears dangerously thin."

There's nothing he can do to hurt Scott, Ben thought, *and a lot he can do to hurt me.* "Okay, you're referring to Scott. What do you want to know about him?"

"I wish to learn the connection between your Scott . . ." Ben sensed the giant's agitation growing. ". . . and these annoying yellow lights that follow you travelers." He raised his fist and shook it at the orb hovering overhead.

A disturbing thought slammed into Ben's brain linking Scott, Colossac and the krang. Ben quickly recovered from the alarming sensation. Knowing it bore him no malice, he continued his conversation with Colossac. "*Connection*; what makes you think there is one?"

Colossac paused thoughtfully for a moment, then said, "I do not know," the giant lied. "That is why I am inquiring of you."

Ben was unsure if this mountain of flesh was telling the truth or just blowing smoke. "I suppose it's possible, but I can't remember anything that would tie the two together."

"Tell me of this one's powers."

"Powers or talents?" Ben inquired.

"Mere words," Colossac said. "You are aware of what I speak."

Ben thought of Eve and what might happen to her if he did not cooperate. "Scott could bring calm to a tense situation. He brought people under his power and made them comply with his direction."

"How was this control accomplished?" Colossac asked, his growing interest now evident.

"That's the weird part." Ben stared at Colossac. "His eyes would flash yellow."

"You have been exceedingly helpful, Ben Adams," Colossac said, scarcely able to contain his excitement. The giant rose and conversed with the remaining rider. Once done, he made his way into the forest and out of sight. The rider moved closer to Ben and stood.

Chapter 94

Orac whirled to the left with amazing speed and caught the dart as it passed by.

Pete's head began to clear, as did his eyes. "Orac," he screamed, then grabbed his head as an agonizing jolt of pain coursed through him, threatening to explode his skull. He felt a hand on his shoulder.

"Are you okay?" he heard a familiar voice ask. Pete raised his head and squinted through the pain. "Eve?" he weakly asked. Then all was black.

♦♦♦

Pete moaned and slowly opened his eyes. "Orac, I had this weird dream. I shot you, and Eve was there—"

"Slow down," Orac warned. "You should not upset yourself so."

"I see your patient is awake," Eve said.

"Eve," Pete exclaimed, grabbing his head. "When am I going to learn not to do that?"

Eve knelt beside Pete. "Orac told me what happened. You're lucky to be alive."

"That's yet to be determined," Pete replied, rubbing his head. He looked at her. "What are you doing here?"

"One of Colossac's cronies nabbed me," she said.

"How did you get away?" Pete countered.

Eve bounced up and down on the balls of her feet, wearing a huge grin. "I peed on him."

"Later, on that one," Pete said, looking puzzled. "What about Ben and Caleb?"

Eve shook her head. "Colossac and the other goon were there. I heard them talking, but I was hauled off and don't have a clue."

Orac joined the conversation.

"Orac," Pete said, "did I hurt you?"

"Worry not, small one, you did no harm."

Pete sighed. "I'm glad I was too out of it to shoot straight."

Orac smiled. "That was not the case," he replied.

"I'm not following you," Pete said. He reached out and touched Orac's shirt. "There aren't any holes."

"I do not understand it myself," Orac said. "I moved faster than imaginable, and with no consideration to that end."

Pete rolled this thought around in his haggard brain. "Are you saying you dodged my shot?" he squinted in disbelief.

Orac nodded, "And captured the dart within my hand as it passed by."

"Could that be the power you were unaware of?" Eve asked.

Orac nodded again. "It was a great surprise, and I am its owner."

Pete labored to push an errant notion through cobwebs and tattered gray matter until it wound its way into his mouth, "The Kumult?"

"I have pondered the same," Orac said.

"And?" Eve asked.

"I do not know," Orac replied. He withdrew into himself and stared into the distance. "If this is so, then what else may lurk within?"

Pete and Eve's eyes locked, as a wave of dread coursed through their bodies at Orac's comment.

Eve turned to Orac. "We're with you no matter what."

Orac looked at her and smiled. "I can ask for no more than that."

The three gathered their things and left in search of the others. They continued on for several miles until Eve noticed a dull light cutting through the falling snow. As they neared the glow, they saw it emanated from the window of a small, disheveled shack. The walls were covered with white paint that was now faded and chipping, with ivy growing up the sides. Two haphazardly placed windows adorned either side of a Z-braced slat door. Uneven rotted chunks were missing from the bottom of the door, allowing light to filter through.

Orac looked at Eve. They both shrugged their shoulders, and then Eve stepped forward and knocked on the door.

Chapter 95

Colossac knelt with both knees on the ground. He cleared the snow away in front of him. "Even after elimination, I fear my one nemesis has returned," he mumbled as he worked. "I have no choice but to enlist that fool Evans once again." He scratched several symbols into the ground and laid the marble-sized passage sphere among them. Throwing his head back, he began to chant, summoning the krang.

♦♦♦

Evans sat in the corner of the lockup, unresponsive. A surge of familiarity pulsed through his brain. He sat up on his knees, his eyes wide with apprehension. Placing a hand on each side of his head, he began to rock back and forth. Beads of sweat popped up on his forehead. "No," he pleaded, "not again."

His motion increased as he pressed his hands tighter in a vise-like manner, trying to force the notion from his thoughts. The ship and the very air surrounding it shook violently and then returned to normal.

"It will do you no good," the now overwhelming influence said.

"What do you want from me?" Evans groaned.

"If not for your incompetence, I would not have had to return." The voice, now clear in Evans' head, snarled.

"Explain what you require and be done with me."

"In time; yet remember you will not fail me."

Evans cowered in his corner as the voice detailed its objective. He then nodded and stood. The same intense quaking ensued as the presence departed. An iron chain around his ankles fell to the ground. The door opened, and Evans was once again free.

Chapter 96

"You okay?" Ben asked.

"I am," Caleb replied.

"Good." Ben shook his head and sighed. "Things sure have turned into a mess."

Caleb pondered Ben's comment. "Perhaps, perhaps not."

"I don't see an upside to any of this," Ben replied.

Caleb smiled. "This is where you must trust in what you cannot readily observe, even though this situation is not within your control. Rest assured it is within the control of the One who will guide it through to its completion."

"The Great One?" Ben asked, already knowing the answer.

"Yes," Caleb replied.

Ben looked at the rider. He stood in the same position, silent and not moving. "You reckon tall, dark and stupid is listening to our conversation? It's almost like he's gone to sleep."

"I do not perceive that to be the case."

Ben touched Caleb's arm. "Let's conduct a little experiment." Ben stood and took a step. Before the step was complete, the point of a sword pressed into his gut with enough pressure to pierce his skin. He held both hands out to the side in a posture of surrender and slowly returned to a seated position.

"Bobo there is as fast as he is ugly," Ben said.

"I do not know;" Caleb said, "however, it would be acceptable to shed my restraints and sit for a time."

The same blade which nearly brought about Ben's demise moments before slashed through Caleb's bindings.

"Guess he doesn't perceive you as a threat," Ben said.

"Perhaps you are correct," Caleb replied, bringing himself to a sitting position.

Ben chuckled and shook his head. "So what do we do now?"

Caleb kept a wary eye on the jailor as he answered Ben's question. "We wait for an opportunity."

The rider standing guard made a barely perceptible movement. "Did you see that?" Ben whispered. "He is listening."

"Yes," Caleb acknowledged, "and take heed you do not forget."

Ben nodded, now more aware than ever of his jailor's power of comprehension.

Chapter 97
Parallel Dimension II

(Aboard the *Morning Star*)

"Gone," Stewart exclaimed.

"Gone," Ben echoed.

"Yes," Vinny answered, "he's gone."

"The generator!" Ben bellowed.

"Do you think?" Stewart replied.

"You and Vinny check it out," Ben said. "Do whatever you must to turn it off."

Seeka turned to leave with the two men.

"Fuzz ball, stay with me. I have a feeling I'm gonna need you."

"You got it, boss man," Seeka chuckled.

"Whadda you see?" Vinny asked.

"Hold on," Stewart said, "I just got here." He searched through the generator housing, fingering leads and wires before shaking his head in resolve.

"Stew, you're not lookin so good," Vinny said. "What's wrong?"

Stewart stepped down the ladder, pausing at the bottom to glance at Vinny. "Can't be done," he said.

"Can't be done?" Vinny echoed, his anxiety growing. "Why not?"

Stewart sat down on a crate, lowered his head and sighed. "It can't be turned off," he said.

"Stew," Vinny urged, "you gotta snap outta this." He placed a hand on each of Stewart's shoulders. "Man, this ain't like you to give up." He shook Stewart. "Now tell me why you can't turn it off."

Stewart raised his head to look at Vinny. "What else is there to do but give up," Stewart said. "The generator has been rewired. I don't know how Evans did it, but I can't reverse it." He lowered his head and then rose to his feet. "Maybe Ben could, but I can't."

An alarm sounded, interrupting Stewart.

"What do we do, Stew?" Vinny pleaded.

Stewart snapped from his complacency. "We get to the bridge."

Stewart and Vinny stepped onto the bridge. Stewart rushed to the console, looked over the instrumentation, and glared at Vinny. "We've got to get to Ben!"

"Ben," Stewart exclaimed.

"Shh," Ben warned. "I've almost got it." He clipped another wire, breathed a sigh of relief, and turned toward Stewart.

"The field can't be turned off," Stewart explained. "Evans has rewired the box."

"Okay," Ben replied, "one down and one to go."

"You don't understand," Stewart said. "The launch sequence has already begun!"

Ben's jaw dropped as the first rocket motor began to fire.

"I guess it doesn't matter," he whispered.

Chapter 98
Parallel Dimension I

(Return to *Deadly Reign*)

Rustling and then uneven stomps could be heard inside, moving closer. All became silent before something slammed into the door.

Orac and Eve both jerked back at the sudden noise. Even Pete, behind them on the sleigh, raised his head before lowering it again.

The door opened, stopping just wide enough for a grizzled old woman to step into the opening. She wore brown, unlaced work boots, scuffed and cracked with age. Scrawny unshaven legs rose out of the boots into a faded plaid, mid-length skirt, tied at the waist with a length of rope.

"What in the name of Jeezy Pete is you two a-doin' out here?"

Eve opened her mouth to speak and was immediately cut short.

"Keep it to yerself," the old women squawked. "Don't make no never mind to me anyhow."

A moth-eaten sweater covered a gingham blouse that clung to her from months of not bathing. Bony fingers held a long-stem pipe. Three brown teeth could be counted as she drew heavily on whatever substance burned in the pipe's bowl.

"I never thunked I'd a seen it, but sure nuff I guess it's here." Her leathery face seemed to pull her features deep into her skull. Black eyes glared from their sockets, and a floppy weather-worn cotton hat sat atop her head. She looked around Eve and noticed Pete huddled on the sleigh.

"Dadburn it all to pieces," she said, grinding her pipe between her gums. She turned around and pushed her fist through a wooden wall behind her. Splinters and dust flew in all directions. "I done and fetched up the wrong count again. They's three of 'em and one of 'em is a-illin' and sittin' out in the snow. Lookie here, ya old buzzard, have ya ever seen such a sight?"

The door opened, revealing an old man, more than a foot taller than his female counterpart. He was barefoot, errant nails twisting several inches from his toes, his hairless legs disappearing at the lower calf into a tattered night shirt. He held a funnel, similar to a miniature gramophone, to his ear. A scraggly gray beard cascaded halfway down his chest.

"Look," Eve said, nudging Orac. "There's something moving in his beard."

Orac focused on the beard and soon could see small brown vermin darting in and out of the hairy foliage. The man's face was old and drawn with a long pointed nose, no discernible teeth and a pipe jutting from his near lipless mouth.

"What in tarnation ya goin' on about, ya old bat?" he yowled. She elbowed him in the ribs.

"I know yer deef," she replied, "but 'er ya blind, too, ya ol' coot?"

He grabbed his side and began to cough up huge balls of phlegm, depositing them on the threshold of the door. Ignoring the old man's distress, she addressed the two and Orac.

"Taint a fit night out fer man nary a demon," she said. "Ya three git yerself up and in here now! They's things out here ya wouldn't wanna run into in the light o' day, much less on a night like this here 'un."

Orac scooped up Pete and followed the old woman into the house. They had to step around the old man, still hacking in the doorway. They made their way down a long, dimly lit hall. The scampering and scratching of small unseen beings was evident from the sounds behind the walls.

Eve tensed. *I wonder which side of the wall they're on?* She imagined long-scaled insects with fangs dripping with venom and mangy rats two feet long jumping onto her shoulders while the bugs invaded her hair.

The trip through the hallway seemed to take forever. Eve entered into a large living area, avoiding the onset of hyperventilation that was overtaking her. She wiped the beads of sweat from her forehead.

"How is Pete doing?" Eve asked Orac.

"With his injuries, it will be a long journey; however, I have no doubt his recovery will be complete."

Two beds lined one wall, and a small dinette with five chairs sat in front of a stone fireplace with a flat rock top. A wooden cabinet, pushed tight to the side of the fireplace, with three shelves and no doors, became a makeshift cupboard. Cut into the stone directly beside the firebox itself, was a rectangular-shaped hole which served as an oven. An unidentifiable hunk of meat crackled over the open flame, and the enticing smell washed over them.

"We gettin' ready to sup," the old woman said. "If ya wanna mouthful, then take a seat; if ya don't, then suit yerself." She yelled back up the hallway, "Er ya comin', ya lazy sack a' nuthin'? Fixins is gettin' cold and I ain't apt to warm 'em back up fer ya."

A garbled "Aye" filtered up the hallway. The old woman walked up to Orac and tapped him in the chest with her pipe. "Ya can make a pallet fer that there sickun on the floor in the corner at the foot a' that first bed. Ya be a-findin' blankets on the shelf just above that very same corner."

She turned to baste the meat on the fire.

Turning back around, she squinted her eyes and pointed a bony finger in Orac's direction. "Mind ya, ya don't put him on my bed. I don't take kindly to strangers lyin' where I lie."

As the old woman tended to the meal, Eve took a moment to survey her surroundings. The floor and walls were made of the same faded wooden planks. Beneath the ancient thatched roof, rafters branched out like an oak rib cage. A multitude of diverse insects could be seen scampering in and out of the thatch. They occasionally rained down on the floor and made a mad dash for the nearest crack or corner in which to disappear.

On top of the sizzling flat stone of the fireplace, the old woman ladled an unknown gruel from a large pot into two smaller bowls.

The old man sauntered into the room, still coughing, having recovered from his partner's jab in the ribs.

"Best get to cuttin', else we'll be here all night," the old woman said.

He began to strop a large butcher knife against a piece of leather hanging from the wall. "I'm a-thinkin you might a busted a couple ribs with that elbow a yern," he complained.

"If'n I did, you deserve ever one of em."

He cut several large chunks of the roasted meat, placed them on a wooden serving platter and joined the old woman at the table.

After several mouthfuls, the old woman wiped her chin with her sleeve and glared at Eve, Pete and Orac.

"I ain't 'yo momma, and I done teld ya once that if ya wanna eat, then eat." She swallowed another mouthful. "An best be quick about it, cuz once I clean up this here mess, ain't nobody eatin' till 'morrow mornin'." She motioned with her fork towards the fireplace, "Now git to it!"

Eve and Orac locked eyes, uncertain what to do next. Their lull soon brought an answer.

"I ain't a-goin' ta tell you nary nuther time!" the old woman screamed. She stood, and grabbing one of the empty plates, slung it at the two surprised visitors. Orac caught the plate before it could smash against the wall.

"Now," she said, pointing a trembling finger and grinding the few teeth she had left, "ya take that dern plate, fill er full o' grub and sit down and et." She stood there glaring at the surprised pair.

Orac gave Eve the plate in his hand, retrieving another from the table for his own use. They both slid sideways around the old woman, keeping a wary eye as they made for the food. The old woman grabbed two bowls and jutted them toward Eve and Orac, causing both to jump, and Eve to almost lose her plate.

"Thank you," Eve said.

The old woman waved her off. "Jest shut up and eat."

Orac set his food on the table, then moved to tend to Pete. He gave him another swallow of the medicine he had concocted earlier. "Here, take this," Orac said.

Pete winced. "That's worse than before."

Orac nodded. "As it ages, it coagulates and becomes more bitter." He looked at the contents in the small container. "In fact, this batch will be solid in a very short time."

Orac laid Pete back down. "Come and take nourishment when you feel up to it," Orac said, patting his friend on the shoulder.

"Where's Pete?" Eve whispered to Orac. "He's not on his pallet."

A bony fist slammed down on the table. "No whisperin' at the eatin' table," the old woman scoffed. "If ya got somthin' to say, then say it so's everbody can hear."

Eve jumped at the noise, filled with irritation for the old woman. "I'm sorry," she said. Her voice rose in volume. "It would help to explain the rules beforehand."

"What's the big idea of eating without me?" Pete asked.

The old woman eyed Pete suspiciously. She took a long draw on her pipe, then slowly released the smoke. "Yer playin' a dangerus game with what yer puttin' inside," the old woman said. "Now sit an et so's I kin get ya freeloaders out'n here."

Pete loaded his plate and took a seat at the table.

A silence that could wake the dead prevailed as the diners clinked their plates with their utensils, bringing food to mouth.

"Miss," Eve asked, unsure what to call the ancient female, "why five chairs when there's only two of you who live here?" Eve pulled back, expecting to be blasted for daring to ask a question.

The old woman swallowed her last bite, wiped her mouth, and sitting back, toked on her pipe, bringing the near dead substance back to life. She eyed Eve for the longest time and then spoke.

"Jest found 'em on the front porch one mornin'."

How strange, Eve thought. *Five chairs, five people . . . preplanned?*

The old woman interrupted any other thoughts that Eve may have conjured in her mind. "Round these parts they call me Hattie Mae." She nodded toward her gentleman friend. "This here's Jakey boy."

The old man stopped eating and raised his head, hearing his name being brought into the conversation. Thick strands of gruel dripped from the corners of his mouth, and as he chewed, globs rolled onto his chin and back onto his plate. The vermin in his beard scampered around, scoffing up the pottage that dripped from his mouth. "What ye say?" he garbled through a mouthful of masticated mush.

"Hush up; taint nobody talkin' to ya," the old woman barked. She turned her attention back to Eve. "As I was sayin', we got hitched." She paused, squinting her eyes in thought and tapped her pipe on the table to loosen its contents. After several minutes, she looked at Eve. "I'm a-thinkin it's been pert near three hunderd year." She elbowed the old man and yelled. "Ain't that bout right?"

He raised his head once again and crammed the hearing device in his ear. "Eh?" he asked.

"Aw, never you mind." She looked at Orac. "You's a mighty big un. Take a lot o' vittles to keep you a-goin'."

"Yes, ma'am," Orac replied.

"Does either of you uns know why yer here?"

Eve began to speak. "We saw the light—"

"I don't mean in this here shack, dagnabbit. I be a-talkin' bout this here sitiation."

"Right now we're looking for my husband," Eve said.

"Not that neither. What I be yakkin' bout is the big reason ya here."

Orac said, "To save this world from the scourge that has overtaken it."

"Sakes alive, ya got it."

Something the size of a small stone hit the floor, bounced twice and came to rest in the middle of the room. It was oval-shaped, two inches long, and a translucent blue that glowed through polished facets. The old lady bent down and picked it up.

"This here rock be attached by a chain wrapped round my neck." She reached in and pulled a slender gold-colored chain from under her shirt. "It stuck to this here rock til the rightful folks that be the ones to use it came round and claimed it. Then it'd fall from the chain and be theirs fer the takin'." She held the jewel in front of her face. "Ya got any idea what to do wit it?" Hattie Mae asked.

Eve, Pete and Orac all shook their heads.

"Course ya ain't, and I ain't apt to tell ya."

"Then what good is it to us?" Eve asked.

"Oh, ya know when the time comes; dat's fer sure." She pulled her pipe out of her mouth, leaned over the table and furrowed her eyebrows. "Now, what I will tell ya is how it came bout to be persessed by me and me alone." She paused and let her black eyes settle on the three travelers. "Now ya listen, and I mean listen close, cuz I don't chew my cud twice."

"I twern't but eight-year-old when my pappy up and died. He left me lone with a step momma that were hard as day-old clabber bread." Hattie Mae pulled her pipe out of her mouth, and reaching across the table, once again tapped Eve, Pete and Orac on the chest.

"Now my pappy had always done and told me if'n things get bad, ya up and run and run as fast as ye can."

"Hattie, Hattie Mae," Greta cried, "ya better show yerself, elsen I'll tan yer hide within an inch of yer worthless life." She stomped around the back of the house and then paused. "Ya can't hide from me, ya useless little scamp."

"I hid on the edge of them thar woods jist out'n sight. When I seen Greta was a-movin' in the wrong direction and getting' further away, I jumped up and ran into them woods as fast as I could run. I runned fer what seemed like hours. I hit the ground too tard to move another step. I curled up 'neath the low branches of a lumbra bush. The leaves were large nuff and drug the ground, givin' me some cover. I could feel the ground underneath a-vibratin' from the workins of the scabbard worms. That vibration put me right to sleep.

When I woked, it was plum dark. I was some kinda scared. I couldn't take no more, so's the panic took a holt, and I bolted from 'neath that tree. I hadn't took no more than ten steps when I bumped into somethin' that plum knocked me back on my keister. It was strong enuff to stop me but soft enuff not to cause me no hurtin'."

"Where is a young one such as you," the obstacle said, "going on such a dark night?"

Something in the stranger's voice told Hattie that she had nothing to fear, and much to her surprise, she answered without hesitation.

"Away," she said.

"Away?" the stranger asked.

"Yes," Hattie answered, "just away."

"What is your name?" The stranger held a staff that glowed bright enough to show a wide smile along with another unusual feature: one green eye and the other yellow.

"Hattie," she replied with a smile, "Hattie Mae."

"You can call me Sarith." He extended his hand, and Hattie placed hers within his.

Eve's eyes grew wide. "Sarith," she said, "you saw Sarith three hundred years ago?"

"One thing we needs to get straight rat now." Hattie took several tokes off her pipe. The smoke from her mouth seemed to curl menacingly around her head. "Ya interrupt me one more time and yer liable to get somthin' ya don't want." Hattie took one more toke off her pipe. "Member dat hole I punched in dat wall when ya first got here?" Hattie paused for effect.

Disappointed, Eve's smile disappeared, and she slowly nodded.

"Slow down little one; no one will take it from you."

Hattie Mae looked up from her plate, her cheeks bulging with food, and with the biggest smile one can manage with a full mouth. The two sat at a small wooden table with a chair for each. They were in the middle of the forest but covered by a clear structure. The edifice allowed one to enter and exit, but remained warm and kept precipitation out.

Sarith smiled. "Carry on, young one."

As Hattie finished her meal, she placed her utensil on her plate and wiped her mouth with the provided cloth napkin. "Much obliged," she said.

"Now," Sarith said, placing his right elbow on the table and nestling his chin into his palm, "maybe I can wriggle an answer out of you this time."

Hattie's eyes brightened. "Sure nuff," she said. "Anybody fix up a plate o' grub like that there, I liable to tell em most anythin'."

"Good," Sarith said. "What is a little thing like you doing out by herself after dark, and if I am not mistaken, running away from something?"

"Yes'm," Hattie retorted. She stood, assuming a more aggressive posture. "My stepmomma twas mean as mean could be. She done and kilt my pappy. No one could prove it, but I knowed better." She wiped the tears that flowed down her cheeks. "My pappy was laid out in this here box in the middle o the livin room. I tried to crawl up to get a good look, when my stepmomma threw me down on the floor and commenced to whuppin' me." She ran her hand and index finger under her nose and sniffed. "Dat's when I did zackly what my pappy had done and told me to do." She looked at Sarith. "I ran."

"That was honorable, indeed; obeying your father's wishes." Sarith stood and waved his hand over the top of his staff.

A blue aura appeared and rotated around the outside of his hand. As it spun, it tightened its spiral until it moved out of sight under his palm. He closed his hand and brought it down as he reseated himself. Rays of blue light showed through the cracks of his fingers, as he brought his hand close to Hattie's face. Hattie's eyes widened as the beams of light swung side to side and up and down, following the edge of Sarith's fingers.

"What dat is?" she asked, mesmerized by the sight of it.

"A gift for you," Sarith replied. He opened his hand, revealing an oval-shaped translucent jewel.

"Fo me?" Hattie said. "Why you give dat to me?"

"It must go to someone pure of heart who also knows the disappointment and abuse that life can bring."

Secured to the stone was a slender golden chain with no visible connection securing the stone to the chain.

Sarith picked up the delicate chain and placed it around Hattie's neck. Hattie kept her eyes on the stone as it moved from Sarith's hand to her chest.

"No one will see this amulet save for you and the ones to whom it is destined to belong."

Hattie shook her head, seemingly under control of the newly acquired blue rock. After several minutes, Hattie looked at Sarith.

"What's it fer?" she asked.

"I do not know; only that you will be the keeper and deliverer when the time is right."

Hattie looked up at Sarith, her eyes asking the question he dreaded the most. He placed his hand upon her cheek and with his thumb, wiped away a tear.

"Yes," he said, his eyes welling, "you must go back." Sarith stood, and taking the little girl by the hand, led her back to the unthinkable.

The old woman handed the amulet to Eve. "Now get out," she said, "and take them two worthless hands with ya."

Eve briefly eyed the stone and shoved it in her pocket. "When we first arrived here, you said it's not a fit night out for man or demon." Hattie and Eve stared at each other for several moments. "What do you know about demons?" Eve asked. "The typical word should have been beast."

"Never ya mind; taint none of it do ya any good." Hattie hocked up a ball of phlegm and spat it on the floor. "Best stick to what ya dun and figgered out fer yerself, an keep dat nose out'n others' business."

Pete was once again incoherent, with his head lying on the table. Orac gently scooped up the injured man, and all three headed to the door.

Once on the outside, the old woman spoke. "Don't 'spect to see ya three round here no more. Ya make sure you do right by that thar stone and do whatever it is yer post to do with it. Ya hear me now?"

The snowfall was picking up as they made their way to their horses.

"And y'all make sure ya take care of that youngun," were the old woman's last words.

With Pete still in Orac's arms, Eve and the giant turned to look back at Hattie and found all traces of the house and its former inhabitants gone.

"Young one?" Orac asked. "Who is young one? Could she have been talking about Yoshi?"

"How could she have known?" Eve replied. She shook her head and reprimanded herself. "Don't ask; just don't ask."

Orac settled Pete onto the sleigh. He plucked a frigid leaf and tucked it under his cloak to use as packaging for the hardened clavian tark. The leaf was supple in under a minute.

"Where do you think your Ben is now?" he asked.

Eve threw a leg over Pete's mount and settled into the soft fur. "With Caleb," she said, "as far as I know, they're still in the same place as when I left."

"That is where we will start," Orac said. He coaxed the horse that was bearing Pete to set out. "We should be no more than one rising of the Great Light by half."

Pete let out a grunt as the sled jerked in response to his mount's motion.

"Sorry, small one," Orac said.

Pete waved him off. "Got any more of that sludge I was drinking earlier?"

"The clavian broth," Orac replied. He pulled a green bundle out of a vest pocket. "However, it is no longer a liquid." He handed the bundle to Pete.

Pete unwrapped the leaf. A thick brown paste clung to the inner surface of the package. "What is this?" Pete said, holding the leaf up and wrinkling his nose in disgust.

Orac chuckled. "The product will never perish; however, to stabilize, it becomes a gel-like substance after its initial liquid beginnings."

"This smells worse than it did," Pete said.

"Take your medicine, you big baby," Eve chastised.

Pete curled his lip at her, looked at the paste, then at Orac, brought the brown goo to his lips, hesitated, closed his eyes and took a bite. He contorted his face in a grotesque expression as he chewed. Moments later his expression relaxed, and he opened his eyes.

"Wow, this stuff is better than the broth." He took another bite and happily chewed away. Pete raised the leaf to his mouth once again.

"No more," Orac stated.

"Why?" Pete asked.

"For the very reason that makes you enjoy it so," Orac replied.

Pete's face fell. "I don't understand."

"It is a substance that can bring great healing if used in the correct manner," Orac said. "Used wrongly, it is a constant series of euphoric highs and unimaginable lows that will destroy the one under its influence."

Pete raised his eyebrows, cocking his head sideways. "If you say so."

Orac turned his attention forward. Pete pushed his finger into the brown gel and placed it in his mouth, scraping the residue from the appendage with his teeth. He made sure he removed any remaining vestige with his lips, producing a faint sucking sound as he extracted the digit. Pete rewrapped the bundle and stashed it within the coverings on his sled. He sat smiling as the drug-induced warmth moved deeper, invading his very soul.

Chapter 99

Ben nodded. Caleb returned the gesture and tightened his muscles for the planned departure. Ben rose to his knees. His palms-down slap on the ground would initiate the plan's execution. He raised his hands, faking a yawn. Caleb nodded a second time, implying readiness. A millisecond before Ben directed his hands toward the earth, an odd vibration filtered through the soil and into his body.

Ben lowered his arms and shook his head, conveying to Caleb that the operation was now off. Caleb acknowledged the signal and then relaxed.

The vibration grew into a steady pounding which shook the ground with each perceived footfall. The concussions now included a discernable break in between and an urgent impression of enraged panic.

Ben soon witnessed the reason for his concern. An aberration he had previously encountered lumbered into the light of the fire. Its mounted beast snorted. Slobber from its rider draped in streams of thick drool, which coursed down the animal's neck.

The rider himself was disfigured beyond recognition, if that were possible, Ben thought. It had no visible means of sight. Its nose and lips were also nonexistent, which caused the steady stream of saliva drooling from its mouth.

Ben shuddered. *That's not saliva,* he thought. A faint, but familiar odor invaded his senses. "That's it," he whispered. "Alcohol . . . they're an alcohol-based life form."

The two riders were now conversing. Ben took advantage of their distraction and slid closer to Caleb. "Are you seeing this?"

"That is Cahotic," Caleb said. "He is Colossac's second. What has befallen him I cannot imagine. What will soon befall you and me is all too clear."

Ben looked puzzled. "What do you mean?"

Caleb creased his forehead, absorbing the negative energy from the disfigured newcomer.

"I sense a great rage in this one. That rage will be spent in our direction; of that I am sure."

Ben nodded. "We're out of water, but there may be another way."

Caleb looked at Ben. "Explain."

"Their body chemistry is based on alcohol. I could smell it when he came into camp."

Caleb shook his head. "What does this alcohol do?"

Ben smiled. "Alcohol burns. That's why they dissolve in water. Alcohol molecules absorb water molecules. It's not the water doing the damage. The water softens the outer shell, then the alcohol pulls the water into itself at an accelerated rate. The byproduct of this reaction is liquefied tissue."

"You said that alcohol burns."

"Yes," Ben replied. "Look at its face."

Caleb turned to scrutinize the blackened, concave indentations in what remained of Cahotic's face. He nodded in understanding. "Yes."

Ben continued, "The entire facial area is cauterized. Apparently, it's been on fire before. Evidently, there wasn't enough fuel to spread the flames, but enough heat to seal the damage."

Caleb looked at Ben. "What is it you propose?"

"We get fire inside of that thing. We do that, and it will take care of itself."

"You are sure of all you have told me?"

Ben shook his head. "No, everything I have said is pure speculation." He paused for a moment. "But it sounded pretty good, don't you think?"

♦♦♦

Eve scowled. "I thought he was dead."

"Soon we will work to that end," Orac said. He pulled a second sword from the stowed supplies. His horse stepped back nervously as the blade cleared its bindings with a metallic "ching."

What appeared to be several hundred karron hovered above, white jet streams marking their position in the sky.

Pete opened his eyes. "Where are we?" he asked groggily.

"Shh," Eve warned, "they'll hear you."

Pete winced at his throbbing head. "I feel like hell," he mumbled. Remembering the package, he dug into his coverings, produced the bundle, quickly unwrapped the leaf, and stuffed a small portion of the gel into his mouth. Immediately, he embraced the tingling warmth encompassing his body, soothing his aching head and instilling an overall sense of well-being. Pete lay back on the sled and smiled.

"You're wielding two of those things?" Eve asked. "I can barely lift one."

Orac scanned the length of each blade and smiled without comment.

Eve sighed. "When do we go?"

"I will say." Orac looked in earnest at the petite figure before him. "And when we go, we must move with all haste. Time grows short for our friend and your husband."

A rumble embedded deep in the earth began to grow, culminating as a strong earthquake. Orac and Eve lost their balance, tumbling sideways, with Orac landing on Eve. Once the quake subsided, Eve stared into Orac's eyes. She looked left, right, and then back to Orac.

"I'm glad you thought to put your arms out;" she said, "otherwise, I'd be so much flattened meat." She took another look at each of his massive arms, and a shudder moved through her body. Eve imagined all of his weight lying on top of her, and another shudder, more violent than the first, surged from head to toe.

Orac pushed himself to his knees, and then standing, took Eve by the hand, lifting her to her feet. "My apologies, fair one."

"Huh," Eve joked. "My thanks." She looked at Orac. "What was that?"

"I know not, but it does not change the need for haste concerning your Ben and Caleb."

"What about Pete?"

"He is no good to us. Leave him to rest." Orac smiled. "We will return to see him."

Eve tightened her grip on her crossbow, a sense of dread coursing through her veins. She began to scold herself when a raspy whisper brought her to the present.

"Now," Orac hissed.

"The blind one will be our primary target," Ben said.

"Do not underestimate his ability," Caleb warned. "I fear his lethality is not as diminished as you may think."

"Your confidence inspires me," Ben replied with a sarcastic tone.

"I only wish to evaluate the situation which looms before us."

Ben nodded with indifference. "We'll need a diversion to distract the sighted rider."

"Agreed; what do you suggest?"

A wide smile crossed Ben's face. "Oh, I don't know," he said with a disturbing air of joviality, "but I think this may help,"

Caleb turned to see a massive blade-wielding blur and a petite screaming banshee enter the encampment. Scores of white fireballs impacted the four remaining targets. A blinding flash of light escaped each time a projectile made contact. The damage they inflicted was minimal, but the distraction invaluable.

Ben and Caleb jumped to their feet and joined the fray.

Orac attacked the sighted rider, his swords circling in such blind fury that a steady stream of sparks rolled off the armored skin. The barrage was so relentless the creature had no choice but to retreat.

Eve sent a constant stream of darts into the devastated facial cavities of the blind rider.

Karron attacked the disfigured divot, igniting small streams of alcohol that drizzled from the wound, producing a short-lived blue flame.

Caleb circled around as Ben moved to the fire. Cahotic's mount positioned itself to its master's left. It moved forward with such stealth, it was unnoticed until it was too late. The creature lifted its great mass over Eve.

"No!" Ben yelled as it dropped to crush the helpless woman.

Eve felt something graze her right ear, causing a lock of hair to fall on her shoulder. The beast hovered for a moment, then systematically dissected and assimilated into the walls of the surrounding vortex.

Eve whirled around. Pete knelt on the ground smiling and waving, his longbow now pulling double duty as a prop. She returned the smile and then continued her onslaught of Cahotic.

Ben pulled a long, slender tree limb out of the pile of collected firewood, breaking it over his knee to a length of five feet. He jabbed it into the hot coals, the frayed end catching fire.

"Now!" Ben yelled.

Caleb leapt onto the rider's shoulders. Ben tossed the burning stick to Caleb, who then jerked Cahotic's head backward and shoved the stick down his throat until it disappeared. As Caleb rolled off the rider's back, Cahotic moved sideways, seizing Caleb's ankle.

"He'll detonate with Cahotic if we don't get him out of there," Ben exclaimed.

Cahotic froze and began to shake violently, his torso extended to the point of bursting. When his outer shell could no longer contain the internal pressure, it gave way, not with an explosive concussion, but more akin to a tick popping. Pieces of flaming goo and body parts spread over a large area.

Ben could hear Orac's barrage on the last rider in the distance. He turned to see sparks flying and the rider's beast moving with the combatants, looking for an entry to help its master.

"They're probably thirty yards offshore," Ben said.

"Is that a problem?" Eve asked.

"The further they go, the thinner the ice will be," Ben replied. "If Orac breaks through the ice, he'll die from hypothermia before we can get to him."

Orac's constant hacking had sliced through both of the rider's arms, the sparks from the blows igniting the flowing alcohol. The scene replicated two rockets, positioned point to point, firing, each trying to push the other out of the way.

The beast, sensing his master's demise, made his escape by moving further out onto the icepack. Covered by darkness, the cracking ice, the ensuing splash, and the dissolution of the wailing monster were heard by all but seen by none. The burning rider fell like a statue. Heat melted the ice, forming a puddle that turned the last aberration into so much slime.

A yellow orb led Orac back to the others. They were helping Pete into the warm light of the fire.

Caleb stood with Cahotic's hand still grasping his ankle, severed at mid-forearm.

"Good to see you, big guy," Ben said. The two men embraced. "Tell me what happened after you and Pete left."

"Well," Orac began, "we—"

Another earthquake, larger than the last, caused the ground to shake violently. The earth rose in an area about thirty feet across. As it cracked and gave way, two giant claws penetrated the soil, announcing their entrance with a loud clacking noise.

"What now?" Ben asked.

Within seconds, the entire beast was free from its burrow and moving toward Ben, Eve, Orac and Caleb.

The marcovian snapped its claws open and shut, clipping through limbs and entire trees. It swung its tail to the left, splintering a tree too large for an average man to wrap his arms around.

"You think he's just showing off for our benefit?" Ben asked.

"Such a display could prove extremely effective toward intimidating their foe," Caleb replied.

"Yeah, well he's scared the hell out of me," Ben said.

Caleb looked at Ben with a puzzled expression. He hesitated for a moment and then spoke.

"We must surround the creature if we are to have any chance to defeat him."

The two, along with Orac and Caleb, circled around the marcovian. Four humanoids and even the beast paused as a fifth figure, covered in fur and carrying a long, slender bronze-tipped object, walked into their midst. The small biped threw its hood back.

"Yoshi," Eve exclaimed.

The marcovian whirled around, snapping at the boy with its right claw. Yoshi jumped back, extending his spear. The tip of the claw clamped down on the bronze spear end. Yoshi grabbed the shaft with both hands, twisted and pushed down on the handle, snapping the claw tip off.

Ben smiled. "It can be hurt." He pulled an arrow from his quill and loaded his bow. "Light him up!" he screamed.

An onslaught of arrows, darts, and karron assaulted the marcovian. The beast reared up, and using its claws to protect its eyes, continued to advance.

Eve noticed that the metal bar she carried hummed at a low frequency. Unable to expend time investigating the implement, she kept firing crossbow darts at the creature.

"This one may just as well be made from stone," Orac said. He swung his blade into the marcovian's leg, causing a nick no deeper than the thickness of a thumbnail.

Ben, along with the karron, bombarded the face and eyes, attempting to turn the creature back.

The marcovian turned one-hundred-eighty degrees, allowing for the usage of its rear claws and tail. The primitive eyes could pick out shapes to attack, as the fire, fueled by the downed timber, spread into a large enough area to afford movement for all.

It was all Yoshi could do to fend off the single claw that snapped at him, and that soon changed. The marcovian snagged the bottom tip of the wooden spear shaft and flipped it out of Yoshi's hands and into the forest away from the firelight.

"Caleb!" Ben yelled, "Yoshi needs us!" The two men made their way toward Yoshi.

"I shall occupy the beast as best I can," Orac said. "Save the boy." He grabbed two of the smaller legs, and pulling them underneath the body, caused the marcovian to fall onto one side. It righted itself as Ben and Caleb reached Yoshi.

"That large outcrop of rocks," Caleb ordered, "now!" Ben, Caleb, Orac and Yoshi moved to the far side of the granite boulders. The marcovian chewed away at the pile, removing large chunks of rock with each swath.

Pete moaned, his head throbbing to the point where it would surely burst. He pulled out the green bundle, unwrapped it and put a small amount of its contents into his mouth. Breathing deeply, he let the air out with a long sigh. As the clavian tark began to course through his body, he noticed an object glowing in the snow just a few feet in front of him. Pete smiled. *So now I get treated to hallucinations*, he thought. Pete stood and wobbled toward the object. Upon reaching it, he dropped to his knees and picked up the spear. He now knew that this was no hallucination.

The marcovian was now through the granite outcrop. Ben, Eve, Caleb, Orac and Yoshi were reduced to pelting the creature with stones fractured from the granite boulders.

A claw swung around, knocking Orac into a tree, rendering him unconscious. As the marcovian moved in to finish the giant, Eve's metal bar vibrated at an increasing rate and whistled at a near deafening pitch. Not sure of what to do, Eve climbed what was left of the largest boulder, took the bar in both hands and jumped onto the back of the marcovian. She knelt and placed the metal object against the shell of the lumbering beast. The vibration caused the beast to shudder and hesitate before it could shear Orac to ribbons.

A blazing rod of fire, which had once been Yoshi's spear, flew underneath the marcovian. The spin Pete applied upon release, carried the projectile up through its shell, uniting the spear with the bar Eve held in her hands. A bright flash of light ensued, knocking Eve unconscious.

When she awoke, in her hands she found a beautifully crafted weapon. It appeared to be a hybrid of sorts, as it could be thrown or wielded as a sword. The octagonal-shaped bronze handle transitioned into a silver blade just over four feet long. A silver counterbalance was affixed on the opposite side of the handle for stability.

Eve jumped to her feet and ran across the marcovian's back toward its head. Caleb, Ben and Yoshi had moved to assist Orac. All four were seconds from death. Eve raised the weapon above her head. "Die, you—" and with all her might, drove the blade through the brain of the attacking beast.

A high-pitched squeal emanated from the crustacean as it shook and collapsed onto the ground. Much to Eve's dismay, the blade snapped off flush with the creature's head. What she held in her hand was the same silver bar she had received from Sarith, but the ornamentation was worn, and several cracks had developed in the piece.

Once Orac regained consciousness, they told him the story of the marcovian's demise.

"Perhaps you would do well to wait until you have achieved success before you celebrate the victory that will never be yours."

Ben shook his head and sighed. "I know that voice," he said.

The three, along with Pete, Orac and Yoshi, turned to see the skinless man mountain.

"Colossac," Ben said.

Chapter 100
Parallel Dimension II

(Aboard the *Morning Star*)

Exhaust from the torpedo filled the area within the stacion field, ending with a bright flash as the rocket started forward. The smoke cleared as the heavier particles settled to the deck.

Ben stood, bent at the waist, hands on his knees, coughing uncontrollably.

"Ben," Stewart exclaimed, "the other motor will fire in five minutes. You've got to disarm it."

"There's no time," Ben sputtered.

"You've got to try," Stewart said. "You won't survive the next launch if the warhead detonates."

Ben rose to an upright position and wiped his mouth. He said nothing, but moved to the second torpedo and removed the access panel. After detaching the last fastener, he dropped the panel and peered into the open cavity. "It's totally different." He turned. Eve was now standing on deck with Stewart, Vinny and Seeka.

"I don't know," Ben said. "It's nothing like the first one."

"You've got to try," Seeka replied. "Even if the island remains safe, the stacion field may not contain the blast. If that happens, the ship will be destroyed."

Ben looked at Eve. "How much time do I have?"

"Just under four minutes," Stewart announced.

Ben returned to work. Upon sliding his hands into the cavity, he heard three consecutive clicks, and the sequence to fire the motor began. He moved away from the torpedo. "That's a short four minutes."

"It may have had a failsafe that fired the rocket if tampered with," Seeka said.

"It's a moot point now," Stewart said.

"We've got to help him," Eve pleaded. She started toward Ben.

Vinny grabbed her and pulled her back. "No!"

Ben moved closer to the stacion field border as Eve screamed.

Away from the commotion and out of sight of its participants, a translucent yellow sphere containing the figure of a young man completed its journey. It rose from the water beside the *Morning Star*, traveling over the rail. The sphere ascended, hovering above the remaining warhead, Ben, and the stacion field.

The group on deck quieted and watched as the anomaly lowered itself into place. Through the haze, Eve noticed Ben expressing recognition toward the newcomer. A thundering blast ensued, blocking the sphere's occupants from view and sending the group outside sprawling on the deck.

Stewart rose first and helped Eve to her feet.

"Where is Ben?" she yelped.

The debris settled, and the smoke cleared, leaving Ben and Skull standing in the space that the torpedoes once occupied.

Eve ran to Ben, nearly knocking him backward.

"Whoa," Vinny said, "you don't want to end up down there." He pointed to the deck behind Ben.

Ben turned around to see a gaping hole in the deck, open to the floor below.

"How?" Eve asked.

"That's the shape the stacion field projected through the deck," Ben said.

Stewart joined the conversation. "Through the deck?"

"The bottom of the field was under the deck," a voice from behind said.

All faces focused on a lone, armed figure.

"You were too busy to notice my appearance," Evans said. "Once again you are mine." He moved in closer. "And just so you're not left hanging, the stacion field was programmed to project through the deck without vaporizing it. In this way, the warheads would have a structure to bear their weight."

"Well, thank you for that valuable information," Vinny scoffed.

"What do you want, Evans?" Stewart asked.

Evans grinned and cocked his pistol, leveling the barrel on Skull.

The yellow orb lingering over Evans dissipated, dropping its sole occupant, an extremely agitated nuckta. Seeka fell teeth-first onto Evans' hand, clamping his jaws tight and causing the startled captain to drop his gun.

Stewart and Vinny took Evans to the ground. The captain went limp, offering no resistance.

"Seeka," Ben exclaimed, "how did you do that?"

Seeka shook himself and ambled over to Ben. He sat down, licked his forepaw and rubbed it from front to back over his head. "Fuzz balls know stuff," he said with a smirk.

Ben shook his head. "The krang is back, isn't it?"

"Well, that too," Seeka conceded.

Eve laughed, knelt along with Ben, and rubbed the nuckta's head. Seeka smiled the best his face would allow.

◆◆◆

"Is Evans secure this time?" Ben asked.

"Oh, yeah," Stewart replied. "He's chained behind a locked door, Vinny is armed, standing guard in the room with him, and Skull guards the door from the outside."

"Sounds like you've got him," Ben said. "At least I hope so."

"I perceive that all you have done may no longer be necessary," Seeka said. "You should at once escort the captain to his quarters and leave him to his own devices. And Eve, please return to your living quarters."

"You want to explain why?" Stewart asked. "Especially after what he's done."

"It is through the knowledge I speak," Seeka said. "The force that influenced Evans in this world no longer does so. I cling to the hope that evil will soon cease to be in the world I claim as my own."

"Can you be sure?" Eve asked.

"No," Seeka replied, "as I have previously stated, it is through hope I convey my desire of the being's extermination. However, in this world, the order of things has been set right. To complete this reset of the ordered timeline, you must move Evans and prepare for visitors who will soon be among you."

The *Morning Star* came to a halt perpendicular to the island.

A surprised Ben turned toward Stewart. "I wasn't aware we were moving."

Stewart returned the gaze and shrugged his shoulders.

"I must now take my leave," Seeka said. "There are pressing matters which require my attention." The familiar yellow orb formed around the nuckta. "I have never been keen for extended farewells." A tear glistened in the corner of Seeka's eye as he ascended.

"Seeka," Eve exclaimed, "how do you know of the coming events you relayed to us?"

Seeka smiled. "Bound in a cave in a later time," he said, and then hesitated. "You told me."

Eve stood mesmerized as the orb carrying an odd furry creature faded from sight.

"Ben, Eve," Stewart exclaimed, "come here, quick."

The pair joined Stewart at the rail. In the distance, a flotilla of wooden canoes made their way from the island toward the ship. They stared at each other in disbelief.

"I'll move Evans," Stewart said. He turned and left the deck.

Eve followed Stewart.

"Where are you going?" Ben asked.

"To my quarters," she replied.

He thought for a moment. "Good idea."

Chapter 101
Parallel Dimension I

(Return to *Deadly Reign*)

"Okay, big boy, it looks like you're on your own," Ben announced.

Colossac grinned. "Indeed, and I wish to thank you for that small detail. You have rid me of the ones who would destroy the one standing before you."

"And now you stand before the ones who will destroy you," Caleb replied.

Colossac circled slowly around his would-be assassins. "Proud sentiments for one who will soon cease to be."

Caleb crouched and mimicked Colossac's movements, crossbow in his left hand and rider's blade in his right. He glared at the man mountain. "Bring it on," he said, glancing at Ben.

Ben smiled and nodded, acknowledging his support.

"Then 'on' it shall be," Colossac replied, lunging toward his verbal assailant.

Caleb took one step back, underestimating the giant's reach. Colossac grabbed the wrist holding the sword, snapping the bone mid-forearm. Caleb groaned, dropping the weapon. A fist sent him sprawling backward.

Orac set Pete down a safe distance away and returned to the battle.

Colossac took Caleb's sword and turned his attention toward Ben and Eve. He drifted through the hail of darts and arrows toward the pair, plucking the projectiles from his weeping muscle fibers as fast as Ben and Eve placed them.

The karron pelted Colossac's face, attempting to blind the giant. His massive hands swatted at the exploding avian onslaught before they could reach their target.

Yoshi ran to the marcovian. He grabbed the weapon Eve used to deal the deathblow and pulled.

Orac, still sporting two blades, stepped in front of Ben and Eve, blocking their way. He now confronted Colossac head on. The barrage of man and beast ceased as the two giants faced off.

The man mountain slowed his advance.

"Well, I see that my dear offspring has come to bid farewell to his father."

"Do not insult me with lies," Orac warned. "We are no more related than the dark and the light, and it is I who will bid you farewell."

"As you wish," Colossac snarled. He raised his blade, bringing it down over the smaller giant.

As large as Orac was, next to Colossac, he appeared as a child. He raised his blade to block the overhead strike. The force of the blow drove the lesser giant to one knee, showering him with an array of purple sparks. Colossac swung again and again, illuminating their patch of forest in a pulsing, lavender glow until Orac was prostrate on the ground.

"And now," the man mountain stated, "as surely as you came in, I will send you out." Holding his weapon high above his head, Colossac made ready to plunge it into his former ward's chest. A sudden, intense burning sensation along his back caused Colossac to abandon his opponent and turn to locate the source of the searing pain. He spotted Ben, Eve and Caleb, firing flaming arrows from behind a large, downed tree.

Taking advantage of the distraction, Orac hacked wildly at Colossac's legs and buttocks. Enraged, the man mountain whirled around to face his foe, only to receive another round of flaming agony in his back. Ignoring the pain, he focused his full fury toward Orac. Dropping his sword, he extended his arms and grabbed Orac by the torso. Orac slashed the giant's forearms and hands until they oozed a thick, pink liquid. Disregarding his wounds, Colossac picked the smaller combatant off the ground, throwing him through one tree and cracking the second as he came to an abrupt halt. Orac, dazed, shook his head, trying to clear the fog that had settled within.

Before he could react, Colossac took one of Orac's legs and sent him flying once again, this time breaking his fall on the frozen ground. A geyser of snow billowed into the air as he landed.

Pete took a bite of the clavian gel before rewrapping the bundle. He watched as his friend was tossed about, losing a measure of life with each incident. Smoldering arrow shafts, some broken flush to the skin, protruded from the giant's back, several still engulfed in flames.

Pete, eyes now clear, loaded his bow and released, striking Colossac in the cheek.

The giant let out a scream full of rage. Ripping the arrow from his face and throwing it to the side, he stomped to the ailing man and brought his flat palm down on Pete as if swatting a fly.

"No!" Eve screamed.

"Pete," Ben whispered.

Orac stood. He shook uncontrollably. Clenching his fists, a cry emanated from the grieving man that shook the foundation of the forest. For a moment, even the mighty Colossac cringed.

Orac began a transformation. His body bulged and extended until he was more than double his previous size. His clothes separated and fell away, leaving him naked against the cold. He took a step, reached down and dislodged a boulder encased in the frozen crust. Holding the stone like a ball, he brought it back over his shoulder. He growled and hurled the rock toward Colossac. The boulder flew true, catching the giant squarely in his forehead and taking him to his knees. Orac picked up one of the discarded blades and lumbered toward his fallen opponent. Standing behind Colossac, he leveled his sword. The metal weapon began to vibrate and crack, turning to dust and raining to the ground.

Colossac recovered from the shock of the boulder. Orac wrapped his arm around Colossac's neck and took him to the ground. He could not allow Colossac to regain his senses and strength, not knowing how long he himself could hold out. With a sudden surge, Colossac threw his head rearward, catching Orac in the chin, knocking him onto his back. Colossac stood and attacked the prone Orac a second time.

Eve's pocket began to glow blue. Remembering the stone, she reached in and pulled out the amulet. She squinted as a thought slammed into her brain. Eve grasped the metal bar she'd received from Sarith, then placed the jewel into the end of the object. The amulet brightened and then disappeared into the metal. At the same time, a five-foot razor-sharp triangular blade shot out the opposite end with a loud "ching."

Colossac was kneeling atop Orac, pummeling him to the point of unconsciousness. Eve, Ben and Caleb fired a relentless barrage of darts and arrows at Colossac, attempting to coax him away from Orac. Colossac, filled with rage, turned his attention toward the four combatants.

"Orac," Eve yelled, "you must get up!"

Orac moaned and raised his head only to have it drop back into the snow.

Colossac continued toward his adversaries. Orac rolled to his side. When he saw the man mountain, he stood and followed. Sensing Orac approaching, Colossac whirled around.

"Have not had enough?" Colossac taunted. "And what would you have me do now?"

The sword sailed over Colossac's head and into the waiting hand of Orac. He winked at Eve.

Orac growled, "Now you die!"

Silence overtook the area as Orac swung the sword. A gurgling sound drifted out from the slice. Colossac jerked, causing his head to wobble and then fall cleanly from his body. A volcanic eruption of fluid spewed from the open stump. As the explosion lost pressure and slowed, it flowed in streams down Colossac's neck, congealing on his body.

Orac picked up the severed cranium. On it was an expression of surprise. The eyes blinked, and the jaw moved, trying to convey a thought or message. Orac brought the lips to his ear. His eyebrows rose as he listened intently. He pulled the head away and stared into the disembodied face.

"That is the last you shall ever say," he whispered, tossing the head to the ground.

Orac began to return to his normal size. He knelt over the form of his friend. Eve came up behind Orac and covered him with what remained of his tattered clothes. Ben, Eve and Caleb gathered around as Orac gently dug his fallen comrade out of the icy depression.

Ben knelt, as did Eve.

"Pete," Ben said.

"Pete," Eve echoed as she cried.

"What!" Pete demanded. "What do you want?"

"Pete!" Eve exclaimed.

"You've said that already," Pete replied.

"Good to see you, buddy," Ben said. "We thought you were—"

"Well, I'm not," Pete insisted. He looked at Orac. "How about a lift to the fire, big guy? I could stand to thaw out."

"With pleasure," Orac replied.

Yoshi, so occupied with removing the weapon from the marcovian, failed to notice that the battle was over. He grabbed the handle and pulled back with all his might. The slight accumulation of snow caused him to slip, landing him on his buttocks. He lifted himself to his feet amidst a string of curses. After several more trips down, he thought to hold onto the weapon to steady himself. Undaunted by the difficult task before him, he began to twist and bend the spear back and forth, loosening it from the shell until he could pull it free. He landed on his butt once again. Yoshi held the prize above his head and smiled. The five people observing the young man's struggle did their best to contain their amusement.

"How's the arm?" Eve asked.

"It is well," Caleb replied.

Orac smiled. "And how are you, small one?"

"Okay, I guess," Pete said, "but now I'm getting hot." He proved his point by shedding his outer layer of fur.

Yoshi lay asleep clutching the spear, exhausted from the day's events.

"It has gotten warmer," Ben agreed, pushing back from the fire.

"I hadn't noticed before, but it has stopped snowing," Eve said.

"That's not all," Ben said, standing and pointing toward a break in the clouds. "Look." All heads moved skyward. Brief glimpses of blue could be seen through the thinning cloud cover.

"The orb has also extinguished itself," Orac said. "The sky once again brightens."

"Then what's that yellow ball over there on the ground?" Eve asked.

The sphere dissipated with an audible "pop" and a four-legged creature trotted toward the group.

Chapter 102

"Isn't that the clavian tark plant?" Pete asked.

"Yes," Orac replied, "there is much of the herb in this place."

Pete looked toward the sky, basking in the comfortable breeze. "It's been close to two weeks since the warmth returned. I guess before long things will be back to normal."

"Perhaps," Orac replied. "However, now we should return to the others. Our supplies run short, and I have promised to teach how to gather food."

"You go ahead. I'll be along in a moment."

"Very well," Orac said. "Do not tarry for long; the daylight wanes."

Pete nodded and watched until the giant lumbered out of sight. He dropped to his knees and gathered the vegetation. Once he had all he could conceal, he sat back on his haunches, giggled and unwrapped what remained of the clavian paste. *Still a few more doses left. That will give me enough time to render this.*

He smiled and lapped at the substance sticking to the surface of the tattered leaf. It warmed him, though not as intensely as before. "Time to meet the others." Pete rose to his feet, leaving the patch of foliage with an unnatural spring in his step.

"What of Yoshi?" Ben asked.

"He is gone," Eve replied. "Yoshi wishes to search for others of his kind and preferred to keep goodbyes to a minimum."

Ben smiled. "I wish the young one success, although it would have been nice to bid him farewell and thank him for his help."

"He knows," Eve said. "Yoshi confided in me moments before he left, so rest assured all is well."

"Pete," Ben said, "you're just in time. I was talking to Caleb about our plans from here on."

"And?" Pete asked.

"They're sketchy," Ben replied, "but we'll get to that later. Orac is about to show us how to hunt for the scoth."

Ben, Eve, Pete and Caleb walked to within a hundred feet of the surf line. An errant wave pushed in, covering their feet before moving back out to sea.

Seeka came to join them, lifting each foot separately to shake the water free, fighting a losing battle as the next wave undid his work.

"Isn't this beautiful," Eve proclaimed. She closed her eyes, allowing the warm, sweet-smelling sea breeze to waft over her face.

"Sweetheart," Ben said, bringing Eve back from her reverie, "we're hunting right now. It would be nice if you would join us."

Orac stood in the ankle-deep water. He thrust his hand into the sand, drawing out an oval-shaped, crab-like creature with sixteen legs. He walked to the shore, depositing the scoth, shell-side down, in front of the gathering. It was slightly larger than a football, with pincers on eight of the sixteen legs.

"This is what we hope to find," Orac proclaimed. "Which one of you would like to secure the next?"

Eve gingerly touched the crustacean, jerking back as the legs twitched. "I don't know," she said, her expression filled with apprehension.

"How about it, Pete?" Ben asked.

"I need more healing time," Pete said.

"Caleb," Ben invited.

Caleb raised his injured arm. "Another time."

Ben shook his head. "I'll do it since no one else will rise to the occasion." He eyed the others. "Looks like I'm the only one without an excuse." Ben stepped to the edge of the shallows, then turned to face the meager assembly. Raising an arm into the air, Ben declared, "Dinner's on me."

The group clapped and hooted, resonating their support. Ben turned and searched the saturated sand for the tell-tale signs of the scoth.

"Look for the triangular offset of the odd bubble," Orac said, extending his arm outward. "It is always to the right."

Ben, facing Orac, looked up from his search. He extended his left hand, telling Orac that he understood.

Orac hesitated for a moment, fearing what his hand signal had done. He yelled, as did the rest, urging Ben to stop.

Ben saw the triangular shaped pattern he'd been looking for. He looked up at his friends. *Wait til they see this one*, he thought. Remembering the direction Orac had pointed, he pushed his hand into the sand.

The warnings ceased, replaced by an eerie, silent anticipation. Eve covered her mouth with both hands.

Ben looked up from his squat position with a wide grin. "Got it," he announced.

Eve moved her hands. Her eyes widened.

"Ben's okay," she squealed.

Ben pulled up, attempting to extract his prey, and with a momentary hesitation, disappeared headfirst under the sand. A sixty-foot long slug-like creature burst from the shore. It was pink and smooth, with no discernable features. It seemed to go on forever as it exited its gritty environment. Once free, the creature moved with amazing speed into the surf and out to sea.

"The lankier," Orac whispered.

Eve dropped to her knees and sobbed.

"He's gone," she wailed. "Ben's gone."

Pete knelt, hoping to console the distraught woman, but Eve would not be comforted. She jerked away and stood to confront Orac. "It's your fault, you overgrown ape," she screamed, pummeling him with her fists. "You did this to him!" She dropped, landing on the sand once again.

Orac took her arms, pulling her up. "Eve," he said, gently shaking her. "There is yet hope. You must compose yourself if we are to help your Ben."

Eve stopped her tirade and looked into Orac's eyes. "What do you mean?" she asked, her expression pleading for any thread of hope.

Pete and Caleb moved closer. Seeka jumped to Caleb's shoulder in order to hear over the relentless sound of the breaking waves.

"There is a chance we can save him," Orac said.

"He was eaten. How do we save him?" Eve implored, "We can't put him back together." She began to cry again.

"Listen," Orac said, "had he been devoured, there would be parts all over this beach." He waved his hand. "Please forgive my choice of words."

"Never mind that," Pete said. "Get to the point."

"Of course," Orac replied. "A male lankier would have devoured Ben here in front of us. Your Ben was taken by a female."

"So he could be eaten later?" Eve asked.

"No," Orac cautioned, "for her young when they hatch."

"What are you saying?" Pete insisted.

"I believe I can answer your question," Caleb said. "Ben has been taken to a place of birthing. He will be held there until the young lankier emerge . . ."

"To feed on fresh meat?" Pete finished. He grimaced.

"Right on both accounts," Orac replied. "However dire these circumstances may seem, there is still hope."

Eve contemplated her husband's fate. "Ben can't survive under water," she said in a whisper.

"The lankier young cannot survive unless they are born out of the water," Orac said. "They live in the air as we do until they are old enough to take their first meal. They will feast and move to their aquatic home. Your Ben will remain safe until then."

"How long before the hatchlings are able to eat?" Pete asked.

"One or two risings of the Great Light," Orac replied. "That depends on the time of their emergence."

"Two days at the most," Pete said. "Do you know where to find him?"

"I know of the caves in which they reside," Orac said. "It is one rising's ride from here."

"Let's go," Eve insisted. "Every minute we waste is another minute Ben loses."

"I must agree," Caleb said. "Time is of the essence."

"I will ask the Great One to walk with you in your travels," Caleb said.

"Thank you," Pete said. "We'll take any help we can get."

"It is not, as you say, any help," Caleb replied. "It is assistance that is truly worth acquiring, and there but for you to ask."

"Wait," Eve said. "Aren't you coming with us?"

"Sadly, my time with you has come to a close," Caleb said. "However, my small friend will accompany you."

"Seeka?" Eve asked.

"Yes," Caleb replied.

"And Yoshi?"

"He is possibly the last of his kind, and his quest will determine this ultimate truth. If so, he will spend his days among my people."

"What will become of you?" Orac asked.

Caleb smiled. "I will live my life, and then I will be no more. For you, I will have ceased to be with your first step on your new journey."

"Does this have to be?" Eve asked.

"Yes, it must be this way," Caleb said. "However, do not concern yourself with my plight. In my time I will live many more years."

Eve smiled and wrapped her arms around Caleb. "Thank you for everything. I will miss you."

"As will I," Caleb replied. "I have recovered the parchment that Belac recorded from the stone tablets in the Andor. See that Ben knows it is in your possession. Now you must not tarry. Great things await your arrival."

Pete and Orac bade Caleb farewell. Seeka was the last to do so. They clicked questions, responses and farewells. When done, Seeka leapt on the back of Ben's empty horse. He curled up and lay down, keeping silent in his grief.

Eve and Pete climbed aboard their steeds, while Orac took the reins of Seeka's mount and the packhorse. One final goodbye and they were once again traveling into the unknown.

Eve turned, looking back. Caleb was gone. Even the area they had just departed looked different—like the changes that many generations would bring.

"How are you doing, Pete?" Eve asked.

Pete quickly shoved a small bundle out of sight. "Fine," he replied, sucking on his teeth.

"And you, Orac?"

"I do well," he said.

"May I ask a question?" Eve asked. "You grew to a great size when we fought Colossac." She hesitated. "Was that because of the Kumult?"

"Even though I cannot say for sure," Orac replied, "that may be the case."

"Do you think it holds anymore surprises?"

Orac stared into the distance. "I do not know; however, it well may. Only by confronting what lies ahead will we know."

End of Book Three

Glossary

Andor A vessel from the Great One that contains the Ten Edicts carved on stone tablets for all to live by, the budding cleric's staff, and food that fell from the heavens each day.

Belac Caleb's brother who assists the three through the journey that is Eden's Wake, willing to give his life for the plans of the Great One.

Ben The original selection in the assembling of the three by the Great One. From a saturation diver in Rising Tide and his marriage to Eve, to leading the three as a mature commander, he begins to see the role the Great One has played from the beginning.

Book of the Chosen The book in which the exploits of the three plus many earlier patriarchs are recorded. A good portion of the book contains blank pages, for the stories are being written as they occur.

Cahotic The true leader of the riders, a rider as well.

Caleb Belac's brother who assists the three through the journey that is Deadly Reign, willing to give his life for the plans of the Great One.

Captain Evans Captain of the Morning Star whose essence alters into Eleazor, then transmutes into evil incarnate.

Clavian tark A medicinal plant used for injuries, especially those dealing with the brain. If abused, the clavian tark can become highly addictive, so much so, that the addict will resort to any means necessary to obtain the drug.

Colossac Was the transformation of Nilrem into an altered state. The monster was skinless, covered with muscle fibers, and a giant among giants. He leads the riders, but only in his inflated ego, the riders having alternate plans.

Companion The presence of the Holy Spirit before Jesus' death and resurrection.

Dark One The pure evil who rules, unseen, from the demon realm. This being originated from the hapless little oaf, Eleazor. (Book two, Eden's Wake)

Deadly Reign Book Three in the Rising Tide series. Ben, Eve, and Pete cross paths with unseen aberrations known as the riders. Earth becomes a frozen wasteland as the three join with allies to defeat the malevolent influence forced upon the world.

Eleazor Originally Captain Evans of the Morning Star, his transformation into manifested evil begins aboard ship, then realizes its completion on the island.

Eden's Wake Book Two in the Rising Tide series. Eve, Ben, and Eleazor continue their journey through the pristine new world. Eleazor realizes his transformation into pure evil while Ben and Eve, along with new compan-ions, enter into a subterranean lair fraught with danger and pitfalls.

Established Place An island paradise, introduced in Rising Tide, the first book in the series of the same name. This anomaly, which shows up on no charts or radar, is home to a primitive yet advanced race of people, The One.

Eve Raised in a cannibalistic society, expects what she wants when she wants it. Married to Ben in Rising Tide, Book One, the two have become inseparable.

Flotilla of Wooden Canoes Denotes the point in time when Rising Tide and Deadly Reign cross paths and the Morning Star is placed back in its correct timeline.

Jhorr Originally in Book One, the elderly leader of an island nation whose people were known as The One. This society was instrumental in guiding Ben and Eve onto their present path. We meet Jhorr again in Eden's Wake, Book Two. Even though Rising Tide precedes Eden's Wake's timeline, Jhorr is now an 8-year-old boy who leads the three through a treacherous subterranean lair.

Karron Small organically jet-powered birds

Keeper The indwelling of the Holy Spirit after Jesus' death and resurrection.

Krang A spherical object that allows one to engage in interdimensional travel, but only with one's essence, leaving the physical body behind. A marble-sized companion to the krang is used for abbreviated trips within a single dimension. This agate may be used in conjunction with its host. Of course, there are exceptions to every rule.

Kumult A malevolent elixir designed for mind control and extraction of information.

Lankier A large wormlike creature that also burrows into the sand. It can grow up to 60 feet long and swallow a man whole.

Living One Jesus

Marcovian An enormous crustacean buried for eons until called into service if needed.

Morning Star The container ship which originally carried Ben, Eve and Eleazor to the Established Place in Book One, Rising Tide.

Narify A race consisting of dissimilar creatures, i.e. flying tree dwellers, insect-like cave dwellers, death squads, and sentries.

Nilrem Surrogate father of Orac, raised him from a youth. The original intent was to feed the yearling a montage of dangerous potions (the kumult being forbidden) to increase Orac's size and turn him toward the Dark One.

Nuckta Resembles a large meerkat that is highly intelligent. Seeka, the last remaining nuckta, communicates with its human counterparts through speech. Among other gifts, Seeka owns the ability to travel to alternate dimensions by use of the krang.

One Who Sees All / Great One God

Orac Raised by Nilrem, this giant of a man once thought evil, joins the three in the fight to rescue Earth.

Orion The decompression chamber that transported Ben from the sea floor to the surface into a category 6 hurricane. He was forced to cut loose from OZ, an oil drilling platform in the Gulf of America. He drifted for days until rescued by the Morning Star. This took place in Book One, Rising Tide.

Parallel Dimensions I and II Parallel Dimensions exist simultaneously apart from one another within the same timeline. Each dimension can consist of totally different environments. Even though they may share many of the same characters, no dimension's development is influenced by another until travel between dimensions is realized. In this case, Parallel Dimension I takes place in the world of *Deadly Reign*, Book Three. The Earth is in its infancy, fighting to stop the influx of evil. Parallel Dimension II takes place in *Rising Tide,* Book One, where Ben and Eve are unwittingly pressed into service by the Great One.

Pete Ben's best friend, once thought killed in an underwater implosion, returns from the dead in Book Two, Eden's Wake.

Riders and Beasts Demonic beings, the riders are naturally armored bipeds equipped with specially forged swords made by their own hands. The beasts, quadrupeds that bear the riders, are 4-legged steeds possessing a high level of intelligence and weapons of their own. Both riders and beasts must avoid contact with water or face death by dissolution.

Rising Tide Book One in the series of the same name. The planet is nearly covered by water. The limited land becomes a focal point for the growth of immorality, culminating in the survival of the fittest.

Scoth An edible crustacean that burrows into the sand on the edge of the surf line.

Seeka The last of its kind, known as a nuckta; it is vaguely similar in appearance to a meerkat. Its eyes partially wrap around the side of its head, giving Seeka an unusually wide field of vision. This unusual animal displays an intellectual prowess superior to most and the ability to speak.

Skull Seems to have come from nowhere, good-hearted, but follows Vinny with very little question. Acts inept, but endowed with supernatural wisdom and power.

Stacion Field An invisible force field that is projected around an object. If the field is breached by a human being, the offender is reduced to a puff of ozone.

Stewart Victim of his upbringing. Determined to seek power and money at any cost. Hired as Captain Evans' second in command.

Tamar A group of nearly indestructible hatchlings brought forth in book two, Eden's Wake. They were beset upon the fledgling earth to spread hatred, greed, gluttony, envy, pestilence, and the like.

The Key The one who is destined to lead The Three (and possibly others) to the completion of their appointed task, which is not yet clear.

The Three Refers to Ben, Eve and Pete.

Vinny Street thug, way out of his element, confused most of the time

Whens Existing within timelines are specific placements of time referred to as whens. The characters' location and reasons for being remain relative to their current place in time, or their whens.

Yellow Orbs Represent the Companion and the Keeper.

About the Author

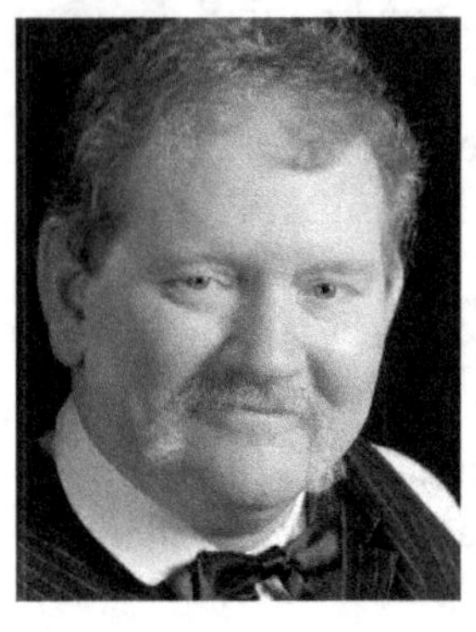 **Lynn Kevin Steigleder** was born in Richmond, Virginia. He spent most of his young adult life as a supervisor in the field of construction and fabrication. During a fishing trip, his son suggested that he consider writing as a career, having enjoyed short stories written by his father in years past. Lynn agreed to the challenge and his first novel, *Rising Tide,* was accepted for publication. Lynn has continued to work on the Rising Tide series. *Eden's Wake* is the second book in the series, and *Deadly Reign*, is the third, with a fourth soon to be published. He is also the author of *Terminal Core*, a stand-alone science fiction novel.

The Rising Tide Series

Available at bookstores and online

in paperback and ebook

Rising Tide, Book 1

Rising Tide depicts a world in which land is at a premium due to the advancing sea, where man's attempt to adapt has led to a decay of morals into survival of the fittest. In the midst of the ocean, a crew of racketeers rescues a stranded diver, Ben Adams. Is the rescue just a fortunate coincidence for Ben, or has he been led to this rendezvous with fate for a common goal? A mysterious island inhabited by a primitive, yet advanced race of people, a devious ship captain's metamorphosis into evil and a ship's container discovered by itself in a billion square miles of ocean all play a role in this tale of rebirth for a world corrupted by the collapse of morality.

Eden's Wake, Book 2

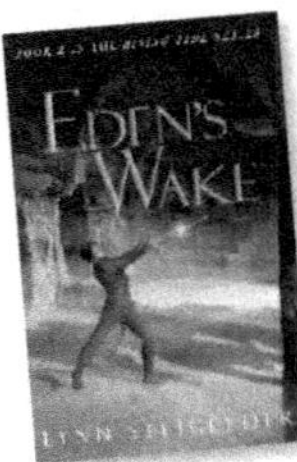

Ben's best friend is killed in an underwater implosion on a dying world. Living to die again, the two men reunite and battle for an ancient artifact—a relic which will ensure this planet's survival. Ben crosses a threshold. The world he leaves—doomed; the world he enters—reborn. His wife, Eve, and their bumbling charge, Eleazor, follow Ben through the doorway and blindly into the void.

Deadly Reign, Book 3

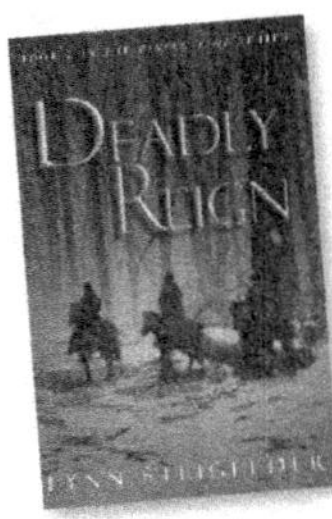

Ben, Eve and Pete continue to push through this new Earth as the world sinks deeper into corruption. They gain new allies, including an intellectual animal equipped with the gift of speech. They are forced to battle six aberrations deemed nearly indestructible. The environment has manifested into a frigid terrain with the sun lost in the ice-filled cloud cover. Swords forged specially for the riders offer another layer of defense to an already superior force

Terminal Core

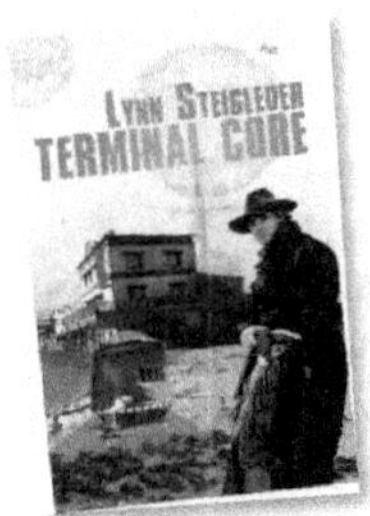

Aon, a solid core planet made from the priceless element in the galaxy, caladium, is under silent attack. Plans are made by off-worlders to dissolve the unbreakable core using crude oil obtained from 19th century Earth. Once the oil is refined, the byproduct gasoline will soften the caladium, allowing it to be collected. It is soon discovered the core is made from living beings created from the caladium itself. The off-worlders employ a band of corrupt inhabitants to carry on this work. They find themselves in a constant struggle with a small coalition of Aonians bent on saving their home world. Both factions clash with the indestructible core creatures. With horrendous beasts one step behind and deadly pitfalls ahead, the coalition struggles to finish its journey, hoping to ensure their race's survival.

www.ingramcontent.com/pod-product-compliance
Lightning Source LLC
Chambersburg PA
CBHW071745190726
48292CB00003B/870